3 4028 06919 8712
HARRIS COUNTY PUBLIC LIBRARY

Summer
Summers, Jordan
Red

$6.99
ocn261939535
12/11/2008

1st ed.

D0030624

Red

Jordan Summers

TOR®

paranormal romance

A TOM DOHERTY ASSOCIATES BOOK
NEW YORK

NOTE: If you purchased this book without a cover, you should be aware that this book is stolen property. It was reported as "unsold and destroyed" to the publisher, and neither the author nor the publisher has received any payment for this "stripped book."

This is a work of fiction. All of the characters, organizations, and events portrayed in this novel are either products of the author's imagination or are used fictitiously.

RED

Copyright © 2008 by Toni Allardice

All rights reserved.

Edited by Anna Genoese

A Tor Book
Published by Tom Doherty Associates, LLC
175 Fifth Avenue
New York, NY 10010

www.tor-forge.com

Tor® is a registered trademark of Tom Doherty Associates, LLC.

ISBN-13: 978-0-7653-5914-8
ISBN-10: 0-7653-5914-6

First Edition: November 2008

Printed in the United States of America

0 9 8 7 6 5 4 3 2 1

There are so many people to thank for bringing this book to life. I'll start with the usual suspects: Kay and Mike Goddard, I wouldn't be here without your love and support; Jill, Jim, and the entire Allardice Clan for welcoming me to Scotland and into your hearts; Teri and Frank, along with their families; the Nickels Clan for taking care of the country while I'm gone; Terri Hendrix, Debbie Gill, Deb Acosta, Dina McMillan, and Betsy Ficarro for being such great friends; Julia Templeton and Sylvia Day for thinking that I was onto something when I penned the first fifty pages of this supernatural thriller; Jeaniene Frost, Vivi Anna, and Charlene Teglia for a third, fourth, and fifth pair of eyes; Kathy Love and Sasha White for the laughs; Paperback Writer for your encouragement and solid advice; Anna Genoese for having the courage to take a chance on this series; Heather Osborn, Melissa Frain, and the entire Tor staff for your guidance and enthusiasm. I owe you all lots more chocolate. My agent, Ginger Clark, for picking up the ball and running with it. You are everything I hoped for and more.

I'd also like to thank my husband, who encouraged me to take the time that I needed to follow my dream. You are my heart and my world.

I'd like to dedicate this book to the readers. I wrote *Red* with the belief that there were other readers in the world like me who enjoy a grittier love story. Thanks for proving me right.

Red

chapter one

Not many people can handle the pain of being ripped apart, of having your limbs twisted and morphed until you are convinced your mind will shatter into a thousand tiny shards.

I can. And I'm tired of hiding my true nature so that humans can sleep better at night, convinced they're actually in control of this tiny blue-brown planet. They need to know the truth—they need to realize that they're not at the top of the food chain.

Far from it.

A permanent shift in power is necessary and I intend to bring about that change one *body* at a time.

Starting now.

Pain sears my flesh, flaying it from the bone. I scream, throwing my head back as blood sprays across the inside of the car, painting the dirty windshield crimson. Pressure explodes beneath my gums, ejecting my teeth to make room for a row of fangs. My arms and legs snap, breaking bone, tearing sinew, to reshape.

The change feels like it is taking an eternity as I drown in a flaming river of agony, but I know it's only been seconds. One last cry rips from my raw throat, and then suddenly I am reborn.

Lungs heaving, I sit up and gaze around. The coppery odor of blood assails my senses, along with something feminine and delicate. Memory evades me. The once familiar vehicle appears alien in origin. The urge to escape its confines is great. Struggling to open the door, I almost miss a twig snapping. My ears perk as I scan the darkness.

It only takes a moment to remember where I am and why I'm here. I raise my nose in the air and inhale deeply. The world comes alive around me as if blinders have been ripped from my eyes. Distant rain wafts on the breeze, along with the sweet, musky aroma of a woman in the throes of heat. The latter draws my attention and holds it.

Ah, that's right. I'd forgotten all about my guest. Where are my manners? I must remember to thank her for accepting my invitation . . . once I catch her.

I watch Lisa Solomon running up ahead, her curly auburn hair blowing in the wind, her long legs flailing beneath her short uniform skirt. She's entering the forest, a relic that once held significance in a green world that no longer exists. She hopes to escape me, find sanctuary among the dead trees, but it's impossible. I give chase.

Branches moan and creak in the darkness, their voices sad and vacant. I can almost hear the ghosts of the leaves rustling in the quiet. I cock my head and listen, loping casually behind Lisa, not even winded. I feel as if I could run for miles, but she can't. The sun-scorched ground is hard and cool beneath my rough pads, perfect for hiding my presence from those who wish to discover my kind.

"Get away from me! Please go away," Lisa says, then screams.

The harmonious sound reaches my sensitive ears as the notes soar into the night, before abruptly cutting off as she labors for air. I yip excitedly, just so I can hear her cry out again. She doesn't disappoint me.

Such beauty.

Such perfection.

And she's all mine.

Lisa's lithe form sways and stumbles as she trips over a stone imbedded deep in the ground, sending her crashing to her knees. She claws violently at the earth in order to regain her footage, leaving deep furrows. Clumps of red clay dirt fly up behind her, before raining down like arid teardrops. Her ripe ass lifts enticingly and then jiggles as she pushes off, scrambling forward, searching frantically for escape.

I love a woman who plays hard to get.

The urge to mate grows strong.

I growl.

Whimpers of pain and fear tear from her throat. "Why are you doing this to me? I thought you invited me here because you liked me. We were friends for God's sake."

Friends? We were meant to be more than friends. Why would she think such a ridiculous thing? I shake my head. If I could laugh in my present form, I would, but I'm too turned on. She has to know what she's doing to me. Perhaps her teasing is a form of human foreplay.

The skeletal remains of a bush lie in front of her. Lisa doesn't even slow as she collides with the fragile limbs. They crackle under her weight, scattering in all directions. By now, her heart must be pumping madly in her chest, painfully slamming into her ribcage, much like the fabled rabbit when confronted by a predator. Appropriate I suppose given what I am. If I close my eyes, I can almost hear her heart's melodious cadence.

Thump.

Thump.

Thump.

I imagine Lisa's pert nipples are rock hard beneath her navy blue quadrant inspector's uniform. It's all I can do to keep from drooling. If I thought she'd appreciate the compliment, I would. I lick my lips and try to recall if she ever wore a bra during the times I'd seen her. Funny how those details slip from my mind's grasp.

All I know is that she's taunted me for the last time.

My tongue lulls out of my mouth as I easily close the distance between us. The sweet warm air brushes over my face and down the length of my enhanced body as I catch a glimpse of her tantalizing flesh.

Lisa's legs are long-limbed perfection, even with the red welts and scrapes forming macabre celestial designs on her skin. A work of sheer artistry. She glances back, her oval-shaped face ashen in the burgeoning moonlight.

Such beauty.

Such frailty.

I try to convey to her with my thoughtful expression that it won't be long now and she needs to ready herself. Her blue eyes widen as she frantically searches for my location in the darkness.

My what big eyes you have . . . too bad they won't help you.

I almost feel sorry for her visual inferiority. It's not as if I'm hiding. There's no cause, since we both know we're destined to be together.

"Dear God. No!" She glances around frantically. "Someone please help me."

My rampant cock grows hard as the waves of her fear lap over my lightly pelted skin like a lover's tongue. It bobs and slaps against my body in a rhythmic beat as I increase my pace. My flesh burns in expectation of our joining.

Hear me coming, Lisa?

I can almost taste her essence and feel the slide of my engorged shaft as it splits Lisa's flesh, knotting and swelling, locking deep inside of her. Doesn't she realize the beauty of this moment and the unmistakable honor I'm about to bestow upon her?

She will.

Soon.

The distance between us diminishes as quickly as the last fragments of her hope. I know this because Lisa's slowing. The wind howls, sending the sweet scent of her sweat-covered body to my nostrils. I inhale, momentarily drowning in the aroma, before expanding my chest to answer its call.

Ahwoo! Ahwoo!

I'm close, I say.

So close.

Lisa darts frantically left and right, her hands out

in front of her as she gropes for a weapon to defend herself. It's a waste of time. My enemies can attest to the fact that I'm not easily killed.

Bark breaks off in her grip, crumbling like ash in her fingertips. She drops it with a frustrated cry and keeps running. I follow her movements with ease. The muscles of my body tense in anticipation.

Should I fuck her first or *after*?

I don't have to decide this moment. I have until dawn, which leaves me plenty of time.

I swipe at her and hear something rip. Lisa screams and manages to dodge away from my taloned grasp. No matter. I allow the tatters from her navy blue shirt to fall to the ground.

Relishing the chase, I permit it to continue.

Lisa stumbles once more, her body making a soft thud as it hits the earth. It's over. This time I have her. I crouch and leap, covering the ten feet that separates us with ease, landing on top of her as she attempts to jump to her feet.

My weight instantly throws her to the ground. Her head and back smack hard, causing blood to coat her beautiful auburn hair. I close my eyes and inhale.

It smells intoxicating. The vintage perfection.

"Get off me. Get off me." Lisa struggles, scratching and clawing and biting at my skin like a wild cat fighting for its life. Her long nails break off as she attempts to penetrate my thick hide.

Doesn't she realize her actions only excite me?

I rip Lisa's useless skirt from her body and toss it aside, before wrenching her bleeding hands above her head. Holding her still, I bury my wet nose between her legs. She stiffens, then her body weeps.

For me only.

I've wondered what Lisa would smell like for months. It's better than my wildest imaginings. The musky spice envelops my senses and my body trembles as I fight to maintain control. I give her folds, hidden by the slight wisp of silk panties, a quick swipe with my long tongue. Ambrosia. I rip them away, exposing her sex. My cock extends and swells as I debate where to part her succulent flesh, so little time, so many orifices to choose from.

With the flick of my jagged talons, I remove the remains of her tattered shirt. I need to see every inch of her fervent skin. The nipples I'd only been able to dream about until now stab skyward. Ripe berries on hills of creamy flesh, waiting to be plucked and harvested. I can't resist one quick lick.

Delicious.

She quivers, then Lisa's screams turn to terrified wails as her gaze shoots from my raging cock to my elongated face. It's almost as if she doesn't recognize me, her own mate. Impossible.

I see that play time is over.

It doesn't matter for I cannot wait any longer.

My need is too great.

I move over her, allowing her to feel the weight of my body as I settle between her ample thighs, until we're staring eye to eye, mate to mate. Tears spill down her cheeks, watering the parched ground beneath her. I lap at them, but they continue to flow like salty treats upon my tongue.

Don't cry, I want to tell her, but I can't. The words come out garbled, guttural, like razors slashing over vocal cords.

"Please," she says, shaking her head back and forth in denial, when I know she wants this as badly as I do.

Why does she continue to deny our love?

"I won't tell anyone your secret. I promise. Just let me go and I'll leave. You'll never see me again."

Let her go. Why would I want to do that? We're made for each other. Doesn't she understand that she's *perfect*?

I peer into her tear-blotched face and watch as acceptance fills her blue eyes. Her full lips part in preparation for my embrace, while her tongue darts out to moisten them. It's all the invitation I need.

The sex could wait. I open my mouth and lower my head to taste her. Colors explode behind my eyelids, a kaleidoscope of emotions whirling in my mind. Disjointed nude images of sprawled limbs cloud my vision, erasing everything but the power gushing through my veins.

So this is love.

Lisa flinches and twists, arching her neck beneath my expert touch. I raise my head and she gasps. One taste is not enough . . . *for either of us*.

I delve in again.

Deeper.

She gurgles.

Lisa's cries stop, along with her struggles, and she goes limp beneath me.

I sit up to get a better look. Her expression seems odd, unnatural. Steam rises from the carotid opening in the darkness.

I nudge Lisa with my moist nose, but she doesn't move. Sightless eyes continue to stare at the star-dappled sky, ignoring the approach of the three-quarter moon. Cocking my head, I wonder why as my mind struggles to understand.

Suddenly, comprehension dawns and I realize she's dead. I have to admit I am disappointed. I chose Lisa to be my one, my only. I had such divine plans for us and the future. We hadn't even gotten to the good part yet.

I dip my head again. There must be no mistake. Blood runs down my chin and onto my hairy chest, burning my throat in an ecstasy unlike any other. Hot, sweet, sticky, and delicious. I fight my instincts, but losing is inevitable.

Closing my eyes, I slowly release Lisa's lifeless hands one claw at a time, and then proceed to gorge myself, taking care to relish each tender bite. My teeth rip and masticate with ease as I feast upon her glorious flesh.

This is how it should be.

How it will be again.

Soon.

The savorous overload sends my body into an unexpected orgasm. My cock jerks above her body. Once. Twice. I shudder. Relief floods through me as my essence spills out, mingling with what remains of my beloved Lisa.

I greedily lap them both, before cleaning my mouth and claws afterward. Sated momentarily, I ponder the question that has been running through my mind for months. I finally have an answer.

Lisa *does* taste as good as she looks.

chapter two

Gina Santiago jackknifed up in bed, her body drenched in sweat, her heartbeat thundering in her head. She gripped her laser pistol, her hand jerking wildly as she searched for an immediate threat in the darkness. Shadows leapt from the corners of the room, menacing her befuddled mind. It took a few seconds for her to focus and realize she was at home, in bed.

"Shit!" She dropped back onto her pillows, the sound of her ragged breathing echoing off the sterile white walls of her living quarters.

She set her gun back on her metal side table with a clank and shot a quick glance at the clock. Damn, it was three in the morning. She'd only been asleep a few hours. Gina punched her pillow and the top of the rest pad to try to get comfortable, then turned to face the wall. Her feet came together with a heavy thump. "What the—"

She glanced down.

"Lights on." Artificial intelligence complied, bathing the dormitory room in a cadmium florescent glow. She looked around the space, taking in the two-seater gray couch, her clothes locker, and her personal food dispensing unit. A blank flat-panel screen blotted one wall like a blemish on a baby's face. The viewer was off, just like she'd left it. The twenty-by-twenty area wasn't big enough for anyone to hide.

Privacy assured, Gina pulled the covers up with trembling fingers until she could see her feet. Why was she wearing her combat boots in bed? She shifted to get a better look and sent red clay dirt onto the sheets. Confused, she whipped the blanket off.

When had she gotten dressed?

Gina gasped, staring down the length of her body in disbelief. Her clothes lay in tatters against her limbs as if someone had fed her through a meat grinder. Scratches and cuts marred her pale flesh and her muscles ached from overuse. Panic slammed her, squeezing her chest until it hurt to breathe.

"What the hell?" she choked.

She replayed the previous evening in her mind. She remembered filing tactical reports, watching the republic news, eating protein-enriched synth-noodles, and then going to bed. The rest of the night was a blank, an endless void in the darkness without beginning or end. She'd assumed she had spent it in deep REM sleep, but now . . .

Gina looked down at her clothes once more. Blood dotted her T-shirt. She frantically pulled the synthetic material away from her stomach, ripping it over her head before tossing it onto the floor. Pressing a splayed hand against her abdomen, she examined her skin. Nothing. She stripped out of the rest of her clothes, adding them to the pile destined for the incinerator. Her gaze swept her body. There were no obvious signs of injuries. Naked and confused, Gina swallowed a lump of fear, feeling its icy tendrils claw their way down her throat.

She curled her knees against her chest and hugged herself as tremors racked her body. She didn't understand what was happening. Where had she been? Gina strained to remember, but no answers came forth, only nothingness. Her gaze strayed back to the crimson mosaic coloring her discarded shirt.

If the blood wasn't hers, then whose was it?

The vidcom chirped, disturbing Morgan Hunter's dream. *Go away.* He pulled the pillow over his head and groaned, trying to ignore the call and get back to the dark-haired woman he'd been about to fuck senseless. He couldn't quite make out his dream woman's face, but he'd know her body anywhere. His hips moved restlessly against the covers, caressing his erection as he sought the comfort of her moist warmth. The vidcom buzzed again, this time louder, more insistent. The dream slowly dissipated.

"Shit," Morgan murmured under his breath, then blindly reached out and pressed a button on a control panel near his rest pad. There had better be a beautiful woman on the other end of the line begging him for his body or else someone was about to get an earful. "Who is it?" he rasped without looking at the monitor screen. "Make it good."

"Morgan, we have a problem," Jim Thornton said, his voice low.

Why was the director of the dissecting lab calling?

And why was he whispering? "Can't it wait until morning?" Morgan asked, removing the pillow, before glancing blurry-eyed at the screen. The image of the red-haired bespectacled man wavered before him.

"No, it can't." Jim's gaze darted from side to side, then he leaned into the viewer until all Morgan could see was two magnified eyes, a bulbous nose, and a thick-lipped mouth. "You're going to want to see this right away."

"What's wrong, Jim? You look . . ." He squinted. "Scared." Morgan came awake in a shot.

"I can't tell you over the vidcom. Come down to the lab immediately." Jim's pudgy face was drained of all color.

Morgan blinked. The hair at the nape of his neck stood on end. What in the hell was going on? "I'll be there in fifteen." He glanced at the clock on his side table. The number three glared back. "Better make that twenty."

"Hurry." Jim abruptly severed the link.

Morgan threw back the covers and sat up, scrubbing his hands over his stubbled face and through his hair before glancing around. The sound of his air-filtering system hummed in the background, comforting like a heartbeat in the womb. No other noise penetrated his living space due to the added thickness of the reinforced tinted-glass windows and concrete walls.

The additional material in the walls served twofold, to protect his home from assault and to make it soundproof. Even in the darkness Morgan could still easily make out his home's Spartan furnishings, a table, two chairs, and a couch. Standard republic issue. Morgan jumped off his bed and padded naked across the sienna-stained concrete floor to the cleansing room, stroking his erection as he went. The slabs were warm against his bare feet despite the built-in cooling system and the double-thick walls.

Pressing a button, Morgan stepped into the chemical shower stall. Injected with a stimulating essence to wake him, the harsh lemon spray rained down upon his shaggy head. He wrinkled his nose and nearly gagged from the odor, but continued to stroke himself until he reached completion, before hitting the shut-off button.

He despised the new A.I. cleansing units with their built-in biomonitors. He didn't need a goddamned machine telling him when he should wake up or soothing him into sleep. He was quite capable of making those decisions on his own.

Sometimes he really hated modern amenities.

Morgan dried quickly and then threw on a pair of black utility pants and a matching shirt. He tugged on his boots, grabbing his gun and badge on the way out the door.

Minutes later he stepped into his vehicle and started it with the press of his hand. A low-level growl came from the engine. He always loved the sound a hydrogen motor made when it came to life. Morgan eased onto the accelerator and the growl turned to a roar. He smiled to himself and flattened the pedal. The power of the car threw him back in his seat as the turbo kicked in.

At this time of the morning, if you could call the middle of the night morning, Morgan could set the car at max velocity without attracting heavy tolls from the Republic of Arizona's automated speed control system.

He pressed the button to roll down the window, and it descended with a pressurized hiss, allowing the desert air inside. The warmth brushed over his face, sifted through his hair, and cleared his head. Morgan went over various scenarios as he drove to Nuria, but none could explain Jim's frightened appearance or the immediacy of the situation.

His gut soured as he neared the dissecting lab. Morgan pulled into a parking space and killed the engine with the swipe of a finger. He pressed his palm to a scanner on the dashboard, setting the doors to lock in five seconds, then exited the vehicle.

Jim Thornton, a portly gentleman with thick glasses and sausage-like fingers, waited outside the door of the dissection lab with a banned smoke stick protruding from his mouth. He puffed heavily, causing wisps of smoke to swirl around his head, before reluctantly throwing it on the ground and snuffing its flame with the toe of his shoe.

"I saw that," Morgan chided, glancing at the crushed remains.

"Who's trying to hide?" Jim shuffled from foot to foot impatiently.

The man's nervousness sent adrenaline surging through Morgan's body. His shoulders tensed and he looked around suddenly uneasy. Normally Jim was the epitome of laid back. Nothing ruffled him. He'd seen more death in his tenure as the director of the dissecting lab than most biodweller directors see in a lifetime. Morgan took a deep breath and released it as something dark and troublesome settled in his gut.

"What is so important that you needed to drag me out of bed? I can't believe this couldn't wait until morning. I'd just finished a twelve-hour shift and had finally managed to fall asleep." Not to mention the world-class dream sex he'd missed out on. Morgan didn't bother to hide his frustration. It was a helluva lot easier than worrying.

"I'm sorry." Jim wiped his beefy hands on his dissecting apron. "But the situation warranted an immediate response." He glanced around the deserted streets, his eyes searching the darkness for unwanted attention.

Morgan tensed, following Jim's gaze without understanding what they were looking for. "Jim?"

The director held his hand up, stilling Morgan's questions. "Once you see *it*, you'll understand why I called." The ominous words fell like ghostly shadows in the night as Jim stepped inside.

Morgan nodded, glancing around one last time, and then trailed behind.

They entered the lead-lined concrete dissecting lab. The odor of disinfectant smacked Morgan in the face, causing his eyes to water. He blinked rapidly to clear them. Bright lights hung above each gurney, illuminating death in a kind of macabre showcase. Several bodies occupied the stainless-steel tables in various stages of dismemberment for the recycling of parts. Disposal chutes lined one wall, while cabinets containing dissecting equipment took up another. Ten large drains dotted the floors in order to catch and recycle fluids that escaped during the dissecting process.

Human remains made up 70 percent of the liquid mulch used for plant growth in the industrial hydroponics chambers. Burials no longer occurred, the practice considered too antiquated and wasteful in a world where survival hinged on conservation and recycling.

Morgan missed the old days. There was something to be said for standing over a grave and paying your respects. How many funerals had he attended during the war? Fifty? One hundred? More? The names were a blur in Morgan's mind. The years had sanded down his memories until only the faces of the men under his old command remained. He'd buried the last soldier a lifetime ago. The rest had stopped dying—thanks to scientific intervention. With everyone accounted for, Morgan burned his captain's uniform and walked away. He hadn't looked back since . . . until now.

Mint-scented antiseptic filled the cold air, attempting to mask the smell of death.

It failed miserably.

Morgan scanned the row of bodies, but nothing seemed out of place until he got to the one at the far end of the room. Instead of being exposed like the others, it lay covered beneath a white medical tarp. Jim never kept the bodies covered. He was convinced that it hindered the dissection process.

"Put these on," Jim said, handing Morgan lab gear.

Morgan donned the protective headgear and gloves, then followed Jim, who hadn't bothered to suit up, to the table at the far end.

"I found her when I was out doing a routine scan of the electromagnetic boundary area for unknowns. You know I like to get to them before it's too late to recycle. She's been dead for about a week, maybe longer," he said, feathering the ends of the tarp through his fingers.

"We have a lot of unknowns turning up dead. That's nothing new. You know as well as I do that illegally crossing the boundary is dangerous. Those who don't die at the fence get taken out by the harsh elements or the animals," he said, bitterness filling him.

Morgan hated the boundary. The electromagnetic barbed fence stretched across the southern half of the North American continent, bisecting what used to be California, Arizona, New Mexico, Texas, Oklahoma, and Arkansas in order to limit illegal crossings from no-man's-land to the republics and keep out unregistered individuals, *unknowns*.

He never agreed with the reasoning behind its construction or the separation it stood for. The division between countries, religions, and humans had been what started the war in the first place. People had been so busy pointing out their differences that they forgot how much they were alike. He shook his head and looked at the tarp in disgust. Just because a person refused to be tagged with a computer chip didn't make him a criminal. At least not in Morgan's mind. But it wasn't his job to create the laws, only enforce them—and he did that because more of them were good than were bad.

"She's not an unknown."

Jim's words slammed into him, disintegrating his thoughts like ash caught in a heavy wind. "She's registered with the Republic of Arizona?" Morgan stilled, his stomach clenched. He stared at the white tarp unable to bring himself to touch it. "Who?" He forced himself to ask.

"It's Renee Forrester."

Oh, hell. He'd dated Renee the year before. They'd split amicably after a few months, their itch thoroughly scratched. She was kind, a tad on the shy side, but well liked. He couldn't think of a soul who'd want to harm her. "Are you sure?" he asked, heaviness settling in his chest as the loss finally registered.

"I'm sorry, Morgan, but I'm positive."

He nodded, his fists tightening on the cover. Morgan took a couple of deep breaths, then pulled the tarp back. The condition of Renee's body punched the air out of his lungs, leaving him disoriented. He'd seen more than his fair share of dead bodies and learned there were a lot of ways a person could die. Yet he'd never seen anything quite like this. Renee had been brutalized. No, more than that, she'd been savaged.

His stomach flipped as he stared at the body, threatening to toss the remnants of his dinner onto the floor. "What the hell happened to her? Where are her eyes?" He swallowed hard, fighting the rising bile in his throat. The smell was stronger now, cloying as it insisted upon entering his protective headgear.

"She's been eaten," Jim said without inflection.

"Eaten? Hell, she's been ripped apart." Morgan stepped back, his attention locking on Jim for answers.

"You know I wouldn't say anything if I wasn't sure."

It couldn't be happening again. No one was that stupid. Desperation clawed at Morgan's chest, leaving him raw and exposed. "No," he said, convinced there had to be a logical explanation. "The zoos never have caught everything that escaped. You and I both know that. Food's scarce. The predators have gotten a hell of a lot more aggressive lately, if the calls from the ranchers are any indication."

Jim's shoulders slumped and he shook his head. "Take a closer look at the injuries, particularly the area near her carotid artery." He pointed to a nasty wound on her pale slender neck.

Morgan stared at the woman with whom only a year ago he'd been intimate. Renee's left arm was missing, along with her beautiful brown eyes and half her lovely face. Blond hair matted with dried blood hung limply next to her remaining ear. Her intestines spilled from her abdomen as though someone had dropped synth-noodles on the floor. He gulped as he bent forward to examine the area Jim indicated. "Tell me that's not a tooth indentation."

"I wish I could, but I've measured the damned thing three times. There's no mistaking the weapon. Trust me, it's a fang."

Jim walked across the room and opened one of the drawers along the wall that held more of his dissecting tools. He took out a small gold case and brought it back to the table. His thick thumbs flipped the latch and lifted the lid, exposing seven perfectly formed incisors made out of plaster. He picked up the largest one and slid it into the wound on Renee's neck with ease. It was a perfect fit.

"Shit! Shit! Goddammit!" Morgan paced a few steps away, pulling off the protective gear so he could breathe. He slammed the equipment onto an unoccupied table. The clanging sound reverberated in the silence. Ignoring his gloves, he ran his hands through his hair.

Morgan shook his head and then strode back to the

dissection table, his steel-toed boots clacking on the concrete floor. "Has anyone else seen the body?" He looked warily at Jim, praying the man gave him the right answer—hell, the only acceptable answer given the circumstances.

"No." Relief flooded through Morgan as Jim pulled his glasses from his face and began wiping them on his shirt sleeve. "As soon as I realized who it was, I covered her. I didn't want any of my lab assistants stumbling upon her."

"Good. Hide the body immediately, but don't dispose of it. We may need her later to identify the killer."

"That's what I'd planned to do after you saw her." Jim said.

"You were right to contact me. I want to handle this personally. We can't afford to have outsiders involved, not with public awareness of our existence beginning to rise. Besides, I don't want to panic the town unless I have to." The thought of the impending hunt chilled Morgan's bones.

"I figured that would be the case."

"You're sure this couldn't have been caused by anything else?" He hated hearing the resignation in his voice.

"You've seen the evidence with your own eyes," Jim said, with the patience of a man who spends his time around the dead. "You know what we have here." He slid his glasses back onto his round face. "Nothing out there has canines this long, not even the wild cats."

Morgan braced his arms on the table, his gloved hands curled into fists around the cool metal frame. He closed his eyes for a second against the gruesome scene before opening them again. "Do you know who did this?" His voice held little emotion, knowing who-ever Jim named would be sentenced to death.

Jim shook his head while gathering the tarp to cover the body. "The tests were inconclusive, but we can safely rule out the vamps."

"Why?" Morgan asked, realizing it would be far easier to stake a vamp than to take out one of his own. "Some of them have long-ass canines, too. Don't they still need blood?"

"Yes, they do, but the amount varies from vamp to vamp. Most prefer to, ah . . . feed during scx. Renee shows no signs of penetration." Jim shoved his hands into his pockets. "Speaking of vamps, I spotted Raphael Vega in town the other night."

"What's the two-legged bat doing back in Nuria?"

"Raphael said he was just visiting friends," Jim said.

"He doesn't have any friends."

Jim smiled indulgently. "I know you'd like to be-lieve that, but he has a lot of female friends. Don't you think it's about time you get over the grudge you've been carrying against him? He didn't steal Karen from you. She went willingly to his bed. Half the town heard her passionate screams when he was—"

"This isn't about Karen," Morgan growled out be-tween clenched teeth. "Everyone knows that lab vamps aren't to be trusted. Hell, even the vamps don't trust each other."

Like Morgan and most of the people living in Nuria, Raphael Vega was one of the many individu-als involved in the old U.S. government's pet project to create a super soldier. The scientists behind Proj-ect Superman had succeeded beyond their wildest dreams.

What had once only existed in myth and imagination now walked the earth and had fought for freedom. The genetically engineered soldiers were stronger and faster than regular men, had greater endurance, and could withstand extreme injury. For all intents and purposes, they were immortal.

At the start of the project, the newly converted soldiers were touted as heroes, but then the war shifted and everyone lost. The scientists and government officials attempted to call back their special teams so they could eradicate them. There was only one small problem—they could no longer control the monsters they'd created.

When their numbers were sufficient, the creatures broke out of their holding cells and had been on the loose ever since. The war destroyed most records and the new governing bodies moved to distance themselves from the whole debacle by denying their existence and disavowing all involvement. This allowed the *Others* to create new lives for themselves among the purebloods. With new identities in place, they'd blended in and built entire societies, but all those gains wouldn't matter if humans rediscovered their existence.

And dead bodies were the ultimate attention getters.

"Raphael has interesting timing," Morgan said.

"So it seems," Jim replied.

He leaned forward. "And?"

Jim shrugged. "You know as well as I do that vamps don't tend to ingest large quantities of meat or any other food for that matter. That was one of the tradeoffs for the boost in psychic ability. Besides, they wouldn't have left so much blood or evidence.

They're very good at hiding their presence and even better at disposing of bodies. You can take the vampires out of the lab, but not the lab out of the vampires." Jim joked, but it fell flat. He coughed, his face flushing under Morgan's steady regard. "We may not know *who,* but you and I both know *what* did this."

Morgan exhaled loudly. Indeed, he did know what had done this to poor Renee Forrester. A pureblood against a predator this cunning didn't have a chance. Let's hope the people of Nuria faired better.

He glanced at Jim. "This is just what we need, especially with Roark Montgomery trying to gain support for his blood purity bill. If word gets out . . ." Morgan's voice trailed off.

"I know, I know. The republic leaders will send orders to IPTT to exterminate first and ask questions later, like during the war."

Ice settled in Morgan's gut as he considered the possibility of the International Police Tactical Team getting involved. He had to put a stop to whoever was doing this—and fast. "We better hope like hell the IPTT doesn't get wind of this or we'll have a bloodbath on our hands." Morgan removed his gloves and tossed them into a nearby recycling bin.

Jim nodded. "My thoughts exactly."

chapter three

Gina Santiago, or Red, as the tactical team re-
ferred to her, slipped one pistol from its holster and looked around. The weapon beeped
softly in recognition of her thumbprint and began to
charge. She hadn't spotted the remaining unregistered individuals—unknowns—yet, but their stench
was undeniable, much like the body lying at her feet.

She inhaled, taking the hot desert air into her
lungs. It scalded like an oven left unchecked.

The coppery-sweet tang of blood and burned flesh
assaulted her nostrils, blotting out the unknowns' odor.
Her black combat boots stuck to the scorched ground,
making suction noises as she shifted her weight from
one foot to the other, in an attempt to displace the dry-
ing blood.

Crap, now she'd have to get a new pair.

The pistol in her hand glowed green and hummed
as the charge reached full strength. Her fingers tightened instinctively, knuckles turning white from her
tense grip. She glanced down at the rookie's lifeless
body, as he lay prone at her feet. The blast had cau-
terized the outer edges of the wound, meaning there

was minimal blood. Somehow that seemed worse than when there was blood everywhere. Like this, Red could almost pretend her colleague wasn't real. As if he hadn't been covering her back and laughing about catching his first bad guy only moments ago. She swallowed the lump in her throat that threatened to choke her. Sympathy right now would get her killed. She'd have to grieve later.

Red watched the smoke rise from the massive hole where the man's chest had been. Another body lay several feet away: just as bloody, just as dead. At least her backup took a few of the unknowns with him before he checked out. That meant fewer criminals to watch out for in the future.

Where in the hell was the rest of the tactical team? By the time they arrived the fight would be over.

Again.

A warehouse rose a few yards in the distance. Its old-fashioned tin roof glowed in the harsh morning sunlight, giving off what appeared to be mini solar flares. A side door of the building stood wide open, swaying with a gentle squeak, betraying where the remaining unknowns slipped through only moments ago.

Red stared at what used to be an agricultural area. She shielded her eyes in order to take in her surroundings. There were lots of places for an unknown to hide, but she doubted they'd survive for long without shelter. If the thinning ozone layer didn't get them, then the animals would. The sun had turned the once green fields into a barren waste. The skeletal remains of a forest lay farther in the distance. She scanned the horizon again for the tactical team, but couldn't see nor hear a vehicle's approach.

Damn, she'd have to do this one on her own.

Again.

She snaked her way into the warehouse, her footfalls silent on the cracked red clay earth. Two unknowns were in here, waiting for Red to make a mistake. But that wasn't going to happen. Not today.

She inhaled the air once again, relying on her nose's sensitivity in hopes of learning their whereabouts. Unknowns always emitted a peculiar odor, like eggs baking in the hot sun. Only about 2 percent of the population could detect it and she was in that small minority. The ability to ascertain their scent had kept her alive on more than one occasion.

Her job was to terminate the unknowns' criminal careers.

Red took her job *very* seriously.

The building was quiet: not even a creak came from the rafters. *Where are you? I know you're in here.* Red cocked her head to listen. Metal and faux wood split near her cheek as a laser blast narrowly missed its target. The clanging sound reverberated under the tin roof, making the noise near deafening. Her ears rang.

"Son of a bitch!" Red bellowed, then dove behind the steel containers stacked near the wall. She rolled forward and came up firing. The unknown shot again, nicking one of the barrels on the end. Something hit the ground with a splat.

Red kicked the barrel closest to her. Liquid sloshed. She didn't dare glance down to check the contents.

"Shit!" She didn't need to be bathed in radioactive material and have to go through detox. Her skin glowed green for a month the last time that occurred. Some days it didn't pay to get up and come to work.

The two unknowns shot simultaneously.

Her mind snapped back to attention and she fired in the direction of the closest laser trail before it faded. The blast illuminated the darkness for an instant. The unknown's eyes widened, then he screamed and crumpled near the rafter.

One down, she thought, scanning for movement.

The second shot came from above and had been close. Damn close. If the bastard's hand hadn't jerked, she would be missing a head. Red stared into the shadows. Nothing moved. Her gaze canvassed the area, attempting to pinpoint the origin of the blast.

"Throw your weapon out now and surrender peacefully. This is your only warning!" she shouted.

Silence met her.

Just once it would be nice if someone surrendered.

The faux wood near the door smoldered as tiny flames licked hungrily at the beam. Red glanced at the flames, willing them to go out. She didn't have time to fight a fire *and* the suspect.

She scanned the loft area. The shot came from above and to her right. At least she was pretty sure it had . . . but at the moment she couldn't discern the unknown from the darkness shrouding the rafters.

"Move, damn you," she muttered. "Give me something to aim at."

Dust motes from the earlier disturbance danced in the sunlight. From where Red took cover, the unknown had her pinned down no matter which direction she moved. Her heart remained calm and her mind focused as she listened for the sound of humming engines.

Where in the hell was the tactical team? She'd radioed "man down" over thirty minutes ago.

A glint of metal caught Red's eye as sunlight filtered through the holes in the roof. With animal-like reflexes, she swung the barrel of her pistol around and squeezed the trigger. Blue light snaked out toward her intended target. The scream that burst forth shattered the silence, but was abruptly cut short by death's embrace. The man toppled from the rafters and landed with a thick thud onto the ground. The showdown was over.

Red didn't bother to check and see if either man survived. There was no point. She never missed.

She stood, slipping the pistol back into the suction grip holster strapped to her thigh and walked to the door. She grabbed the canteen clipped to her belt and doused the wood frame. Smoke coughed into the air as the flames gasped for breath. The fire sizzled, hissing one last time, before extinguishing.

Red stepped out of the warehouse into the heat and the smell of death dissipated. The second her boots made contact with the dirt, the hair on the nape of her neck rose. She released a heavy breath, her hand resting on her pistol. Red turned to find the rest of the tactical team approaching her position from the north.

About friggin' time.

"I see we're late again," Lieutenant Bannon Richards quipped as he looked at the bodies on the ground. "This was supposed to be an *eyes only* patrol in the southwest quadrant. I sent you and the rookie to this part of the boundary because I thought it would keep you out of trouble. I see I was wrong again."

At first glance, Bannon seemed attractive with his blond crew cut squaring his jaw, deeply tanned skin, and a body mass three times her size. But there was a hint of cruelty lurking behind his pale blue eyes. That look could leave any woman with a case of frostbite.

Bannon never missed the opportunity to throw his weight around or remind Red that he was the one in charge. Technically, he wasn't her commander, since she was a lieutenant, too. Unfortunately on-site, due to a one-month difference in seniority, Bannon had final say . . . and control of the patrol schedule. That's why Red had been spending more and more time on bogus patrols that took her hours away from tactical team headquarters, when she could've been sent out on real calls.

She glanced at the bodies lying around them. Okay, maybe today's assignment hadn't been a waste of time. And the dead rookie was certainly real enough. Yet those tiny details did not make up for all the other days she'd spent driving for hours, staring at sandy rubble, and it certainly didn't earn Bannon her respect.

"There are two inside. One perched near the rafters, the other on the ground." She pointed, not bothering to spare Bannon a second glance. She covered the short distance to where her backup lay lifeless next to an unknown. Flies buzzed and landed on the bodies. It wouldn't be long before they planted their

larva. Red swallowed hard, forcing her mind to clear.
Nothing killed an appetite quicker than a body full of
maggots.

Bannon barked orders to the various team members. Red listened with one ear as he began directing
the scene investigation so it would be finished before
the cleanup crew arrived.

"It's nice to know you're still living up to your rep,
Red," he called out from somewhere behind her.

She grimaced, shifting her feet once more, debating whether to ignore his gibe. Her shoes were sticky
from the crimson pool. The unknown's lifeblood
dried quickly in the sun's harsh rays. Soon he'd be
nothing but a hard shell, not worth recycling.

Bannon approached, his head bent as he looked at
her backup. "McCallan was a good man." He paused.
"They *all* were. And you wonder why no one wants
to work with you." His biting tone hit its mark.

"Screw you, Bannon," she snarled, checking the
charge on her weapons. "I get the job done. If you
guys hadn't taken your sweet-ass time getting here, I
wouldn't have been left to clean up your mess."

"Mess? Is that what you call this bloodbath?" Bannon crowed, looking around at the carnage, his mallet-
sized fists resting on his hips. "That's rich coming from
someone who got their nickname from all the blood
they manage to spill. If it were up to me, you wouldn't
be on this team."

"But it's not, is it?"

Bitterness infused his tone, "No, the commander
wouldn't allow it. Not his precious little—"

"Leave him out of it," she snapped, cutting him
off.

Bannon sneered, his thin upper lip curling in disgust. "Next time, try waiting for backup."

Red glanced at the soon-to-be-recycled body on the ground. Her stomach churned with barely contained rage as she fixed Bannon with a flat stare. "If I'd have done that, my body would be right next to McCallan's and we wouldn't be having this conversation."

"That's a chance I'm willing to take." He grinned, causing the scar on his chin to split obscenely.

Red bit back the reply forming on her lips. Bickering with Bannon, the bastard, was always a waste of her time. He'd been a prick ever since she told him she didn't fuck outside of her species and refused to sleep with him. He wasn't going to change anytime soon.

There were reports to fill out and weapons to check. The cleanup recycling crew would arrive on scene any moment. Once they got here, she'd be able to leave. Until then, Red would try to be civil.

The unit worked around her, documenting the crime scene. Lasers measured distance, while DNA scanners attempted to identify the unknowns' bodies. So far, trace found soil samples from the Republic of Arizona in two of the unknowns' shoes.

Red raised her hand, flipping open the navcom on her wrist to reactivate voice capabilities. The mobile A.I. unit, or navcom, linked by satellite to the main compunit at headquarters, allowing her instant access to information.

The screen glowed eerily, then blanked.

"You've broken me again," the unit's artificial intelligence told her in a slightly nasal sounding female voice.

Red punched button after button and grimaced.

"Hitting me repeatedly will not fix the problem."

"Shut up, Rita," Red said, addressing the unit by the name she'd given it as a child. Her grandfather had the unit custom made for her. Instead of upgrading to the latest navcom model, Red insisted that Rita be repaired. She knew one day the tech department would run out of parts, but until then, she'd keep the old girl running.

"I sense foreign material on your boots," the machine piped up again.

"I know. Not now."

"Are you talking to that machine again?" Bannon asked, drawing the attention of several team members. "No one has talking navcoms anymore—except you. Why don't you upgrade your equipment and come into this decade like everyone else?" He laughed. "Forgot who I was talking to for a minute."

Red scowled.

Bannon pressed the button on his navcom. "Listen," he said. Other than a bleep, there was no other sound. "You know what that is?" he asked.

"No," Red said.

"It's the sound of progress."

Murmurs started around her. Red heard them as clearly as if they'd shouted.

"How many dead rookies does this make . . . She's losing it . . . I don't want to be around when she explodes . . . She acts like the navcom is a real person . . . How did she ever pass the psych test?" Red bristled under the onslaught and pressed another button. For some reason she couldn't bring up the mapping section. Lucky for her, the rest of the files seemed to be in working order.

Scrolling through the menu, she found the UID report she was looking for.

"Do you want me to send the report?" Rita asked.

"Yes."

"Very well, it's done."

The proper document would be waiting for her in the mini compunit on her desk when she returned to headquarters. From there it was a matter of a couple of clicks to file the report.

Just once, Red would like to be able to fill out an Unknown Individual Apprehended—UIA—report, instead of a UID, Unknown Individual Deceased. But that wasn't going to happen today. The criminals hadn't cooperated.

She inhaled deeply as a breeze shifted the stifling air. The sickly sweet odor of perfume embraced her, followed by something far more sinister. Her stomach tightened and she wrinkled her nose and sneezed.

"Do you need an antihistamine?" Rita asked, running a diagnostic on Red.

"No, thank you." The last thing she needed was an antihistamine shot directly into her bloodstream, now that she was finally coming down from the adrenaline rush.

Red turned to Bannon and sniffed. The scent wasn't coming from him unless he kept quite a secret. Her lips canted at the thought. *Fat chance.* He was wholly male and not the good parts. "This is the only crime scene, right?" she asked reluctantly.

Bannon raised his arm in order to view his navcom. "Yeah, according to dispatch's satellite images, this is it."

"The firefight started the second we cut the hydrogen engine, so we didn't have time to look around when we arrived. Are you sure?"

He glanced once more at his navcom before shutting it off. "I'm telling you this is it."

"Gina, your heart rate is accelerating," Rita chimed.

"I know."

"You need to calm yourself."

"Shh, I'm trying to concentrate. I can't do that with you talking to me."

Bannon turned. "What did you say?"

"Nothing, I was talking to Rita."

He snorted. "Nice to know you have a *friend*."

Red cringed inwardly at how close to the truth that statement hit. Rita was more friend than machine. She'd shared everything with her. It was much easier to do that than to face the constant rejection of the team. Red stepped around the body and away from the blood to clear her senses. The perfume still wafted on the air and the taint of death strengthened. It might be nothing, but . . .

She swiveled to face Bannon. "We have another crime scene. One that's not been reported yet or maybe not even discovered."

He scowled. "I don't think so. The initial scan of the area only showed five unknowns."

Red shot Bannon a look that she hoped said *You can shove that navcom up your ass, because I know what I'm talking about,* before sprinting across the field.

"Where in the hell are you going? Get back here! That's an order, damn it!"

"Gina, you really shouldn't disobey a direct order," Rita chastised. "It could impair your spotless record."

Red hesitated at Rita's words, then shook her head and kept going. Bannon continued to shout. She ignored him, following the flowery scent of the perfume as it zigzagged in the air. She stopped when she lost the trail, waiting for the wind to shift so she could pick up the scent again. She could hear Bannon's heavy breathing coming from behind her, his footfalls near silent, given his size.

Good.

At least he wasn't pigheaded enough not to follow her. The rest of the team wouldn't be far behind. Procedure dictated they fan out and search if a team member suspected a secondary crime scene.

The scent became oppressive as Red entered the edge of the dead, leafless forest. What few animals' sounds remained quieted at the team's presence. A ghostly shiver started between her shoulder blades and traveled down her spine. This place was creepy and . . . *familiar*. The urge to turn around and flee was strong. Her sense of duty was the only thing that kept her rooted in place.

A shout came from the right, confirming Red's worst suspicions. Damn! She'd been hoping to be wrong, even if it meant losing face.

Red made her way toward the team and immediately spotted the corpse. "What in the hell happened to her?"

The body of a young woman who appeared to have been mauled by animals lay sprawled on a barren patch of blood-stained ground. Her curly auburn hair matted against her head from where the blood and brains had dried. Her ears had been ripped off, leaving two gaping holes behind. The tips of her fingernails were scattered around a ten-foot radius, letting the tactical team know she'd fought hard for her life.

"Good for you," Red murmured.

There was a wide aperture where her throat used to be. Bits of flesh were ripped from her body, exposing bone and sinew. There was no way to determine her weight; too much of her was missing. Her clouded blue eyes remained open wide, capturing her frightened expression.

Red turned away as a wave of grief swept over her. Someone was without a sister, a daughter, or a mother today, their lives changed forever. Unfortunately, she knew how that felt firsthand. Red pushed her thoughts aside. She couldn't afford to lose her objectivity.

Bannon's gaze narrowed as he watched her survey the scene. "How in the hell did you know about this?" he muttered between clenched teeth, pointing at the woman's body.

She glowered. "Gut feeling." Red ran a trembling hand through her thick black ponytail. What was she supposed to say—that she smelled her on the wind when no one else had? Not a chance. She didn't know how she knew certain things, only that she did. Doctors blamed it on possible radiation poisoning in the womb, but Red wasn't so sure. A lot of kids had gone through exposure during gestation and turned out perfectly normal. *Special,* her grandfather had said.

Red didn't feel very special at the moment: more

like a freak of nature, which was exactly how her team viewed her. She looked at the men gathering evidence. Wary eyes stared back.

The fact that she had special abilities should've scared the shit out of her, but it didn't. Red accepted it, as much as she could truly accept societal shunning. Her abilities were one of many reasons the team kept their distance from her. She scared them and she knew it.

Being a woman didn't help.

Bannon turned to face Red. "The *only* reason I'm not reporting this incident to the commander and naming you as prime suspect is because your DNA isn't at the crime scene."

She slanted her head. "I'm sure your decision wouldn't have anything to do with the fact that the commander is my grandfather, would it?"

Bannon's face flushed. "I always knew you were a bitch, but this is ridiculous."

Red snorted. She'd been called worse throughout the years.

"It's not natural to be able to sniff out a body. You aren't a goddamned dog. So explain to me how in the hell you did it if you didn't have prior knowledge of the crime."

"Who said I smelled her?"

"I'm not a fucking idiot," he snapped. "I saw you sniffing the air."

Red wasn't about to touch that one, no matter how tempting. "Let me get this straight—you think I killed this woman and then pretended to find the body? Is this before or after I planned the shootout with the unknowns?"

"Fuck off." He raised his thick middle finger for emphasis.

"You really *are* an asshole, Bannon."

Bannon opened his mouth to respond again, but Red cut him off before he could utter a single word. "We're near the northern half of the Republic of Arizona, correct?"

He nodded.

"In all likelihood, the unknowns crossed the boundary to the south, given the trace recovered thus far."

"That's a fair assumption."

"So what's the name of the nearest border town? I'd like to check it out and see if they've been having a problem with feral animals, along with illegal boundary crossings." She shrugged. "You never know. I might get lucky."

"Why don't you ask your *friend* Rita to check for the town name? She seemed to have all the answers a minute ago."

"Rita's geographical locator file is currently malfunctioning." She flushed.

"Fell on it again, huh? How many times does this make?"

"Exactly forty-six," Rita chirped.

Red closed her eyes and counted to ten before opening them again.

Bannon grunted out what may have been a laugh, then punched a button at his wrist. He shaded the screen with his hand and squinted. "The nearest town is Nuria. It's thirty klicks south of here, not far from where Old Phoenix used to be. The local sheriff is a man named Morgan Hunter." He chuckled. "Good luck getting help from him. He's not exactly known for being cooperative with IPTT. In fact, if this report is correct, he's a territorial bastard like most republic sheriffs."

"Leave that to me."

Bannon snickered. "I suppose you could always spread your legs for him . . . if you remember how."

The team members around them laughed, then tried covering the noise with coughs when she met their gazes.

"Your blood pressure is rising, Gina. You must calm down," Rita warned.

Red turned back to Bannon. Her fists hurt from clenching them. Was punching a senior officer in the face worth a mark on her record? No, damn it. "Only you would come up with something so vulgar."

"What can I say? It's a gift." Bannon grinned, flashing white teeth against his tan skin. "But hey, if you want to go traipsing around in the backwoods of some boundary town, be my guest. We're a tactical team, not pest control."

She lowered her voice. "You've heard the rumors floating around about the existence of the *Others*."

His brow rose. "You can't be serious."

Red mirrored his expression.

Bannon's face twisted. "You're talking about myths. Faceless monsters that don't exist. The old government did *not* experiment with people's DNA. It was just a story passed around by a bunch of paranoid conspiracy theorists. Next you're going to tell me you believe in the bogeyman."

"That's uncalled for."

"You're the one who suggested it." He threw his

arms up in disgust. "Hell, I can't believe I'm surprised, since you spend your time conversing with your navcom like it's a real person."

"I'm merely suggesting alternate possibilities. Everyone knows that radiation poisoning has caused minor mutations."

"Is that the excuse you're using these days?" he asked.

Red glared.

Bannon sobered. "You are not talking about minor mutations. You're talking about genetically engineered monsters that no one has ever seen." His expression turned to utter disbelief. "I don't know why I bother."

"But—" Red said.

"Let me finish." He gave her a look that brooked no argument. "We've identified no human DNA on site, except for the victim. The fluid scan gave us a positive hit on a Lisa Solomon." He looked at the vidscreen, then back at the body. "The image looks the same, give or take a few missing pieces." Bannon smirked. "At least they left the good parts," he said, glancing at the woman's exposed genitals. "The findings are conclusive enough for me. As far as I'm concerned, once cleanup arrives, this case is closed."

"You can't do that."

He laughed. "Oh yes I can."

"I know these bites resemble an animal attack, but the bite depth seems off."

"Are you suddenly an expert on carnivorous mammals?" Bannon asked.

"No, but I know enough to know that there's something odd about this whole scene." Red waved her arms around to encompass the area. "Look around. There are no fur deposits or fecal spoors nearby. The animals didn't *fly* here."

"You may have noticed there aren't any footprints either. The ground is too hard to leave any behind." He stomped his booted feet for emphasis. No dirt rose up from the cracked earth. "See what I mean?" he asked.

"But she's been ripped apart, including her clothes."

Bannon groaned in frustration. "That's what animal packs do. They feed. Haven't you ever viewed the vid-footage?"

Red shook her head. "They don't eat clothes."

"We've located her clothing. It wasn't eaten. Well, at least not much. It had traces of canine saliva on it from multiple donors. Solomon probably wandered too close to the woods. Many people like to come to places like this and reminisce about the 'good old days.' God only knows why," he scoffed, running a beefy hand over his buzz cut.

Red ignored his explanation. "Don't you think there's something strange about this crime scene? I don't believe this woman would come into the woods alone without at least carrying repel spray."

"Sorry, but being stupid isn't a crime," Bannon said. "You may not like it, but the evidence rules out foul play having been committed here. You're the only person who has a problem with this scenario. I suggest you let it go. That's an order. You know, one of those things you refuse to follow."

Red's gaze narrowed. "I can't let it go." She took a step forward and stared down at the remains of the woman. "She deserves better than to be a feast for a roving pack of predators—not that I believe for a second that's what happened here. Her family deserves the truth."

"You don't even know if she has a family. According to the navcom—" He pressed another button. "—she's single."

Red's fists clenched again as she fought the urge to bloody Bannon's nose. "That doesn't mean her parents aren't wondering where she is."

"Parents? Hell, a labor farm could've created her. Without the bar code, you can't tell the difference these days. I came this close," he pinched his thumb and forefinger together for emphasis, "to fucking one of those clones and didn't even know it." Bannon shuddered in mock horror.

"She *has* family," Red whispered, rubbing her hands along her arms and ignoring his asinine comment.

"We'll know soon. If we hadn't been able to identify her by her registered DNA, we would've removed her and tagged her as an unknown. More and more are turning up these days, the filthy little beggars. Worse than cockroaches if you ask me. That's what they get for sneaking past the boundary and refusing to register with a republic. There's a reason we have rules for everything." Bannon turned and bellowed an order to an underling to do a background check on Lisa Solomon to see if she had any connection to the unknowns.

"She's not affiliated with the unknowns," Red said.

"Funny, I never took you for being an unknown sympathizer."

"I'm not and you know it." She snarled.

"There's no room for crusaders on this team," he said.

"You and I both know this isn't right." Red crossed her arms over her chest. "You're burying this case so that you don't have to do any real investigative work."

"There's nothing to investigate. The facts refute your theory," he said, tapping orders into his navcom. "Give me one strand of evidence. Anything at all to back your claim."

She remained silent.

"That's what I thought," he said.

Red reached out and grabbed his arm, stopping his movement. His muscles flexed and heated beneath her fingertips. "You're not being fair," she said softly.

He glanced down at her hand and something flared momentarily in Bannon's pale blue eyes. Shocked by what she'd seen, Red released him abruptly.

Bannon's expression cooled. "Life's not fair, but what are you going to do? If you want to stay, suit yourself. You'll have to look into this on your own time. I'm not wasting the team on a wild animal chase."

chapter four

S ituated in what used to be grasslands, the gold dome of the International Police Tactical Team (IPTT) Headquarters rose like a 150-foot-tall leviathan out of the dead prairie. Massive concrete dormitories, which housed a thousand people each, jutted out like spokes on a bicycle wheel from a central hub. Living quarters were broken down between officers, trainees, and team members, with officers receiving a spacious twenty-by-twenty private living area.

The dome protected the entire complex from the brunt of the sun and regulated the ambient temperature. Carefully cultivated plants dotted the landscape within the biosphere to give life inside the bubble a semblance of normality.

Red entered the imposing military structure via a twenty-person EDS shuttle, since her two-seater transport had been damaged in the firefight. The electrodynamic technology had been developed in the twentieth century for Maglev trains, which used high-temperature superconductors in conjunction with magnets in order to run. The EDS technology had been altered several times since then in order to eliminate the use of tracks and increase speed. The added boost allowed the tactical team to get anywhere on the North American continent within five hours or less. From the Republic of Arizona it had taken three hours to reach IPTT, located in what used to be northern Montana and Alberta, Canada.

Three very long hours with Bannon bitching in her onboard headset the whole way. Red rolled her neck, trying to ease the tension knotting her shoulders as she strolled out of the docking area toward the central hub. The man loved the sound of his own voice.

Rows of stainless-steel beams, like silver incisors clenching a kill, marked the entrance to headquarters. The thick sloping, lead-flaked outer glass walls appeared vaguely pyramidal in origin, but the reality was much more mundane. The glass filtered the sun's harsh rays while the sloped walls helped dissipate blasts from hydrogen car bombs and other projectiles.

Started in the year 2010 during the last world war—which brought about the dissolution of countries and the formation of self-governing republics—the IPTT was in its 150th year of existence. The agency's main job was to curtail open aggression between the republics.

At one hundred thousand square miles each, the republics took up 70 percent of the land mass in the world. The other 30 percent encompassed no-man's-land, a place of lawlessness and utter chaos. These areas were so dangerous that boundary walls had been erected around them to keep the peace.

Due to the constant threat of upheaval each republic

created its own unique computer chip, which was used to identify its citizens. People could travel freely from place to place as long they were registered with one of the republics. If too many registered individuals from one republic crossed a border checkpoint into another, it would be considered an act of aggression and IPTT would step in, whether the republic wanted its help or not.

This didn't help its popularity around the world, but since the team had gathered 90 percent of the weapons left over after the war, no one said much in protest.

Along with peacekeeping duties, the tactical team was also responsible for boundary patrol and handled most of the unusual criminal cases.

Murder, having been all but eliminated, qualified as unusual. Killing unknown individuals fell into the acceptable action category and wasn't considered murder due to the unknowns' lack of registration with a republic. As far as the world was concerned, unknowns did not exist.

Red strode to the weapon detectors, noting the extra guards posted nearby. It wasn't drill day, so what were they doing here? She began to disarm, crinkling her nose at the sharp mint odor the A.I. filtration system pumped into the air to keep everyone alert.

She laid her laser pistols down first onto the conveyor belt, followed by Rita, her malfunctioning navcom, her pencil bombs, emergency oxygen inhaler, ultrasonic whistle, throwing knives, and rib splitter, then stepped into the arched scanner.

A green beam shot down from above, slowly traveling the length of her body before shutting off. A machine located on the other side of the scanner spat a printout through a thin slot.

Red slipped Rita back on and grabbed the synthetic paper before gathering her weaponry. She scanned the document. Her vitals were on target. The only marker readings that spiked were from her bloody combat boots. She paused to stare at the readouts that represented McCallan's and Lisa Solomon's DNA. Neither one had deserved to die.

She glanced down at the offending objects on her feet. She'd have the boots incinerated immediately. Red didn't want to consider what number this pair would make. Pretty soon the commander, grandfather or not, would dock her pay.

A hatch to her right opened. Red removed her boots and dropped them inside the container. The unit closed with a slight hiss. A pair of sterile blue booties sprung out of a tube next to the incinerator. She slipped them on and continued inside, heading toward her desk, trying hard to ignore the snickers coming from her fellow team members who'd caught sight of her feet.

"Gina, your feet are not properly protected," Rita chastised.

"I know, *Mom.*"

"I am not your mother. It is biologically impossible for me to have created you."

Red rolled her eyes. "I'm aware of that," she said, shaking her head and crumpling the readout in her fist. She dropped the document in a recycle bin.

The console to her compunit sat atop the flat three-by-five metal table that served as her desk and work space. A cursor blinked, reminding her that the UID report waited for her to fill it out. Red sat down and tapped a finger on the keys as she considered what to write. Maybe some synth-chocolate would help her think.

She opened the drawer, pushing aside her personal items to see if she'd buried any chocolate near the bottom.

"Your body is giving off a cravings signal," Rita said.

"It's not a crime to need something sweet."

"If you're searching for the chocolate, you've already eaten it . . . along with thirty-five other bars in the past two weeks."

"Terrific." Nothing like a diet reminder to kill a craving, Red thought, taking one last look under her throwing knives just to be sure.

Pushing the blades back into place, she spied her comlink, which allowed anyone in the building to contact her directly without having to route the call through the old phone systems. Red considered ignoring the device, but thought better of it. It *was* mandatory after all, and she did follow *some* orders. She slipped the oval plug into her ear, then removed the navcom from her wrist.

"Rita, you need to wait here," she said, placing it in the drawer.

"I cannot assist you if you are not wearing me."

Without her, Red felt naked. "You can't assist me period when you're broken," she said, rubbing her empty wrist.

"That is a valid point, but—"

"I'll put in a call for repairs. Be back in a few." Red slammed her chocolate-free drawer shut, cutting off

Rita's rebuttal, and began to type in a repair order. She didn't need to put in any details, just her name. The tech team would know what it was about the second they received the request.

The comlink earpiece clicked on. She heard a deep intake of breath and knew who it was before her grandfather spoke. "I want you to come to my office immediately. We have to talk." His clipped voice left no room for argument.

Red weighed her options. She could sneak out and claim exhaustion. She was truly beat, so it wouldn't be a total lie. She stood, eyeing the distance to the nearest exit. Maybe if she moved fast enough she'd make it.

"Don't bother trying to slip away, Gina. I know you're at your desk and I know you can hear me." Humor softened his tone.

The man must be psychic.

Red rested her hands on the keyboard and closed her eyes. She wasn't prepared to discuss the case with her grandfather. He would only agree with Bannon. And she wasn't ready to hear that right now. She opened her mouth to respond, but he cut her off.

"That's an order, young lady."

She groaned and blew out an exaggerated breath. The officers around her looked up and then quickly away as Red made eye contact. What did they think? That if they stared at her too long she would turn them to stone like a raven-haired Medusa? If she had that kind of power, Bannon would already be the new centerpiece for the lobby, peeing out recycled water.

"Right this minute!" the voice in her earpiece barked.

She jumped. So much for putting off the inevitable.

Red rounded the corner of the long hall that led to her grandfather's office and froze, her gaze locking on the dark-haired man shaking Bannon's hand. Was that Roark Montgomery? *The* Roark Montgomery? What was he doing here? It must be important if he took time out of his busy campaigning schedule to drop in to IPTT. She took a deep breath to steady her nerves and stood a little straighter. She didn't want to get caught slouching. It wasn't every day you encountered a living legend.

One of the best marksmen to ever grace the halls of the tactical team, Roark had single-handedly changed the training system so its members could become the most elite team in the world. His accuracy record remained unbroken. A terrific speaker with charisma enough for ten men, Roark had parlayed that success, using his strength and natural leadership to move into politics. Rumor had it that he was trying to unite the republics.

Roark's dark head dipped toward Bannon as the men shared a private joke. The laugh he expelled rumbled like a sonic boom of pure energy. If anyone could bring the republics together, it would be him. Montgomery certainly had her vote.

Red tilted her chin higher and squared her shoulders before continuing down the hall toward her grandfather's office. The two men hadn't noticed her yet.

"You have my support," Bannon said, releasing the politician as Red neared.

"I appreciate it, Lieutenant. The continuation of the tactical team is a top priority for me. I won't forget you when I unite the republics. I can always use a man like you as extra security."

"Thank you, sir." Bannon grinned, his eyes flashing with the myriad of possibilities his new position could bring.

Power-hungry bastard.

Red's stomach clenched as something close to envy wound its way into her system. She walked down the lead-encased corridor, her footfalls whispering softly on the ancient marble floor.

Roark Montgomery looked up and smiled at her. "Lieutenant," he said in greeting before dropping his gaze to her feet. "Nice booties."

Red flushed. She'd forgotten all about her shoes. So much for making a good impression. She continued on without a word, wishing that the floor would open up and swallow her.

A set of wooden doors marked the end of the hall. Her grandfather often spoke of how prevalent wood was back in the *old* days, before the thinning ozone coupled with the last war all but annihilated outdoor forests and the oxygen generating machines became a necessity.

She ran her hand over the smooth surface, the intriguing sensation both familiar and foreign at the same time. What had the dead world looked like covered with trees? She closed her eyes a moment and tried to imagine. All that lovely green must have been a remarkable sight.

Red straightened her black uniform, then raised her hand to knock on the door. A camera popped out of the wood in front of her face before she made contact and scanned her retina.

"Come in, Gina."

The door swung open with a barely audible swish. The harsh mint scent from the A.I. system fell away, unable to cling to her as Red stepped into the spacious old-world room. She glanced around the commander's office, admiring the holographs of the long extinct animals lining the walls. So many colors, so many species. Such a waste.

Floor-to-ceiling bookshelves held volumes of rare work, tomes made of paper and bindings. Nothing like the e-books she grew up reading. Red loved the smell of this room. Modern, yet ancient in origin. It was like a living, breathing extension of her grandfather.

Commander Robert Santiago sat behind a large maple desk, his silver-haired head buried in the synthetic documents clenched in his hands. He inhaled and his chest widened.

Red watched, smiling to herself. The man gave the best hugs. Not that he was free with his affection while on duty. Quite the contrary. He regarded her as he did any other tactical team member. If anything, he held Red to a higher standard than the others.

She stared at his face. A mole the color of his alabaster skin dotted his right cheek, giving him a perpetual tilt to his mouth. When he laughed, the contagious sound electrified the air. You couldn't help but join in. Red would carry that joyful sound with her forever.

He looked up as she strolled closer. "Where's Rita?" he asked, using the name she'd given the unit.

"I left her in my drawer."

"Why?"

"She's currently malfunctioning."

"Again?" Robert arched a brow. "When are you going to get a new A.I. unit? You've had that one for nearly twenty years. I'd be happy to have another one designed for you."

Red stiffened. "I like Rita. She'll be fine after a few minor repairs." Or at least Red hoped she would.

"Sometimes I wonder if that navcom knows you better than I do," he said, his eyes warming with affection. "Is there anything else you'd like to mention?"

"No, sir," Red said, knowing she wasn't going to get away with that answer.

He frowned as he glanced at her blue-bootie-covered feet. "Where are your combat boots?"

Red shrugged.

"Gina, not again. Do you know how many pairs this makes?"

She shook her head. Rita would know the answer.

"I'm going to have to dock your pay if you keep this up. Have them sanitized next time."

She pointed at the door and changed the subject. "I passed Roark Montgomery in the hall. What was he doing here?"

"Looking for support, like every other politician."

"He's better than most." Red smiled. "At least he supports the continuation of the tactical team. That's more than I can say for the other guy."

"Yes, he certainly backs our job. No surprise there seeing as though he used to be one of us, but I still couldn't in good conscience endorse him," he said, avoiding her gaze.

"What? Why? Roark is trying to unite everyone.

He's the best thing that's come out of the republics in years. Surely you can see that."

"I'm well aware of his credentials." Robert Santiago released an exaggerated breath. "But I have my reasons."

"I don't understand. The tactical team's backing would practically ensure his victory. How can you withhold that? The other guy wants to shut us down and leave law enforcement solely to the republics. It would be chaos."

"We're done talking about this, Lieutenant. You won't change my mind."

"But?"

"That's an order," he barked.

Red debated whether to argue, but then caught sight of his expression. Gone was her grandfather, in his place sat the commander. "Yes, sir," she said, biting her tongue.

He dropped some of the synth-papers he held onto the desk. "I've been reading Bannon's UID report. He seems to differ with your account."

"My account of what? I haven't finished my report yet." She shifted. "Besides, Bannon has an overactive imagination."

"As I recall, the same could be said about you." He arched a bushy white brow, his gaze growing distant. "I remember when you were five and were convinced that a dragon lived under your rest pad. I told you I would slay it. Your little lip trembled as you stopped me and said you'd take care of it yourself." He chuckled, shaking his head. "Some things never change."

"Grandpa . . ."

"Please take a seat, Gina."

Red sat in the burgundy monstrosity her grandfather called a chair. She sank two inches the second her body made contact with the cushions. Her bootie-covered feet dangled above the area rug, making her feel like a child. The same child who'd been frightened of the dragon under her bed.

The chair's thickness reminded Red of her rest pad and it took concerted effort not to doze off while he spoke. It had been a long day and it wasn't like she'd gotten any sleep after she awoke last night covered in blood.

Red shuddered, pushing the memory aside, when every fiber demanded that she report the incident. She loved her grandfather and normally shared everything, but relaying this bit of info was out of the question. The team already considered her an explosive about to detonate. The last thing she needed was to add fuel to their fears.

"Are you listening?"

Red jerked at the sound of his voice. "I'm getting ready to submit my report now," she said as she sat a little straighter and prayed that's what her grandfather had been discussing.

"Could you explain what occurred out in the field before you file your *permanent* report? I want to make sure your thoughts are concise. The review board looks at every duty-related item in an officer's background before promoting them to commander."

"You're not going anywhere for a long time, Grandpa."

"I can't run this place forever," he said, suddenly looking much older than his seventy-five years.

Red knew he warned her out of love, out of his need to protect. Couldn't he simply trust her judgment?

Robert Santiago had been grooming her since childhood to eventually take over his position. He'd pushed, cajoled, and fought for her when it came time to make the team. Red had pushed herself to the limits in order to please the only person she could call family. He had always told her that once their dreams came true and she became commander that Red would be safe and in charge of her future.

There was only one problem—being commander was never her dream. Not that Red would ever tell him. It meant too much to her grandfather. The truth would break his heart. And that was something that she refused to do . . . even if it meant putting her dreams on hold.

Her expression must have betrayed her thoughts because he added, "Please tell me exactly what happened. You know how I love a good story, particularly when it comes from my special girl."

Red shifted under his appraisal. He'd called her *special* again. Normally she relished his endearments, but not that one. She didn't want to be special. Not then. Not now. Not ever. She wanted to be normal like everyone else.

"I'm not making anything up or imagining things, if that's what you're suggesting," she said with certainty, needing to convince him. "My gut tells me there's more to Lisa Solomon's death than what the evidence states."

"Why do you think so?" He leaned forward and rested his chin on his hands. Red recognized the open expression. He was giving her the benefit of the doubt.

"The look of the scene, maybe. Perhaps, the alignment of her body. Her horrified expression." She paused to gather her thoughts. "The attack looked personal, and animal attacks aren't ever personal."

His face soured. "Yes, I've seen the photos. Quite gruesome. But we know death is oftentimes not pretty or clean."

"I'm used to seeing death." All emotion fled from Red's tone, until it was flat and lifeless like the void inside of her. "It doesn't bother me." *Anymore* floated in the air between them, left unsaid.

"Trying to save your mother and sister again?" he asked quietly. "Heaven rest their souls." There was no reproach in his voice, only sadness and resolve.

"Someone should have." Guilt swamped her. If only she'd been older, been at home instead of with her grandfather, then maybe they'd still be alive. Even as the thought filled her mind, Red knew if she'd been there she would be dead, too.

Robert Santiago sat back. "You can't save them, Gina. You never could," he said finally. "They're dead and recycled, so please stop trying."

Red's chest squeezed tight. She bit the inside of her mouth and tasted blood. "I know they're dead." The words choked in her throat nearly gagging her. There wasn't a day that went by that she didn't think about her family and what might have been. "I know I can't save Mom and Ann any more than I can save Lisa Solomon, but I can find out what happened to her. I can give her family some closure, even if I'll never have it myself."

"Is that what this is all about?"

She considered his question carefully. "No, it's not about me. It's about finding out the truth."

He nodded briefly. "Bannon says he believes Lisa Solomon was killed by wild animals. He even notes trace amounts of canine saliva. Said there were multiple contributors."

"That may be, but I don't know many animals beyond the two-legged variety that would take the time to undress their victims." Red shook her head. "Hell, even her ears were missing."

"Watch your language, young lady."

"Sorry, Grandpa." Red's face heated, but she continued. "Something out there frightened Lisa more than death. The crime scene is screaming at me to pay attention." She came to her feet, resting her fingertips on the edge of his desk. "I can't let this go."

"Okay." He held his hands up in surrender. "Before you make any rushed decisions, there's one more point I'd like to bring up."

Red gestured for him to continue.

"Bannon says you suggested the Others might have done it."

Crap! Red nearly croaked. "It was just a theory—I was desperate," she lied. "I couldn't let him dismiss the scene without further consideration."

He tsked. "You know that the Others don't exist. If they ever lived—and I'm not saying that they did—they'd all be dead by now."

"Just because their existence hasn't been proven yet doesn't mean they don't exist. Some of them had to breed. That means their grandkids or great-grandkids could still be around."

"If I remember the old stories correctly from childhood, the Others couldn't conceive," he said, his gaze dropping away from hers.

Red frowned. She'd never heard that before, but it didn't matter because she wasn't the only one who thought the Others might still be around. "Even Roark Montgomery has hinted at the link between the Others and the unknowns. He believes the Others are assisting the unknowns with illegal boundary crossings. They can't do that, if they don't exist."

"Another good reason not to endorse him. The last thing we need is a return to our hate-mongering days." Regret and something else colored his features. For the first time, her grandfather seemed evasive. "I'd like to believe you. You know I would, but I'm afraid I am going to have to side with Bannon on this case. You've presented no facts or DNA evidence here that would indicate murder by a human being. Bannon explained his theory on the woman's missing clothes. You've given me impressions and feelings. The law doesn't recognize those. I can't act on your gut, Gina." Robert Santiago stood, his gaze filled with compassion. "I know you understand."

"Yes, sir," she replied reluctantly. Red understood all too well. He couldn't have the future commander entering reports about the Others. She'd lose what little credibility she had. Unfortunately, that logic didn't douse the fiery passion for justice burning in her stomach or the tightness in her chest that kept telling her that she had to do something. The woman's frightened face flashed before Red's eyes. She could not turn her back on Lisa Solomon—even if everyone else did.

"I'll expect your report to concur with Bannon's," Robert said, straightening the papers in front of him.

Red stepped back, smoothing a trembling hand over her hair. "I understand that you're only doing your job, but now I have to do mine," she said, feeling the emotions churn inside of her, threatening to overwhelm. "I have some break time coming to me, do I not?" The question was a courtesy. She'd never taken recreational time off, so she had a lot accrued.

"You're certainly long overdue for a vacation." He punched a button on his compunit. "You have six weeks available. The max you can accumulate."

"Good, three days should do it."

He stilled. "You're not thinking about doing anything impetuous, are you?"

"No, of course not, Grandpa."

"Glad to hear it. For a second you had me worried." He gave her a nervous smile.

She snorted. "You know me."

"Yes, I do." He laughed. "That's why I asked."

Red reached out and squeezed his hand in reassurance. "I think I'm going to check out Nuria—in the Republic of Arizona—to see if they're having any problems. You know how lax those boundary towns are about reporting incidents."

His laughter faded. "Do you think that's wise? Republics don't like the tactical team sticking their noses into their business, especially when they haven't been called."

"I know, but I have to do it for my own peace of mind."

He sighed, rubbing a hand over his face. "Please be careful. Boundary towns aren't exactly welcoming places and you will have *no* jurisdiction. If you go there, you have to go as Gina Santiago, not Lieutenant Santiago."

"I understand. I'm only going to give it a look-see. Strictly hands off. I'll be back before you've noticed that I've gone."

"I doubt that."

Red smiled reassuringly, but his expression remained shrouded in worry. "You know I can take care of myself. I slayed that dragon, remember? Besides, I learned from the best." She winked and released her grandfather's hand. "You taught me all there is to know about the criminal element. I'm not concerned about encountering unknowns." *Or Others,* she added silently.

"I didn't teach you everything, special one." She heard him murmur softly as she headed for the door. "There are worse things in this world than unknowns. I pray you don't find them—and that they don't find you."

chapter five

Situated in a low desert valley, surrounded by the rubble remains of bare mountains, Red smelled the dying town before she caught sight of any of the buildings. The odor of decay wafted in the air, polluting her nostrils and burning her throat. Located twenty miles north of what used to be Phoenix, Arizona, the municipality of Nuria resembled every other small dusty boundary fence town that was scarce on jobs and brimming with poverty.

Solar panels twinkled like displaced stars from the rooftops, giving the appearance of life, but several of the buildings sat empty, closed signs barring their sealed front doors. Windows had been shattered, leaving glass skeletons behind. All the town was missing was the sound of a death rattle. Red was sure that if she tried really hard, she'd be able to hear one. There were no biospheres here like the ones built to enclose and protect IPTT and the larger cities from high levels of radiation exposure. Nuria had been left to fend for itself like all the other boundary towns, which explained why the architecture reflected a different time, a different age.

Red was amazed they'd managed to survive the last world war with so many of the original buildings intact. Not many places could boast of such a feat. It was as if the world had forgotten about them.

Although the houses appeared antiquated with their whitewashed window frames and brick walls, Nuria's streets were paved with the latest synthetic green tarp scientists had designed to accommodate the sun's punishing rays and protect the tread on most civilian hydrogen vehicles.

Red couldn't really blame them for choosing that practical option over the more expensive biodome. Nuria might not have many businesses, but the ones that did exist needed a way for their employees and customers to reach them.

She hadn't been able to find much information about the town before she left. Most of the buildings weren't recorded in her navcom, so it made using Rita damn near useless. Nuria proper didn't exist on any map. That was the trouble with small towns, they popped up overnight and faded just as quickly. It was a waste of manpower to keep track of them, so IPTT didn't. And obviously neither did the Republic of Arizona, since it wasn't listed there either beyond its care center.

Despite the oppressive heat and the sweat trickling between her breasts, Red smiled. Her grandfather would feel at home in this place that time forgot. She could almost picture him strolling down the sidewalk, a blissful smile brightening his face as he perused the architecture.

At some point, the town must have had a booming economy, but you couldn't tell that by looking at it today. The fringe owned it now. It wouldn't be long before Nuria took its last breath and expired, swallowed by the ever-present boundary area and encroaching desert sands.

As if on cue, a strong wind blew dust over the road, covering a portion of the green tarp. Red hit a button inside her car to clear the grit off her windshield.

She drove into the heart of Nuria, bypassing the quaint side streets. She wasn't here to sightsee, no matter how tempting. The main drag through town brightened considerably. Shops lining the road aimed their wares at weary travelers and locals alike. Cheerful hand-painted signs hung above each building, indicating what could be found inside. They were a marked contrast to the sealed storefronts she'd driven past moments ago.

Specially treated one-way lead mirrors stood in place of traditional windows, allowing shop customers inside the ability to look out, but preventing anyone from gazing in.

Supposedly the material served a twofold purpose— it preserved privacy and kept the radioactivity from passing through the windows. Red decided the mirrors had more to do with privacy, since humans either were born immune to the higher doses of radiation or received gene therapy in the womb to counteract the poisoning. Being naturally curious, she found the visual impairment an annoyance.

Red parked her vehicle and pulled the sunshades from her eyes, peering at the townsfolk. Several people passed by and smiled, nodding their heads in acknowledgment. She frowned and looked behind her. There was no one there.

Confused, Red slowly turned back to face the

people. She had never encountered a small town where the residents were actually friendly to strangers. Quite the contrary. The last time she'd entered a boundary town a laser pistol firefight resulted. She'd prepared herself for outright hostility, not an open welcome. As much as she appreciated the change, Red wasn't quite sure how to handle the situation.

She glanced at her clothing. Her black T-shirt and pants screamed tactical team and didn't exactly conceal her pistol. Yet the people seemed unfazed, like they were used to the tactical team's presence, which was impossible, considering it had been twenty years since the team's last operation in this area. She'd had to look it up to be sure, since Red had been an eight-year-old child at the time.

Another couple strolled by, their faces just as open, just as friendly. Dressed in typical boundary town clothing, the couple's sand-colored fatigues blended seamlessly into the surroundings. Red bobbed her head in acknowledgment. There was something strange about this place. Pleasant, but strange.

Red slipped her shades back on and strode down the sidewalk until she reached what she assumed was the town center. A small park with benches and faux trees formed a perfect square. There were play areas set up for children and picnic tables for family gatherings. No one was around. Most people avoided afternoon sunlight due to its intensity.

She glanced at the swings, which squeaked lightly in the hot desert breeze. Red could almost hear the ghosts of laughter echoing in the emptiness. She was about to return to the car when the sensation that she was being watched hit her.

The skin at the back of her neck prickled as she felt a heated gaze scroll over her shoulders and down her body. Red straightened immediately, tension thrumming all the way to her toes. Her hand automatically reached for her weapon, but she stopped short of withdrawing it from its holster. She wasn't in hostile territory surrounded by enemies—she was in Nuria's town center. She would do well to remember that.

Yet someone was watching her, following her movements as she strolled around the square. She took a deep breath, but smelled nothing. Whoever it was had taken care to remain downwind. It could be one of the people she'd passed, who'd gotten curious and had come back for a second look, but Red didn't think so.

This *seemed* different, more intense.

It felt . . . predatory.

Male.

She paused in the middle of the sidewalk and rolled her shoulders, letting whoever was watching know that she was aware of his presence. Red forced herself to release her weapon. The stalker wasn't a threat—at least in the physical sense.

She fought the instinct to turn and confront the individual. Her body trembled from the effort. The last thing Red needed was a skirmish upon arrival in town. She knew better than to piss in someone else's water reserve, especially when that someone may have the information she needed.

Breathe. Let it go. You have no jurisdiction. You're here to look around, remember?

Red pressed on reluctantly, ignoring the urge to glance back. She refused to give whoever it was the satisfaction of knowing that she was rattled. Besides,

she had things to do. Locating shelter was the first order of business. She had plenty of credits saved, so
finding refuge shouldn't be difficult.

Even small boundary towns housed a variety of
share spaces. Once Red secured a room, she'd track
down the local sheriff, Morgan Hunter. If there were
murders or strange things happening in his town, he
would know about it. After a cursory glance at his stats
back at headquarters, she wasn't looking forward to
the meeting.

Some people on the tactical team considered republic law-enforcement officers inferior to their international counterparts, but not Red. She knew better.
Some of the best tactical team enforcers she'd met on
the job were recruited from small towns within the
various republics.

Morgan had been recruited by IPTT, but ultimately turned the position down—something all but
unheard of at tactical team headquarters. Instead,
he'd returned to Nuria and took the position of sheriff. He'd been on the job ever since.

She pulled Rita out of her tote and slipped the
newly repaired navcom on her wrist. Once again Red
opened the electronic file on Morgan Hunter. She
needed to know more. What he looked like would be
a good place to start. His documentation listed that
he'd been on the job for the past fifteen years; a long
time to spend with no opportunity for advancement.

Red pressed the screen and an image of the sheriff
popped up. She blinked in disbelief, then hit the re-
fresh button. The picture remained unchanged. He
wasn't exactly what she'd been expecting, after Bannon called him an *uncooperative territorial bastard*.

He was younger—much younger—and handsome in a wholly exotic, battered warrior kind of way.

Red stared at the image, taking in his rugged cleft chin, savage mouth, dark wavy hair, and stern no-nonsense expression. His nose appeared to have been broken at some point and reset the old-fashioned way. He hadn't bothered to use enhancers to hide the injury as most people with imperfections routinely did. *This is a typical enforcer image,* Red told herself, ignoring her heart's sudden acceleration and the sweat forming on her palms.

She rubbed her hands along her pants, then highlighted his face so that the image would zoom in. The move brought his golden eyes to the forefront. Red had never seen a color so vibrant and rich. Like molten honey that had been kissed by the sun, they practically glowed. There was no way they could be real, but she knew that they were . . .

Captivating.

The word came to Red's mind before she could brush it aside. Strange, she'd never thought of a man as captivating before. She gazed at the image, allowing herself time to study his features. What made Morgan Hunter so different? Red tried to recall the last time she'd noticed a man. Her mind blanked like a virus-ridden compunit screen.

If she couldn't remember the last time she'd noticed a man, Red didn't even want to think about how long it had been since her last physical joining. Twenty missions ago? Forty? More?

She grimaced. It had been too long since she'd experienced anything other than a computerized body toy. Not that they weren't good, with their advanced

A.I. orgasm-inducement system, but they'd never replace the real thing. There was just something about having a man's sweaty body resting above her as he rolled his hips, impaling her with his . . .

Red quivered at the thought, her eyes unconsciously drawn back to Morgan Hunter.

After Bannon's smart-assed comment about her spreading her legs, Morgan was the last person she needed to be thinking about in that way. She'd just have to stick with the body toys awhile longer. She wasn't here to get laid, so her dry streak wouldn't be ending anytime soon, captivating man or not.

"Gina, I'm noting a change in your autonomic system," Rita chimed. "Should I be concerned about outside stimuli? I can have the team dispatched to Nuria within three hours and two minutes. You'll have to manually input your coordinates. I am unable to pinpoint your exact location."

"No! That won't be necessary." Red grimaced at being caught ogling what would probably turn out to be an old image. Boundary town law enforcers were notorious for not updating their pictures. Some were nearly thirty years old. "But I can't find you," Rita said. "There do not seem to be markers or streets. You are in Nuria, correct?"

"Yes, I'm in Nuria. It's okay, Rita. The town hasn't been mapped."

"How will I assist you in locating markers, if the town has not been properly recorded?"

Red laughed. "You won't. I'll have to do it the old-fashioned way and use my eyes."

"This is highly irregular," Rita said, sounding

more than a little perturbed. "I recommend reporting this situation to headquarters immediately. You could be in danger."

Red shook her head. She wasn't in danger. At least not yet. There was no way she would report this non-incident to headquarters. Her grandfather was looking for an excuse to send in the troops and bring her back. "Power down to standby. I promise I will call you if I need you."

"Very well." The A.I. unit made a chirping sound as it powered down. Red shut the viewer screen, ignoring the flare of disappointment she felt as Morgan's image faded. She chided herself for having such foolish thoughts in the first place. She was here to find out who—or what—killed Lisa Solomon. Nothing more, nothing less. And she'd do just that, right after she located shelter for the night.

During the day, boundary towns were generally unfriendly. At night, they could be downright hostile.

Red began to explore the town. If Nuria had amenities, she wasn't seeing them, but she had managed to pass the same fake bush four times. She should have come better prepared. Eventually, she ferreted out a few necessities—an extra water canteen, a small food dispensing machine, and a crude area map, which highlighted the local emergency care center. It didn't look far, so she decided to take a detour. She wasn't expecting trouble, but you couldn't predict those sorts of things.

She still hadn't managed to find a suitable share space yet, but she would. The first two she'd encountered had no cleansing units, and offered little beyond a communal sleep area. Red was used to staying out in the field on occasion with the tactical team, but not with a room full of strangers. What if someone accidentally woke her suddenly and she shot him? What if it was a child? Worse—what if she had another missing time episode? She still didn't know what had happened. She hadn't had one since, but that didn't mean they were gone for good.

She just couldn't take the chance.

Red glanced up and realized she was standing in front of the emergency care center. The entrance was plain with small gray letters indicating the building's purpose. She watched as people filed out, dressed in their medical uniforms. A few glanced her way. Most moved directly to the parking lot, more concerned with going home than with worrying about a stranger in town.

She entered as the last group exited. The main building seemed to consist of three wings lined with rooms. There were four emergency treatment areas off to the side and a nurse's station. The facility was large for a town this size.

It must treat the entire republic, not just Nuria. No wonder it was the only thing noted by the Republic of Arizona.

Red walked up to the first nurse she encountered, a jovial woman with short auburn hair and a round laugh-lined face, and asked to speak with the doctor in charge.

"What is your emergency?" she asked, eyeing Red from shoes to nose.

Red grinned. "I'd rather speak directly to the doctor, if you don't mind."

"You and all the other women in this town," she said, her eyes glittering with speculation.

"What?" Red asked, confused by the woman's statement.

"I'll page him," the nurse said, then pressed her ear and began to speak. Red hadn't noticed the com-link tucked there. It was all but hidden beneath her shaggy hair. "You can wait here. Dr. Hunter will only be a moment." She pointed to a row of uncomfortable-looking seats.

"Thank you."

Thirty minutes later a dark-haired handsome man with a casual rolling gait approached. He was talking with a child whose arm was in a sling. Tall and broad-shouldered with big hands, the man looked more suited to hard labor than to caregiving.

Maybe his job was to cleanse this building, Red thought.

"I better not see you back here again," he said, mussing the boy's brown curls.

"You won't, Doctor," the boy said, then rushed past Red and out the front door.

The man stopped in front of her. Red stood so he wouldn't tower over her. It didn't help. She craned her neck to look at him.

"You asked for me." He smiled, giving her clothing a cursory glance. His gaze hovered on her breasts a little longer than needed, before moving onto her face. "You don't look injured."

"That's because I'm not." She stepped forward. "You're Dr. Hunter?" Red asked, surprised that this man was a boundary town doctor. Most young medical professionals left for the cities the first chance they got. It was impossible to make a decent living otherwise. What was it about this town that made people want to stay?

He laughed. "Not what you expected, eh?"

"I didn't say that."

His smile spread. "You didn't have to. It's written all over your pretty face."

Red opened her mouth to contradict his assessment of her, but he cut her off before she could utter a word.

"Please, call me Kane."

"I'm Gina Santiago," she said, extending her hand.

He shook it, lingering, his warm palm enveloping hers. "Nice to meet you."

Red tried to pull back, but he didn't release her until he was ready. The brush of his fingertips sent a wave of awareness through her.

Kane grinned. "What can I do for you, Ms. Santiago?"

"I'm with the International Police Tactical Team. I thought it best to check in."

His smile wavered, but did not fall, much to his credit. Most people didn't bother to hide their distrust, but Kane did. "I'm honored to have the IPTT stop by our facility. Greta forgot to mention that small detail." A different nurse approached Kane and asked him to sign a comp-chart. He did so, but his gaze remained unerringly on Red.

His overt attention was a little disconcerting and Red fought the urge to step back. Her years of training were the only thing that kept her in place. There probably weren't many eligible females living in Nuria. That could explain the undue attention she'd received earlier from the townspeople and now from Kane. As a single female tactical team member, Red was used to being an oddity. Some things were the same no matter where you went.

Red waited until the nurse left before she continued to speak. "Actually, Dr. Hunter—"

"Kane," he corrected.

"Kane." Red acknowledged. "I'm here alone—in an unofficial capacity."

"Nuria is an odd choice, if you're trying to get away from it all. It's not exactly a travel destination. I mean it's quaint, if you like deteriorated historical structures, but—" He grinned. "—otherwise nondescript."

"Long story." She waved her hand dismissively. "I won't bore you with it. Suffice it to say, whenever I travel I like to meet the local doc in case I need patching up."

"Patching up? Are you expecting trouble?" His brow scrunched, then slowly lowered. "I can assure you that Nuria is a law-abiding town. We get mostly farm-related injuries."

"I have no doubt. No one is saying otherwise." Red hiked her bag higher onto her shoulder. "But I like to be prepared. So here I am."

"I suppose you're right, anything can happen this close to the boundary." Kane nodded. "If I can assist you in any way, let me know."

"I will, but to be perfectly honest, I hope I don't need you."

He laughed. "Fair enough."

"No offense," she added quickly.

"None taken." Kane winked.

Red turned to leave, but stopped short. "You wouldn't happen to know of a good share space in town, would you? My navcom is drawing a blank."

"Understandable, since we haven't been mapped. The republic has been threatening to do it for years, but it hasn't happened yet," Kane said. "Try Jesse Lindley's place. It's down a couple of blocks. Turn right on Evergreen, and then hang a left on Spruce. She's not the friendliest person you'll ever meet, but her share space is clean and well kept—the best in town."

"Sounds good, thanks." Red walked toward the front entrance. The doors slid open as she approached.

"Maybe I'll see you around," he called out after her, hope filling Kane's voice.

"I'm sure," she said with a shrug. "It's a small town."

He coughed. "That wasn't exactly what I meant."

Red glanced over her shoulder and grinned. "I know." She left the emergency care center to go find the share space. As handsome as Dr. Kane Hunter was, Red still found her thoughts drifting to the brooding image of Morgan Hunter.

Hunter? Hunter? She wondered if Kane was any relation to Sheriff Morgan Hunter. There was nothing in the file about it, but the boundary town files, as she knew, were woefully incomplete. Not that it mattered. She doubted the sheriff would be near as welcoming.

Red purchased a protein pack from the automated food dispenser she'd located earlier to still her growling stomach, and then headed to Jesse Lindley's place.

Jesse was a stocky cantankerous woman who ran a

water trader business along with the share space. She looked to be in her mid- to late fifties with gray hair, a deceptively open expression, and an eye patch. Red didn't bother asking how she got the latter. The fact that she had an eye patch and looked like a pirate out of the history e-books was all Red needed to know.

Jesse agreed to give her a room for fifty credits a week—a steep price, but well worth it. Red didn't bother to haggle for two reasons: one, the woman appeared to desperately need the credits; and two, a room above a water exchange was the best place to be to catch local gossip. Eventually everyone in town would come to get their water supplies.

Red climbed the stairs two at a time. The hall that led to her room was swathed from floor to ceiling in yellow and pale pink flowers. They'd been painted or stenciled on the walls. She couldn't tell which.

Several thick animal hide throws buffered the floors, silencing footsteps. She stared at the fur a second, but couldn't identify the species. Red resisted the urge to touch them and kept walking. The place was not quite what she'd been expecting after meeting Jesse. Somehow the words *soft* and *feminine* didn't quite capture her true essence.

She arrived at her door a moment later and placed her palm against the scanner. It hummed as it ran her IPTT identity through the Republic of Arizona's registrar system. A beep sounded when it finished. The door in front of her opened a second later.

Red entered the large square room with its cheery bright yellow walls and dropped her black duffel bag on the rest pad in the far corner. She sat beside the bag and bounced, testing the rest pad's firmness. It was hard. Not her preference, but it would do for a night or two.

She glanced around the space, shocked to realize her entire housing unit could easily fit inside this place with room to spare.

Another area jutted off from the main living space. Red walked to the doorway and ran her hand over a panel in the wall. A light came on. She could hardly believe it. Jesse had attached a cleansing unit to the room. This gave her an unusual amount of privacy for a public house. Water rationing had all but done away with old-world ideas of modesty.

Murmuring voices from below reached her sensitive ears. Several patrons had been gathering on the first floor when she checked in, making small talk while they waited at the chest-high bar for Jesse to fill their supplies. Red left her room and made her way down the stairs, hoping to catch them before they left.

She glanced around at the growing crowd, recognizing a few of the people she'd passed on the street earlier. Suddenly jumping into the fray and firing off questions, didn't seem like such a good plan.

Contrary to what she wished, this was not a sanctioned investigation, only a fishing expedition. At least she had six weeks of leave—not that she'd need them, but it meant there was no reason to hurry.

Direct questions wouldn't work here. One thing all boundary towns had in common was their tight-lipped mentality. Nuria may be friendly on the surface, but they didn't need or want help from the outside. Whatever happened here stayed here. That included wild animal troubles—and murder.

chapter six

Morgan Hunter smelled her long before he laid eyes on her. Like a cool breeze that alleviates intense heat, she blew into the gray dissecting unit, dispersing the odor of disinfectant and death, leaving the scent of lush, moist woman in her wake. All he could do was stand there and stare, what he was about to tell Jim Thornton completely forgotten.

The tension in the air thickened as his gaze locked with hers. Her eyes shined an unusual color—greenish gold. How long had it been since an unattached female entered his town, his territory? Morgan couldn't remember. He inhaled, closing his eyes a second as he reached out to her with his senses. There was something tantalizingly familiar about her. He nearly groaned.

Her gaze caressed him, starting at his boots and leisurely traveling up his legs and over his chest before settling back on his face. She might as well have raked him with her claws. His cock hardened instantly.

Beside him, Jim Thornton laughed, quickly muffling the sound with a cough.

Morgan stiffened. For a moment, her lush scent and dark beauty had distracted him from the fact that she was a tactical team member, but that moment had now passed.

He approached her, his long legs and casual gait eating up the distance between them. She made no attempt to acknowledge his position in the community by bowing her head or lowering her gaze. Strange and intriguingly alpha.

"Can I help you?" he asked, his voice rumbling close to a growl. Before he could stop himself, Morgan circled her and sniffed twice. She was beyond ripe.

"Do you have a cold?" she asked, following his movements with her eyes. He blinked. Why would she think such a thing? "No." Morgan's brow furrowed as he stopped in front of her. She hesitated, then stuck out her hand. "My name is Gina Santiago."

Morgan shook her hand, surprised by the calluses he could feel etching her palm. She obviously didn't work at a desk. He released her reluctantly, when every fiber of his being screamed to draw her close. "Is there something I can do for you, Miz Santiago? We don't normally get much attention from the tactical team. Looking for a donation? If so, I could've saved you a trip."

"Not hardly, but I'll keep you in mind for next year." She smiled and Morgan's knees almost buckled. "So you're aware of what I am."

"Of course." Morgan stepped closer, crowding her. Gina held her ground, showing no signs of submission. Her inaction both surprised and pleased him. "I spotted you coming a mile away. Even if I hadn't, half the town has called me since you arrived." His lips quirked. "You're big news." He gave her a cursory glance. "And now I see why."

Gina crossed her arms and glowered.

"I take it this isn't a social call," he added quickly.

"No." She glanced around the tiny room, her gaze landing on several of the lab assistants huddled in the corner.

Morgan followed her line of sight as it focused on the small viewing screen highlighting Roark Montgomery. Today he appeared to be pushing his platform on protecting the "blood purity" of the human race. He tried not to listen to the politician spew his racist venom about separating "true society" from the Others.

"Turn that crap off," Morgan snapped, glaring at the lab tech holding the remote.

Gina flinched.

A second later the screen dimmed and tense silence permeated the room.

"I guess I know who you'll be voting for come election time."

Morgan shot her a sharp glance. She couldn't possibly support that monster. Yet, from the expression on her face, he knew she did. Something wasn't right.

"Is there somewhere private we can talk?"

Morgan paused, not sure what to make of this woman. Finally, he nodded toward the door. "We can speak in my office."

He turned to leave. Her fingers curled around his bicep, sending warmth rocketing through his blood. His heart slammed against his ribs. Her touch was so soft, caressing—*familiar*. He tensed under her grip.

A vision of the erotic dream he'd had flashed in Morgan's mind. It couldn't be. Yet there was no mistaking his body's reaction.

If she could do that with a touch, what would happen when he spread her beneath him?

Morgan stilled. When had he decided he'd have her? Was it when he'd heard that she'd entered town or when he first laid eyes on her? He wasn't sure, but he had no doubt that he would.

"Before we go, is there anything of interest in there I should know about?" She pointed to the double doors leading to the dissecting lab.

Her question dashed his ardor and made him decidedly uneasy. "No, why?"

Gina rose to her toes and tried to look through the scratched windows. What in the hell was she doing now? Morgan squared his body, using his shoulders to block her view.

"Are you sure?" she asked.

If it wouldn't raise suspicion, he'd kick her cute ass out of town right now. Morgan quelled the urge. "Not unless the tactical team is suddenly interested in becoming involved with tracking the movements of the unknowns or our illegal boundary-crossing problem."

Gina bristled and slowly lowered her heels to the ground. "We do our best to patrol the area."

"Yeah, and we do the rest," he said, before adding, "Follow me."

Morgan led Red out the door and into the street. She half expected him to tell her to go to hell. She wouldn't have blamed him if he had. She probably would've if their circumstances were reversed.

They walked past a couple of outfitting shops before reaching his office. She barely glanced at the storefronts as they passed by. Her eyes had zeroed in and refused to leave his perfectly compact ass.

Morgan was a lean man with sinewy muscles, but in no way skinny. His shock of dark hair hung to his shoulders in wild disarray, a blatant disregard of law-enforcement grooming standards. Red wondered what other rules he ignored.

"Gina, your heart rate is accelerating again and the temperature of your skin is rising. Do you need assistance?" Rita chimed.

He glanced over his shoulder in time to catch her staring at his ass, and arched a brow. His spun-gold-colored eyes glittered with amusement. Their intensity sucked the breath from her lungs.

"Your palms are beginning to sweat and your nip—" It took two tries for Red to hit the right button and shut Rita off.

"She's been malfunctioning lately," Red lied, hoping that Morgan believed her.

The look he gave her made Red decidedly uncomfortable. What was it about the men in this town? She wasn't used to men looking at her *that* way. For that matter, she wasn't used to men noticing her at all. Most couldn't see past the uniform.

Kane and Morgan Hunter didn't have that problem. They paid far too much attention. For a heartbeat, Red feared what Morgan might see. Yet when he met her eyes again, his expression had changed.

Until that moment, Red hadn't known that it was

possible to simultaneously convey resentment and sexual desire. She found the ability disconcerting, especially since she had no doubt he'd done it on purpose.

And that, more than anything, pissed her off. She wouldn't allow him or anyone else to intimidate her. Red didn't scare easily. He would find that out the hard way. She opened her mouth to tell him, but he interrupted.

"I haven't seen one of those talking navcoms in years," he said.

She bristled.

"They don't make them like they used to. I wish I would've hung onto mine," he said, taking the fight right out of her. "We're here."

Morgan opened the door and waited for her to step inside, then led her to his office. The show of manners reminded Red of her grandfather, despite the decades' difference in their ages.

He signaled to a clerk and one of his deputies in the other room, before pressing a button to shut the door. "Please take a seat, Miz Santiago." He drew out her name, swirling it on his tongue like a sweet until she shivered in response. "Can I get you some water?"

"That would be great," she said, sitting in the chair nearest the desk so she could keep her back to the wall and her eyes on the door. An old habit that had kept her alive on more than one occasion.

Morgan's office was streamlined, much like the man. There were no personal touches, only the bare minimum in the way of furnishings. Whatever it took to function and nothing more.

White paint splashed the walls, while gray trim out-
lined the window and door frames. A row of vertical
buttons lined one wall, making the room look as if it
wore a shirt. Thin pad-less metal chairs banked a faux-
wood desk, leaving little in the way of comfort. A
couch that had seen better days was shoved in the corner, almost as an afterthought. Either Morgan didn't
receive a lot of visitors or he didn't want any.

Red decided it was the latter.

He pressed a button on the wall and a refrigeration
unit popped open with a hiss. Morgan reached inside
and grabbed two waters, then held them out. Their
fingers brushed as he handed her a canteen. Red's
hand shook and she almost dropped the water as tin-
gles from the innocent caress shot along her arm.

Red looked from her hand to his face, then pulled
away. It had been a long time since she'd felt more
than basic physical satisfaction from a man's touch.
The fact that Morgan's innocent caress managed to
affect her left her on edge.

"Thanks." She nodded, before taking a huge unla-
dylike gulp.

Morgan watched Gina Santiago from beneath his
lashes. He couldn't help but do so. She was stunning
and unclaimed—a very rare combination for a woman
her age these days. One that made her more valuable
than water in his mind.

His sex twitched at the thought of drinking her up.

He'd thumbed through a file on her history before
she'd come to the dissecting lab. The document didn't
compare to the woman. She'd pinned her ebony hair

back in a severe ponytail and wore no enhancement whatsoever, but those things did little to diminish her impact.

He inhaled again, unable to get enough of her ripe scent. Although slightly different from anything he'd ever encountered, it nonetheless drove him insane. The aroma filtered through his senses, encircling his cock as surely as if she'd closed her tight fist around him.

Her civilian clothing purposely resembled the uniform the tactical team wore. The black fabric that was nearly painted on her luscious curves left little to his already strained imagination. Her hard nipples bore into her shirt, teasing his eyes and mouth. One taste would quench his curiosity, but would it sate his hunger? His gaze traveled leisurely down her long, slender legs, visually feasting upon her muscled limbs.

Even if her clothes hadn't been a dead giveaway about her profession, her shoes would've been. No one outside of law enforcement was issued black combat boots. He looked at the shine. They were new, if the lack of scuff marks was any indication. Yet he knew from her file that she wasn't a rookie.

Nothing about the woman's appearance explained the strange nickname he'd found tucked discreetly within her file. Why did they call her Red?

She shifted, her womanly curves undulating beneath her clothes.

Morgan fought hard to keep from drooling. He doubted that she'd take it for the compliment that it was. This wasn't good. Gina Santiago's presence was a distraction he could ill afford. Not now. He needed to get rid of her and quick, before he did something embarrassing like bend her over his desk and mount her from behind.

"So what interest does the tactical team have with my little town?"

"None." Gina shook her head, and a strand of hair cascaded down to rest next to her delicately curved ear. "I'm here unofficially."

Morgan's hands tightened on the arms of his chair as he fought to keep from reaching out and touching the silken mass. "Mind explaining?"

Gina sat forward, accidentally giving him an unexpected glimpse of her modest cleavage. "We found a body in the woods thirty klicks north of here yesterday. The victim, Lisa Solomon, appears to have been attacked by animals. From soil samples gathered at the scene, we suspect she came through the Republic of Arizona. Quite possibly Nuria itself. Does her name ring any bells?"

Morgan tensed as her words registered, all desire forgotten. She wasn't here because of Renee Forrester. That fact should make him feel better, but it didn't. There had been another murder. "No, should it?"

She shrugged. "I don't know. You tell me."

"It doesn't," he said firmly. "She isn't from Nuria. If she was, I'd know. But that still doesn't explain *your* presence."

"I thought I'd check to see if any strangers have passed through or if you've received reports of similar incidents."

"You think I'm leaving deaths unreported," he challenged, knowing full well he *had*—but he'd be damned if he'd tell her that.

"No," Gina said hastily.

"Good." Morgan sat back, resting his hands behind his head in attempt to appear more casual than he felt. "You know it's against regulations for me to fail to report any unusual incidents that result in death to the tactical team."

"I know that and no one is saying you've done anything wrong," she reassured. "I wondered if perhaps something might have slipped by you."

Morgan let out a pained laugh. "Of course." He shook his head. "You think we locals can't handle little things like crime solving or reporting problems when they arise. How did I make it through training without the IPTT there to babysit me?"

Her voice rose. "That's not what I'm saying!"

"Then what exactly are you accusing me of?" He sat forward until they were nearly nose to nose. Her hot breath brushed against his stubbled face, leaving fire in its wake. Awareness flared between them. "Need I remind you that all republics are self-governing, and the Republic of Arizona is no different. The tactical team has no jurisdiction here unless a murder has been committed and you said yourself it was an animal attack."

Gina stood, breaking the contact. "Listen, I didn't come here to fight. I'm here on my own time. My commander closed the case on Lisa Solomon, even though I think there's more to her death than a simple animal attack." She clenched her jaw as if she'd said more than she intended. Her face flushed and her lips pursed.

Damn if she didn't look sexy when she was mad. Morgan schooled his expression. "I still don't understand why *you* are here."

"I came here because I thought maybe you could help me, but obviously it's too much trouble."

Relief flooded Morgan. With her case closed, he was free to hunt the killer in his own time. "I'm not sure how you expect me to assist you on a nonexistent case, so I guess we're done here. You'll probably want to be on your way. I'm sure you have a long ride ahead of you."

"Trying to get rid of me, Sheriff?"

Morgan chose to lie. "Not at all."

"Good, because I thought I might stick around for a couple of days and explore your town. It's quaint. I've never seen anything quite like it."

"Suit yourself." Morgan reached for the nearest water canteen. He tilted the jug and took a deep swig. Gina stared at him. It took him a second to realize he'd grabbed her canteen. Too late now. He tipped the container again. Water poured out of its spout.

He could almost taste the impression her full lips left behind on the opening. If a trace of her mouth tasted this sweet, what would the real thing be like? His body shuddered at the thought. Morgan tried to recall the last time he'd fucked one of his own kind. His mind blanked.

It had been too long since he'd had a *real* woman.

Red watched the columns of Morgan's throat work as he swallowed the water. Why she found the action so fascinating, she couldn't say. As though reading her mind, he grinned, flashing stark white teeth against a naturally tanned face.

Was he flirting with her? Did she mind if he was?

Bannon's words about spreading her legs filtered through Red's mind. Was that what Morgan Hunter expected from her?

The thought chilled any desire she might have felt. Red's face grew hard, her body rigid. She sat once more. "Have you seen or heard anything out of the ordinary?" she asked, her voice brisk.

Morgan snorted, placing the canteen back on his desk. "This is a boundary town. What do you think?"

"You know what I mean."

"Yes." He sighed. "I know what you mean." Morgan ran a hand through his long hair. "Nothing unusual, but you'd be the first person I'd tell if I had. Our kind need to stick together."

"Our kind?" Red frowned. "What exactly do you mean by our kind?"

Silence filled the space. His eyes widened a fraction, before settling back into a mask of mundane. "I meant law enforcement."

"Oh, it sounded like . . . Never mind. Doesn't matter." Red shook her head, not believing for a second that was what he'd meant. His pat answer troubled her. She'd noted the change in his demeanor. Hell, with them being so close together in this small space, she'd caught the subtle change in his scent.

Morgan Hunter had just lied and Red had no idea why.

chapter seven

The main food dispensing station sat on the corner of Pine Street and took up half a block. The building itself resembled the images Red had seen of theaters back in the twentieth century when viewing entertainment was made of film. Faded vintage movie posters hung on the sun-bleached walls advertising *Harry Potter, The Trouble with Harry,* and *Dirty Harry.*

Red wasn't familiar with these particular movies, but she was sure her grandfather had seen them, if any copies survived the last war. Metal double doors marked the entrance, muting the sounds of the crowd inside. Red's stomach fluttered and she tensed, reaching down to rub the wrist that Rita normally occupied. Bare skin met her fingertips. She shouldn't feel naked without her navcom, but she did. Red took a deep breath and squared her shoulders.

She still couldn't believe she'd allowed Morgan to talk her into coming here. This was a mistake.

They pushed their way inside. The doors closed with a whoosh behind them. The place was busier than she'd expected. Customers gathered around a couple of dozen stainless-steel tables, talking and laughing. The tables were squeezed in tight squares to accommodate the crowd. Wait staff dressed in white uniforms distributed a steady flow of food and drinks.

It was probably a good thing that she had left Rita in the room. The last thing Red needed was for her navcom going off every few minutes because of the change in her vitals.

Somewhere in the prep area, behind a set of swinging doors, Red caught bits of Roark Montgomery's clipped voice coming from a broadcast. The man seemed to be popping up everywhere lately, his popularity building like the wind before a storm.

The unknowns are being aided by the Others and I intend to prove it. We can't allow these criminals to continue unpunished.

Red considered his words. If what he said was true, that would certainly explain the increase in boundary crossings that the tactical team had been dealing with lately. Morgan's gentle touch to her elbow brought her out of her reverie. Roark's broadcast faded into the kitchen clatter. She glanced his way.

"Are you ready?" he asked. Morgan stared at her as if he knew she was about to bolt. She gave him a firm nod and stepped forward, leaving the shadows of the entryway behind. The place fell silent; even the waiters clearing the tables stopped banging plates. Curious glances shot their way, along with smiles and the occasional nod of approval. Heat poured off Morgan's body, bathing her in warmth. Oddly, she found his nearness reassuring instead of overbearing, and took a step closer.

Red glanced around at the captivated crowd, her discomfort growing. "It doesn't look like there's anything available," she said, hoping Morgan would take the not so subtle hint. She wanted to leave and go somewhere less public. The attention was making her uneasy.

Morgan didn't answer her. Instead, he stared at the patrons, slowly making eye contact with each one. Several looked away or cast their eyes down. He coughed, emitting a low guttural sound that barely registered as human. Then everyone suddenly began speaking like they'd never stopped.

Red found the reaction strange, but was too grateful to have the crowd's attention elsewhere to care. The sheriff obviously wielded a tremendous amount of control over the town. Odd, but understandable given Nuria's relative location to the boundary fence. At least she'd be able to enjoy a meal now without her stomach knotting.

"Follow me," Morgan said, leading her to an empty table near the back.

"Was this here a moment ago?" Red asked, sure she hadn't seen it.

"They can add tables with the press of a button in this place." He tapped his boot on a seam in the floor to indicate where the table had come from. "It can come in handy sometimes."

"Like now?"

Morgan grinned. "Yeah, like now. Is this okay for you?" he asked before pulling her seat out for her.

Red glanced at his hand, so unaccustomed to the polite gesture that she almost forgot what to do. She nodded her acceptance and then sat as he scooted the chair in. Had anyone other than her grandfather ever treated her this way? Red couldn't recall, which probably meant no.

"Why are you doing this?" she asked without thinking.

Morgan stopped next to his chair, gold eyes locked on her face. "Maybe I'm trying to change your opinion about *us* locals."

"You think it needs changing?"

He shrugged. "Couldn't hurt."

Red smiled, not convinced for a second that's why he'd invited her to dinner.

Morgan took his seat.

A list of offerings filled the screen of the mini compunit on the table. Red watched as Morgan scrolled down the screen. While he perused the menu, a waiter dropped off two canteens of water.

"Does anything look good to you?" he asked.

"Meat is fine. That is if Nuria receives bovine and pork shipments," she added quickly, since a lot of towns couldn't afford fresh meat and had to settle for genetically engineered protein packets. "Whatever is available. I'm not picky. I'll eat anything."

Morgan grinned. "Relax, we have plenty of fresh meat. We just received a shipment the other day. How do you want it prepared? Bloody?"

She laughed. "Perfect."

He nodded and punched in their choices. His gaze lingered longer than necessary on the mini compunit. "How long have you been on the tactical team, Ms. Santiago?"

"Please, call me Gina."

His eyes rested on her. "Okay, *Gina*. Are you going to answer my question?"

"I didn't realize this was a working dinner," she said, debating whether to leave now or once the food arrived. Her stomach growled, deciding for her. Red didn't like being on the receiving end of questions, even when they were couched in politeness.

Morgan brushed at invisible crumbs with the back of his hand. "Just making small talk."

"Sure, whatever you say." She sat back.

"How about we start this conversation over?" Morgan suggested.

"Why, when it's going so well?"

He chuckled. "Have it your way. I believe you were about to tell me how long you've been on the team."

"You've read my file. How long did it say?" she volleyed back.

"Files rarely tell the whole story. I'd rather hear it from you, if it's all the same."

Red snorted. "Wow, that's a new one."

"What is?"

"Someone actually taking the time to ask me about my job."

Morgan frowned. "Why is that surprising?"

She shrugged. "I just didn't expect it."

"There still aren't many women on the team, are there?" he asked.

"It is what it is. I'm used to it by now." Red reached for her canteen. He was too perceptive for his own good.

Morgan quirked a brow. "If you say so."

Her gaze leveled on him. "I do."

"Fine." He reached for the lid of his canteen and slowly unscrewed it, but didn't drink. "Truth is I didn't want to know about your job. I wanted to find out about you."

"I thought this was a working dinner," Red said.

"You said that, not me."

Her eyes widened in surprise before she could school her features. Red hadn't expected that kind of candor. She shifted uncomfortably as if her seat had suddenly grown lumps; no one had ever been interested enough to ask about her, not even the men she'd joined with.

"I've been with the team for ten years. What else would you like to know?" she asked, surprising herself and Morgan, if the startled expression on his face was any indication.

"You can start by telling me why they call you Red. It can't be because of your dark features or your hair, since it's black." He sat back, his large frame relaxing into the chair.

"No, it's not due to my appearance." Her stomach dropped and her face blanked. "You know why. It's all in the file."

"Actually, that part's a little vague. I can guess, but I'd rather you tell me."

"Sure you want to know before the food arrives? Might ruin your appetite."

"I have a pretty strong stomach, so I'll chance it."

"Suit yourself." She projected bravado that she didn't feel. "I tend to spill a lot of blood when I go after an unknown. Very few surrender. I don't set out to kill anyone. It just happens. I guess I don't appreciate being fired upon."

"You don't miss." It wasn't a question.

"Never. My grandfather says I'm like a modern-day Annie Oakley, whoever that is."

Morgan sat forward. "Where's your backup when all this is happening?"

Red snorted. "What backup?"

"I see." His jaw tightened.

"Actually, I doubt you do."

"You're probably right. What does a boundary town sheriff know about violence and unknowns?" he asked flippantly.

Red's stomach clenched. She hadn't meant to sell Morgan short. Sheriffs like him were the front line of defense against the unknowns. She knew that better than most, since his work aided hers. "Sorry," she said.

"You should be."

They sat in silence for a few minutes, neither willing to be the first to yield. Finally Red gave in. She wouldn't garner Morgan's cooperation if she continued to piss him off. Time to do a little male ego repair.

"How did you get into law enforcement?" she asked, changing the subject.

"I guess you could say it's in my *blood*," he said, casually as he glanced around the room, taking in the other patrons. Red followed his perusal. Several people looked away as Morgan made eye contact.

The first time she witnessed this she'd chalked it up to control, but now Red wasn't so sure. There was something weird happening here that went beyond respect for local law enforcement.

Morgan slowly turned back to her. "Is anything wrong?" he asked.

"Do you always get this kind of reaction from the town when you go out?"

"No." He chuckled. "This doesn't happen when I'm alone," he answered, flicking a gaze at the crowd.

Heat filled Red's face.

"I suppose lack of privacy is part of the joy of small-town living." Sarcasm dripped from his words, but his eyes sparkled with mirth.

"I wouldn't know. I've never lived in a small town."

"Biodweller, eh?"

Red giggled unexpectedly at the disdain in his voice and her tension began to ease. "Born and raised."

"I love it when you do that," he said, staring into her eyes a moment before gazing at her mouth.

"Do what?" Red licked her bottom lip. He was giving her that look again. The one that said he'd eat her alive given half the chance. Self-conscious, she brushed at her face.

His gaze widened a fraction before he lowered his lashes, effectively concealing his amber eyes. "Laugh," he said finally.

"Oh . . . I knew that's what you meant." Red actually felt the heat rising from her neck, trailing over her cheeks, until it reached the tips of her ears. She couldn't believe he'd managed to make her blush. It hadn't been his words as much as the infused meaning behind them.

Morgan opened his mouth to say something more, but the food's arrival stopped him. He acknowledged the server delivering the trays and then turned back to Red. "Where were you sired?" he asked, cutting into the rare factory-raised beef he'd ordered. Bloody juice dripped from his fork as he brought the steak to his mouth and bit down.

Red watched him chew, ecstasy clearly written on his face. Her mouth went dry and she reached for her canteen before answering. "I was born in the New Town biosphere, but I grew up in various cities. We moved around a lot when I was young, before returning to my birthplace." She took a bite of her steak and groaned as the savory juices burst into her mouth before melting on her tongue. "This is great," she said.

"I'm glad you like it." Morgan smiled. "Do your parents still live in New Town?"

The food in her mouth turned to ash. "No." Red shook her head. "They're dead."

"I'm sorry."

"Don't be. It happened a long time ago. I barely remember them," she lied.

Morgan watched her, his gold eyes probing into the tender places she hoped to hide. "Who raised you?"

The question brought a smile to Red's face. "My grandfather, Robert Santiago."

"The tactical team commander?"

"That's the one," she said.

He nodded, understanding dawning in his expression.

"See," she chided playfully. "I knew you'd read my file."

"Guilty." He grinned.

"Now that you know my story, what's yours?"

He looked around casually, but the sudden tension in his body betrayed him. "This is it," he said.

"I may have read the file, but I doubt I know your *whole* story."

"Smart lady." He raised his canteen in salute before taking a drink and setting it back on the table. "There's not much to tell."

Red began to regret sharing her past with this man. What did she really know about Sheriff Morgan Hunter?

Nothing. The answer came back swiftly in her mind.

He'd played her, not that she'd told him anything that couldn't be found in her data file. It was the thought that she'd relaxed enough around him to carelessly spill personal information that truly angered her. And she'd done so after only a few kind gestures and words. This just wasn't like her at all. She didn't go to dinner with men. She didn't share her life. And she certainly didn't flirt. Red was about to excuse herself from the table when he spoke.

"I come from a very large extended family, some of whom still live in the area."

"That explains the same last names around town."

He acknowledged her statement. "My family has lived in this area for generations. I guess I never saw a need to leave."

Red could barely comprehend what it would be like, feel like to have lived in one spot. With her parents dead, she only had her grandfather and they'd moved often. It seemed like every time she got settled someplace he'd find something wrong with the area and decide they needed to leave. She learned early not to get attached to anyone that she met. That's why she clung to Robert Santiago so desperately. Once he was gone, she'd be alone. Not that she wasn't already. Her existence required isolation—or so she kept telling herself.

She watched Morgan Hunter's face as he regaled her with more stories about his childhood while they finished dinner. He'd grown up with loving parents, close friends, and an uncle who liked to read fairy tales to him while acting out the characters. His life had been idyllic. She envied him that. Red pushed aside the melancholy thought and smiled at the trouble he managed to get into during his youth. It was a miracle he and his cousins had survived.

He was in the middle of another story when Red caught a jerky movement out of the corner of her eye that didn't match the pattern of the people around them. Her head whipped around out of instinct to face whoever approached. She didn't realize she was gripping the knife until Morgan stared at her hand. She released the utensil.

"Sorry. It's habit."

Morgan stopped midsentence, his gaze going from Red's hand to the man who'd just stepped from the shadows. "Kane." He nodded, acknowledging the town physician.

Red's attention shifted, too, along with the rest of the women in the room. Out of uniform, Kane Hunter was without a doubt one of the most handsome men Red had ever laid eyes on. She'd thought so when she met him at the emergency care center earlier and her opinion hadn't changed.

His dark hair glistened like it emitted its own light from within. A black shirt encased his broad chest, before nipping in at his narrow waist. Loose tan pants draped his lower body, accenting his long strides. The only wrinkle came from what looked like a portable heart monitor poking out of one of his pockets. Otherwise, the line was flawless, like his features. No wonder all the nurses at the emergency care center were crazy about him. He was a prime catch for any woman.

Too bad he really wasn't her type. She'd never gone for the nice guy who always saves the day, and she wasn't about to start now. If something needed saving, Red planned to do it herself. Besides, nice guys always wanted far more than she was willing to give. And there was no doubt in her mind that Kane would demand a lot.

Red glanced at Morgan, then back at Kane. They had similar facial structure and coloring, although Morgan was a bit rougher around the edges. His jaw was scruffier and he seemed less inclined to preen. Of course, the real difference came with their personalities.

She had never really understood until now the archaic saying comparing the difference between night and day. Kane flirted with abandon, his easygoing manner contagious. He welcomed people with warmth and caring, while Morgan's closed nature warned everyone away. So why was she drawn to the one who at any moment might reject her?

Kane slowed as he neared the table, grinning as he glanced from Morgan back to her. "You work fast, cousin."

Red blushed a second time in one night. She shot Morgan a pointed glance.

"Ms. Santiago's in town for a short visit," Morgan

said, reverting to a formality that they'd disposed of earlier.

"So I heard. I didn't think that you had time for dinner." He raised a brow and his lips twitched in amusement.

"I—"

"It was my idea," Morgan interjected. "I thought a little interdepartmental courtesy was called for."

"Is that so?" Kane extended his large hand. "It's nice to see you again, *Gina*."

"You, too." Red shook it, feeling the rough calluses on his palm and fingertips before releasing him. A doctor who got his hands dirty. That's something you didn't find every day. Her respect for him rose a notch.

"I didn't realize you two knew each other." Morgan tensed, but still managed to force a smile. It had never bothered him before, but now, with Gina, Kane's overly familiar tone had him on edge.

"We met briefly when I was finding my way around," Gina said. "Kane pointed me to Jesse Lindley's share space. Thank you by the way. The room's perfect."

"How civic minded of him," Morgan said without inflection, watching Kane from beneath hooded eyes.

"Now, cousin. Your hackles are showing," Kane quipped. "You can thank me later, Gina." He waggled his eyebrows at her.

Gina's color bloomed and her heart accelerated.

Morgan scowled, fighting back a full-fledged growl. He loved his cousin like a brother and hadn't had any problems sharing women in the past. In fact, he'd taken great pleasure in doing so. But Gina was bringing out his alpha side. The hair on his nape rose as he met Kane's gaze. It was childish to pull rank, but Morgan couldn't seem to stop himself. The need to exert his dominance pounded in his veins, sharpening his senses until the urge to pounce made his muscles twitch.

Kane's expression changed to one of momentary surprise. "Well isn't that interesting," he said, holding Morgan's gaze a second longer than was respectful, before slowly dropping his eyes to the floor. He peeked at Gina a moment later and grinned, effectively dissipating the tension.

A waiter came by and removed their empty plates.

"How long have you worked at the center?" Gina asked.

"Forever it seems. The place would shut down without me." He winked. "Don't forget to let me know if you need anything examined. It would be on the house, seeing as you're one of u—"

"Kane keeps this town going," Morgan interrupted, glaring at his cousin. "He's the only full-time doctor in these parts. We have a few part-timers, but none choose to stay for long. Kane pulls shifts at the emergency care center, makes house calls, and visits the elder care facility at least twice a week. He's a regular humanitarian," Morgan said jokingly, even though it was the truth. "Nuria would've succumbed to the maladies plaguing all small boundary towns without Kane's care and nurturing of its citizens."

Kane blinked as if he hadn't heard Morgan correctly. "Why, thank you, cousin. I didn't think you'd noticed." Humor glittered in his eyes, along with speculation.

"Nuria is lucky to have you," Gina said.

"Did I mention that he's also a notorious flirt?" Morgan added.

"No, you didn't. I could see that." She grinned.

"Don't pay any attention to him, Gina. His bark is far worse than his bite."

Kane flicked Morgan a curious glance, then turned his attention back to Gina. "Now, cousin, quit lying to the woman. We both know that's not true."

Gina glanced at both men and laughed.

"I'm really a pussycat," Kane said, showing off his dazzling smile.

She shook her head. "Somehow I doubt that." Her lips parted slightly, revealing the pink tip of her tongue.

"Like I said, smart girl." Morgan stared, unable to look away from her lush, inviting mouth. The urge to kiss her and see if she tasted as delicious as he imagined rode him hard. He gripped the arms of his chair to keep from acting on the impulse.

"Sure there isn't anything we can do to convince you to stay longer?" Kane asked smoothly. "We can be quite persuasive given the chance."

Morgan's attention snapped to his cousin. He'd all but warned Kane away from Gina. What did he have to do to get it into his thick head, grab him by the scruff until he showed his belly?

"Sorry, I'll only be here a day or two. Not enough time to socialize," she said.

Kane made a show of glancing at her, and then at Morgan. "Funny, it looks like you're doing a bang-up job to me."

Red's expression turned to one of panic. "This isn't . . . I'm not . . ."

An awkward silence fell upon the table.

Kane licked his bottom lip. "If this isn't social, then I see no reason why you can't go out with me before you leave. At least give me a chance to show you not everyone in Nuria is like my stuffy cousin here." He nodded in Morgan's direction. "What do you say?"

Red tore strips from her recycled napkin while her gaze darted around the room. Instead of stepping in to save her like he wanted to do, Morgan waited for her response, a mixture of dread and hope filling him. Women didn't turn Kane down. Would Gina be the first?

He and Kane had always been highly competitive, whether they were hunting, fighting, or chasing women. They both played to win and sometimes shared the spoils. Gina was taking too long to answer. This didn't bode well for him. Morgan's gut clenched and his ribs squeezed. Sweat broke out over his brow. He tugged at his collar and took a drink of water.

"I have no doubt that you could be quite convincing, but there really won't be time. I hope you understand. Thanks anyway," she said.

Relief flooded Morgan and his muscles relaxed. He shouldn't care whether Gina wanted Kane because she'd be gone soon enough, but he did. For some reason, her answer was very important to him, and possibly to their future.

"Don't you have somewhere you need to be?" Morgan asked, unable to hide the triumph in his voice.

Kane shook his head. "No, dear cousin. You

should know that I have all the time in the world to talk to a beautiful woman."

"Well, that's too bad, since we were just leaving. You can have our table, if you like." Morgan stood, his gaze going to Gina.

"It was nice to seeing you again." She followed Morgan's lead and was on her feet before he had a chance to finish pushing in his chair. "It's all yours." She flicked her wrist, stepping away from the table.

The moment she did, a panel opened up and the table disappeared. The floor gently vibrated and gurgled beneath their feet.

"What's happening?" Gina asked.

"The table is being cleaned and disinfected. It'll return in a minute," Kane said.

Gina stepped back and collided with Morgan's chest. She gave a startled squeak and tried to scoot away. Morgan caught her elbow and brought her against him before she toppled the chair beside her.

Gina's scent changed on contact, drowning his senses, firing his blood. His grip tightened involuntarily and he briefly closed his eyes. Morgan took a deep breath and willed his fingers to relax. She stepped slowly out of his embrace, as if she were reluctant to move.

Morgan exchanged glances with Kane. His cousin's nostrils flared a second before his expression soured. He'd just caught the sudden change in her delicate fragrance that signaled arousal. Gina had made her decision without even realizing it. Tension crackled in the air as the two men faced off. The voices around them dropped to hushed whispers. Everyone, including Morgan, was waiting to see if Kane would concede.

The table popped up, glistening from the thorough cleaning.

Gina jumped and let out a nervous laugh.

"All yours." Morgan swept his hand above the shiny surface. "Enjoy your evening, Kane."

"You, too, cousin." Kane gave Morgan a curt nod before turning his attention to Gina. "Always a pleasure," he said, taking her hand and bringing it to his lips.

Gina's pulse jumped in her throat.

Morgan saw it and tensed.

Kane's gaze fell on him and he grinned. The devilish glint in his eyes told Morgan that he hadn't given up on Gina yet.

Morgan walked Gina outside. The night was warm, but bearable. Certainly comfortable enough for them to take an evening stroll. He pushed thoughts of Kane out of his head. He'd talk to his cousin tomorrow. If need be, he'd order him to back down, but Morgan hoped it wouldn't come to that.

"Thank you for dinner," Gina said, bringing him back to the present.

Morgan smiled. "It was my pleasure."

"I'm sorry," she said, but she sounded like she wasn't sure what she was apologizing for. "Kane caught me a little off guard. I'm not used to men . . ." She shrugged, her unease apparent.

"Don't worry about it. Kane has that effect on people—well, women mostly, but he's harmless." Morgan gave her hand a quick squeeze, then released her. "I have to say this is the first time I've ever seen a woman stand firm and not fall at his feet."

"Really?" she asked.

"Oh yes." He nodded. "Can I ask why you turned him down? I mean it's obvious that women find him attractive."

"Kane's certainly easy on the eyes. There's no denying that. And he genuinely seems like a nice guy. The kind of guy that you'd want to settle down with, if you're into that sort of thing." Her teeth tugged on her bottom lip.

"And I take it you're not," Morgan said. Disappointment settled heavy on his shoulders.

"I didn't say that." She shook her head. "Look, my priorities are different. I took an oath to serve the republics. Men like Kane . . . well, they don't understand things like that. So it's easier in the end to avoid those types of complications. I guess in that respect I'm just not like most women."

He regarded her for a moment to gauge her sincerity. "Truer words have never been spoken," he murmured.

Gina was unique, and not just because of the blood running through her veins. She'd chosen a rough path for a woman to take by joining the IPTT and had proven herself repeatedly. Morgan respected anyone with that kind of tenacity and sense of honor. The fact that those traits were coming from a woman just made her all the more appealing.

His heart hiccupped and began to race. Morgan hadn't been this nervous around a woman since his teens. He knew Gina was attracted to him at least a little. She'd proven that in the food dispensing station, when her scent changed after he'd touched her.

The fact that it hadn't when Kane kissed her hand only reinforced his beliefs. Suddenly Morgan wasn't sure what to say—or do.

They walked on, the sidewalks nearly empty as Gina made a right toward the share space she'd rented. Morgan sensed danger before spotting it. His head snapped up and he tensed, ready for a fight. Shadows shifted and morphed, swirling menacingly. Suddenly, Raphael Vega appeared. The lab vamp glided down the sidewalk toward them. Gina's body stilled.

"It's okay," Morgan assured her, convinced he could reach his weapon in time if necessary.

Raphael stopped three feet away, his flat doll-like prosthetic eyes moving from Morgan to Gina and back. He inclined his head. "Sheriff," he said in way of greeting.

"Raphael. What are you still doing around here?" Morgan's question was cordial, but his tone revealed the underlying tension between the two men.

The vampire ignored his question. "Aren't you going to introduce me to your *friend*?"

Gina glanced at Morgan.

He exhaled loudly. "Gina Santiago, Raphael Vega. He's our resident rat catcher."

Raphael laughed, the twinkling sound filling the air. He approached Gina and held out his hand. When she extended hers, he flipped it palm down and pressed a kiss to the back of her knuckles. "It's a pleasure." He smiled, his gaze predatory. "Your perfume is divine."

Gina's brow creased. "I'm not wearing any."

"My mistake. It must just be you," Raphael said smoothly.

Morgan knew that Raphael was smelling her blood. It took every fiber of his being not to pound the vamp's face in. "Gina's a member of the tactical team," Morgan said casually.

Raphael dropped Gina's hand like it had scalded him, hissing as he stepped back.

"Did I say something wrong?" she asked.

Morgan grinned. "No, I did. You'll have to excuse Raphael's rude behavior. Not everyone in town is as fond of the tactical team as I am."

Gina bust out laughing. "Actually, I'm used to his kind of response. It's the rest of the town's behavior that I find odd."

"We'd better get going. Raphael was just leaving, weren't you?"

"My apologies, dear lady. I seem to have forgotten a previous engagement." The vampire smiled and bowed to Gina, then turned to face Morgan. "Sheriff," he said, amusement infusing the word. "I had no idea you liked to play with fire."

"There's a lot you don't know about me, Raphael."

"Indeed. Good thing I have all the time in the world to find out." The vampire faded into the night as if he'd never been there.

"Don't bet on it," Morgan muttered.

Gina tilted her head to look at him. "What was that all about?"

"We have a lot of eccentric people in this town. They like the fact they can be themselves here."

"I've never seen anyone so pale. His skin is almost translucent. From the looks of him, you'd think he never saw the sun."

"Now there's a thought." Morgan smiled, remembering the first time he'd witnessed a full-fledged laboratory vampire meeting the dawn. They didn't burst into flames like the old legends suggested. Instead, they hardened and began to expand until they exploded into thousands of pieces of living shrapnel. You had to stand back or they'd take you with them into the next world. They were the perfect weapon, dead or alive.

Many enemy soldiers and the vampire hunters who'd followed learned that lesson the hard way.

"The boundary brings in all types, eh?" she asked

"Oh, yeah." Morgan nodded. "And Raphael is one of the odder ones. You may want to give him a wide berth."

"No problem.

They continued on for a few minutes in silence. The air had grown cooler now that they were farther away from the town's center. Gina rubbed her hands along her arms and looked his way. "I could still use your help."

Morgan cocked his head. "With what? I thought we already established there was nothing happening in Nuria."

"You may have, but I haven't. I need to talk to the townspeople, particularly the ones living outside of the city limits. I would like to find out if anyone has seen or heard anything unusual."

"They haven't." Morgan reached out and stopped her. "But you don't need my help for that. Just ask them."

"You and I both know no one is going to talk to me. I'm a stranger. An outsider. And if that wasn't bad enough, I'm a tactical team member. Hell, look what

just happened with Raphael Vega." Her lips quirked.
"I am like poison. I'm surprised people didn't run
screaming from the food dispensing station at my
mere presence."

Morgan laughed. "It would take more than your
presence here to scare those folks away."

"It didn't seem to take much for Raphael to re-
coil."

He glanced at her. "I can honestly say Raphael
Vega is *not* like most people in town." They continued on.

"Okay, so Raphael Vega is an exception," she said,
bypassing a crack in the sidewalk.

"He's something all right."

"The people know and trust you. They may say
things to you that they'd never tell me. I'm asking as
one fellow law-enforcement member to another. Will
you help me?"

"Professional courtesy?" He stopped again and
turned to look at her, not bothering to hide the disappointment in his voice. "Is that all this is?"

She tilted her chin, confusion marring her features. "Isn't that what you told Kane?"

"Yeah, but—" He shook his head in frustration.
What did he want from her? Morgan wasn't sure. He
knew that before she left Nuria they'd share a rest
pad, but he couldn't exactly say that. He also knew
that there was something more, something deeper at
work here. He just wasn't ready to identify it yet.
"Fine. Have it your way. If the townspeople tell you
that nothing's happening will you believe them? Will
you let this go?"

"Yes, I will." Gina nodded. "If there's nothing here

to see, I'll be on my way. I just have to know for sure. I don't want anyone else getting hurt because I failed to do my job."

"I don't either." He strolled on. This time his pace was brisk. "You may not believe it, but I take my job just as seriously as you take yours."

"I know you do." Gina trotted beside him to keep up. "I have good instincts when it comes to reading people."

"Obviously." Morgan balked. "Seeing as though you almost knifed Kane."

Gina grimaced. "With this job it's easy to think the worst of people. Anyway, he surprised me."

"Remind me never to surprise you." Morgan glanced at her and smiled. "I suppose you're right about the job. You definitely don't think the best about people after a few years of cleaning up society's crap." He paused at the street corner. "Well here we are." The share space stood across the street. The faint yellow porch light glowed in the darkness, but did little to illuminate the area. "Would you like me to walk you to the door?" Morgan lifted his foot to step off the curb, but Gina stopped him.

"There's no need. I've got it from here." She flipped her shirt up an inch, revealing her concealed pistol.

"You came armed to dinner?"·

She quirked a brow. "Didn't you?"

"Touché." He snorted. "I still wouldn't want anything to happen to you in my town."

Gina smiled. "Sheriff Hunter, I assure you that I can take care of myself."

"If we're going to be around each other for a few days, you might want to start calling me Morgan," he said, returning her smile. He could drown in those light hazel eyes so easily. "As to your abilities, I have no doubt that you are a one-woman fighting machine, Ms. Sant—Gina, but humor me."

"Will that get me your assistance?"

His eyes flashed in the darkness. "Among other things."

chapter eight

"Took you long enough," Roark Montgomery said, glancing up from the documents in his hands as his assistant scurried like a mangy rodent into his office.

Oily black hair molded Mike Travers' scalp, giving sharp relief to his cadaverous face. Obsidian eyes that absorbed the light peered out from beneath lashless lids. His navy suit clung precariously to his bones much like his pale skin. The fact that his lips were unusually red always struck Roark as strangely out of place on an otherwise blank canvas.

Mike stiffened under his perusal.

"Take a seat." Roark cleared his throat. "Any word on where the Others are at?"

Mike sat. "No, sir. We've narrowed their location down to three republics." He worried the cuffs of his suit with his fingertips. Roark rolled his stiff shoulders, ignoring the bile rising in his throat at his assistant's effeminate actions. If he didn't need the man's unscrupulous talents, he'd fire him on the spot. Despite Roark's distaste at being subjected to Travers' presence, he'd keep him around until after the election. "Are you going to tell me which three republics or do I have to guess?"

Mike pressed a button on his mini compunit. "Republic of New Texas, Republic of the Floridian Islands, and Republic of Arizona."

Roark sat back, his fingers going to his chin to form a steeple as he pretended to ponder the options. "I think we can safely rule out the RFI. The Others aren't hiding on the islands. There would be no way to escape in the event of an attack, unless they've suddenly become amphibious."

"No, sir. I believe we're still dealing with land mammals."

"Then they're smart enough to avoid being surrounded." Roark nodded at his own assessment. "Remove RFI."

"Yes, sir," Mike said, deleting the Republic of the Floridian Islands from his list.

Roark rocked back in his chair, his gaze locking on the squirrelly man. It was so hard to find worthy people to employ these days. The last war did away with all the quality human stock. All that remained were the scavengers like Travers.

He was amazed he'd managed to put up with the man for all these years. Fortunately, people like Travers were expendable. That knowledge was the only thing that kept him in the same room with the man.

Once he gained office and united the republics, he'd introduce a law to protect the pure-blooded humans from the less-than-acceptable stock. Travers, although pure-blooded, fell into the latter category, along with the Others.

Roark reached over and punched a button on his

compunit. He stared at the maps a few moments, running his fingers over invisible lines, before returning his attention to Travers. "The other two locations are much more viable. They're on the boundary, which gives the Others quick access to no-man's-land."

"I suppose that sounds reasonable."

"Of course it's reasonable. How many times have I told you that you have to learn to think like the enemy?"

Mike opened and closed his mouth a couple of times before squeaking out one word. "Several."

Roark stopped rocking and sat forward. "Must I do everything for you? Next you'll have me wiping your ass."

"Yes, sir. I mean—no, sir. That won't be necessary."

"I want you to have both locations scouted. I want anything out of the ordinary reported to me. You can start with—" Roark flicked a glance at the map. "—the Republic of Arizona." He hid a smile as he realized everything was falling into place.

"Don't you think we should start with the Republic of New Texas? It's twice the size as ROA and will take more time to cover."

Roark rose like an angry grizzly from behind his desk. "Are you questioning my orders, Travers? I won't tolerate insubordination."

Travers cowered in his chair. "Understood, sir. I'll get right on it." He paled and scrambled to his feet, stepping back until he was out of arm's reach.

"You're dismissed." Disgust filled Roark's voice.

Mike nodded, walking backward until he reached the door to the office. He pressed a button and a panel slid away, revealing a hall. He stepped outside a second before the door hissed closed.

Roark waited for the light on the panel to register red to verify it was sealed, then moved to his telecom. Normally Travers handled office communication, but this was too important for a lackey to be trusted with.

Roark told himself he shouldn't risk a call, but insubordination and uneasiness in an assassin worried him—even though the killer came in the guise of a meek assistant. Right now Roark needed reassurance from the only person who could give it to him.

He jabbed five numbers into the unit and took a deep breath. The link crackled and popped, giving a final gasping beep before connecting.

"Hello?"

"Is everything going as planned?" Roark asked, impatience scratching like glass in his throat.

Silence met his question.

"Are you there?" Panic filled Roark's voice.

"I told you never to contact me, unless it was an emergency. Your pitiful insecurities don't count."

Roark covered the mic and growled in frustration. "I don't need your permission. I'm the one running this operation, remember?"

There was another long pause on the line.

"Did you hear me?" Roark asked, kicking himself for making the man angry. He needed him. At least for a while longer, then it wouldn't matter.

"Yes, I heard . . . every word." His jaw snapped shut, causing his teeth to clatter.

Roark's pulse jumped in his throat. He stacked synth-papers on his desk to fool the man into thinking that he didn't scare him. When he was done, he asked casually, "Why haven't any bodies been discovered?"

"At least one has, but the authorities don't realize what they're dealing with."

Roark frowned. "How do you know?"

He laughed. "Let's just say I have an inside scoop."

"I haven't heard a thing through my connections."

"Perhaps you need better connections."

"Or maybe instead of worrying about me calling, you could use your sources to make the authorities understand."

A growl rumbled through Roark's comlink and he instinctively jerked back. "That's the only warning you're going to get."

"Don't threaten me. We have a deal," Roark spat. "Or are you reneging?"

"No, I'm still in, but we may have another problem."

Roark mangled the documents he'd been holding. "What kind of problem?" he asked, tossing the papers aside. The last thing they needed were problems. Not this close to the election. Everything had to be perfect.

Voices murmured in the background, slowly growing in volume. Roark listened as they reached a crescendo, then gradually faded. His chest stretched with tension.

"We have a tactical team member nosing around town."

Roark swore under his breath. "What in the hell is he looking for?"

"He is a *she*."

"There aren't many women on the tactical team. I'll give headquarters another impromptu visit and see what I can find out. She may have orders to do reconnaissance."

"Doubtful."

"You can't be sure," Roark said. "It wouldn't hurt to look into it."

"Poking around could raise a red flag. You can't afford to be involved any more than you already are, so I'll take care of it." The man's heated whisper scorched Roark's ear.

"We don't need tactical team interference this close to obtaining our goals. Do I have to remind you what that would do to our cause?"

"I said I'd take care of it," the voice snapped with a whip of impatience. "She won't be a problem."

"How do you know?"

"Because she has a few secrets of her own." Roark couldn't see the man grin, but he could hear it in his voice. What wasn't he telling him?

"I need more reassurance than just your word."

The man scoffed. "My word will have to be good enough."

"Remember your ass isn't the only one on the line. If I go down before this plan is fully executed, I'm taking you and your *people* with me," Roark vowed.

A soft tinkling of laughter filled the connection. "Is that a threat?" Roark shivered and said nothing, wondering again why he'd gone into business with someone so deadly.

"I didn't think so," the man said smugly. "You do your job and I'll do mine. Don't contact me again or the next time I'll be the one paying you a visit."

The line went dead before Roark could respond. The coiled tension filling his shoulders threatened to rip muscle if he moved. At least they were on target. With the help of this insider, the republics would fall into line. Fear caused even the bitterest enemies to join ranks. And he'd be there to lead them . . . right after he destroyed the abominations known as the Others.

Mike Travers held his head against the door of Roark Montgomery's office, ears straining to hear. He knew it was wrong to eavesdrop, but his boss had been acting strangely for the past few weeks, looking at him with something akin to loathing in his eyes.

At first Mike had considered Roark's behavior election jitters, but he had been around long enough to recognize those symptoms and this wasn't it.

He slid down the door as if that would make it easier to hear. The voice grew muffled. Damn it! Mike stood again, returning to his previous position. His gaze darted down the hall to ensure no one was coming. The last thing he needed was to be caught spying.

He couldn't hear what the person on the other end of the line was saying, but the stress in Roark's voice was apparent. Who was he talking to? Why hadn't he asked him to place the call?

Montgomery rarely did anything for himself, enjoying the thrill of ordering underlings too much. Mike played the part of timid assistant to perfection. His act was so good he'd even convinced himself at times. So why the sudden secrecy?

This change in protocol made Mike decidedly uneasy. Six more months and the elections would be over. Six more months and he'd reach full vesting, allowing for a pleasurable retirement. One that didn't involve assassinating the competition. Sweat dotted his upper lip and his heart began to pound. He pressed a hand on the door to hold himself in place.

"Is everything going as planned?" Roark asked.

Mike glowered. What plan? Was Roark going to dump him now that they were on the verge of winning this final campaign? Was he contracting another killer to dispose of him? Rage ignited within him, spreading the acid of hate through his veins.

He'd given this man fifteen years of his life. Fifteen years that had cost him everything he held dear. Mike pictured Raphael's luminous face, smiling during happier times, and his heart clenched. Not a day went by that he didn't mourn his brother's death. He'd tried—and failed—to save him when the genetic testing labs were destroyed.

The pain had been so great that he'd actually changed his last name from Vega to Travers. All that was left were the memories. Without Raphael, Mike had no life outside of campaigning and Roark Montgomery. He'd poured his soul into his work. And he wasn't about to let Roark stop him from escaping this nightmare that he'd created.

His jaw clenched, causing his incisors to grind together and slash his gums. A not so gentle reminder of his days spent strapped to a gurney pumped full of drugs that forever changed his DNA. The pain was quickly replaced by cold.

Mike wouldn't put up with that kind of behavior

from Roark Montgomery or anyone else. He'd worked too long and way too hard to get to where he was and he wouldn't lose it now that his goal was in sight.

He straightened the front of his suit. His hands curled into tight fists, his nails ripping the skin of his palm. Mike ignored the blood as he strode down the hall to his small utilitarian office. He entered the room and slammed the door. The walls bowed from the energy rolling off him in waves.

Mike took a couple of deep breaths and tried to calm down, but he couldn't see beyond the red haze clouding his vision. Items on his work space shook violently before plummeting to the floor. The air crackled and his chair slammed into the desk. No one would be replacing him.

No one!

It was time to find out who his competition was and eliminate them.

"Travers, get in here," Roark Montgomery bellowed in his comlink, the sound nearly splitting his eardrum.

Mike forced himself to calm and a minute later entered his boss' office, looking a little worse for wear.

"What the hell have you been doing?" Roark asked, scowling.

Mike kept his hands behind his back, wishing he could ask him the same question. Instead, he reverted to his cowering persona. "Research like you asked, and I was cleaning."

Roark frowned. "Well forget all that. I need you to do something else. I want you to find out how many female tactical team members there are at IPTT."

"Sir?" *What was he up to now?*

Roark ignored his question. "After you do that, run a background check on all of them. I want to know who their families are, where they were born, rank, and their current location."

"I'll get right on it, sir."

"I want it by tomorrow," Roark added.

"Are you sure this is more important than locating the Others? We have a lot of territory to cover."

Roark's features flattened. "Yes, and the next time you question my orders, you're fired."

Mike swallowed hard, then gave him a curt nod and left. He didn't know who Montgomery was after, but he felt bad for whoever she was.

Red arrived at the sheriff's office the next morning at six. She wanted to talk to the townspeople before the heat of the day baked the desert and sent everyone scurrying inside until the late afternoon. She wasn't sure how long it would take to reach the outer limits of the town, but she wanted to give them plenty of time to access the remote areas.

She parked her car out front and stepped onto the sidewalk, not sure if they'd be taking her vehicle or his. The sun was already near blinding and it had barely poked its bald yellow head above the horizon.

Morgan Hunter exited the building, carrying a thermos. Dressed in taupe khakis and combat boots, he signaled for her to get into his vehicle. "I thought we could use some synth-coffee because it's going to be a long day." He smiled as he slipped on his sunshades.

"Good idea." *Why did he have to be so thoughtful?*

They drove out to the homesteads, leaving behind pavement for gravel roads. Miles separated the settlers. Out here near the boundary fence, they were exposed, unprotected, yet somehow survived.

Red shivered at the desert's vastness. Could she live in a place so remote? Face every day not knowing whether she'd survive to see the next? A strange peace settled in her bones as she realized she could. She'd put her life on the line every time she went to work. At some point over the years that had become normal. Life here would be no different.

Morgan pulled into the nearest home, a cloud of dust trailing in his car's wake. A woman in her midtwenties exited the house, holding her hand above her eyes to stave off the glare. She wore what appeared to be a stained green coverall over tanned fatigues with tattered brown leather shoes. Her hair was short, mannish in style. If it hadn't been for the apron cinching her waist, Red would've thought she *was* a man.

"What can I do for you, Sheriff?"

"Nancy, this woman has a few questions for you. I'd be grateful if you'd answer them the best you can."

The woman glanced at Red's black combat boots and instantly stiffened. "What does the tactical team want with my family? We're law-abiding, registered folk."

"Nothing, ma'am," Red replied. "I just have a few questions about the area."

Her wary gaze went from Red to Morgan and back again. "I suppose you should come inside, so you can get out of the sun."

They followed Nancy into her flat-roofed home, which consisted of four rooms that Red could see. The space was clean and well kept. Modest gray republic-issued furniture filled the inside, leaving little in the way of comfort. The woman had done what she could to add color by sewing pieces of red fabric to the understuffed squares that passed for pillows. It brightened the room and made it feel more like a home than a hovel. If she didn't look out the window, Red could almost forget that they were out in the middle of nowhere.

Living on the fringe of society left most families existing on the bare necessities—food and water. The woman had done a good job with what she had, Red noted.

She motioned for them to sit. Red and Morgan did so, then accepted glasses of water from the woman's trembling hands. Red wanted to reassure her, but she didn't know how.

"Gina, this is Nancy Dupray. She and her husband own this plot. They domesticate wild pigs, which are perfect prey for a *marauding pack of animals*." Morgan's gaze shot to Nancy and she fumbled with her apron.

Red leaned forward. "It's nice to meet you." The woman reluctantly shook her hand. "I only have a few questions to ask and then we'll leave you in peace."

Nancy nodded jerkily.

"Have any of your stock come up missing?"

Nancy's face flushed and she looked to Morgan again.

"It's okay, Nancy. You can answer her."

The woman shifted, her boots clunking on the floor. She sat suddenly, the cushion deflating under her weight. "A few sows have gone missing and some water rations, but that's nothing new in this area. We suspect some of it's caused by the unknowns that come across the boundary in search of a better life. Can't say as I blame them. They need something to eat after that journey."

Red frowned. "You haven't noticed *anything* else unusual."

"Nope, that's about it." Nancy shrugged. "What are you looking for?"

"Animals."

"I don't understand," Nancy said, glancing between them. "There are all kinds of animals around here. We have packs of wild dogs, coyotes, and wolves. The latter are rare. They don't tend to come around these parts much. Even seen some of those big cats they used to keep in zoos before the war. That's just how it is in the outback. You either accept it or move to town."

"Let me be blunt" Red said. "These animals I'm after may have killed a woman."

The color drained from Nancy's face. "D-don't know nothing about that." She rose, wiping her hands on her apron. "I think you'd better leave. Don will be home soon. I have to fix his midday meal so he can take it with him when he heads back to work." She glanced around anxiously, her gaze straying more than once to the kitchen.

"Midday meal? It's six-thirty in the morning," Red said.

"Most folks around here work from midnight to

noon, so that they can avoid the hottest part of the day," Morgan answered, before she could reply.

Nancy gave him a half-smile and her shoulders relaxed.

"Are you sure you can't help us?" Red asked. "You haven't even seen her picture yet." She tossed the photo onto a table in front of them.

Nancy jumped back as if she'd been struck. "We don't know anything about that woman." She shook her head. "You'll have to look somewhere else. We didn't do anything wrong. I think you should leave."

"No one's accusing you of anything—"

"Please leave." Nancy sniffled, then ushered them to the front door.

"Thanks for all your help, Nancy," Morgan said.

Red couldn't help but replay the woman's reaction when she told her what she was after. Nancy knew something, but there was little chance she'd get her to talk. The woman had made that perfectly clear when she'd practically tossed them out of her home. Red didn't want to think about Morgan. He'd been no help at all.

She spun on the sheriff after they stepped off the porch, her hands resting on her hips. "Why didn't you question her? She obviously knew something. Her body language practically screamed liar. You did notice that, right?"

"What? Maybe I missed something." Morgan tilted his head until they were nearly nose to nose. His warm breath brushed across her cheek with each exhalation, causing Red's nipples to bead in response. Moisture that had nothing to do with perspiration trickled between her thighs.

She ground her teeth and clenched her fists to keep from reaching for him. A few more inches and their lips would meet. Out of self-preservation, she jerked away, breaking the strange tension coiling around them.

"The second I told her about the woman's death she suddenly remembered she couldn't talk to us. Her body language closed."

"I'm not surprised. Is that how the tactical team operates when questioning a potential witness?" Morgan held up his hand to prevent Red from answering. "Your scenario of the way things went down in the house is not how I saw it. Nancy didn't know anything. Then you tossed the body out there in front of her and she acted like any other civilized human being would act—she got upset. She would've vomited if you'd brought the photo image any closer to her face. Nancy may look stout, but she's as soft as they come on the inside. She'll probably have nightmares for months. What in the hell were you thinking?"

Red cringed. Had she caused Nancy Dupray's reaction? She grimaced. It was entirely possible. She wasn't exactly known for her tact. It also didn't help that she'd never interrogated anyone before. No one had lived long enough to answer questions. Red hated to admit her inexperience. She didn't want Morgan to lose respect for her, but she also knew that they couldn't continue like this all day. Maybe if she trusted him with this information, he'd begin to trust her. After a minute's reflection she said reluctantly, "I'm sorry if I got carried away in there." Red paused, knowing that she had to tell the whole truth. "Nancy is the first person I've ever managed to question."

Morgan blinked at the news, then his features soft-ened. "That explains a lot. From here on out, do me a favor."

"What?"

His lips canted. "Follow my lead."

The rest of the day was much like their first visit to the Dupray home. People skittered away from the topic of wild animals and missing livestock. Red wasn't sure why she'd expected anything different, even with the sheriff leading the questioning.

On a couple of occasions she'd actually thought Morgan had cued the townsfolk with a slight nod or tap of his finger, but since it was so subtle Red couldn't be sure. The question of why hovered in the air. There was no obvious reason, so therefore she had no real clue.

Red and Morgan drove back to Nuria in silence. She appreciated the fact that he hadn't said "told you so" after the last inquiry. Red wasn't so sure she'd have been as gracious.

Night settled onto the town, blanketing it in dark-ness. Except for a few scattered solar-powered street-lights and indoor lighting, the place was like pitch. Red was no closer to discovering an answer than she'd been the day she found Lisa Solomon's body. If today was any indication of how things would go, she wasn't sure she'd ever get an answer. Or at least the answer she wanted to hear.

Red's three-day break had come and gone without so much as a single straight response from the Nurians. As soon as they saw her coming, people suddenly remembered appointments or work that couldn't wait a moment longer. The ones who couldn't get away gave pat replies—as if they'd comlinked their neighbors and asked what they should say.

Worst of all, she'd had to contact her grandfather and extend her leave for another day. He'd been very unhappy to hear the news. It broke her heart to have to reject his pleas to return—but for the first time, she wanted something more than she wanted to make him happy.

Red wanted justice for Lisa Solomon.

Standing up to her grandfather had been both frightening and exhilarating. Here in Nuria she was carving her own path, making her own decisions without worrying about the wrong thing ending up on her permanent record. And it felt good. Yet with this small victory came frustration. Frustration with the people of Nuria. It ate at her as she climbed out of the vehicle once more and dusted off her clothes. If she didn't get a lead tomorrow, Red knew she'd have to let the case go unsolved. At least . . . Lisa Solomon's death would remain so in her mind. It didn't matter what the reports said.

But the thought sickened her. She wasn't accustomed to giving up. She didn't *want* to give up.

The truth was here somewhere, just out of reach, hiding in the shadows of ambivalence . . . or perhaps fear. Red wasn't sure which. All she knew was that she needed more time, but she had little left.

She shut the vehicle door and headed inside the share space to her room. Morgan's eyes never left her back. She could feel the heat of his gaze as it scorched her skin.

Red swallowed hard, ignoring her body's immediate response.

Morgan was growing impatient. Well, impatient wasn't entirely accurate. More like *aware*. He'd been nothing but polite while driving them around town and into the outback areas, but she could sense the tension lurking below his calm exterior. She'd offered to go alone or with one of his deputies to ease Morgan's discomfort, but he'd flat-out refused, snapping at her like a kicked dog for even making the suggestion.

Not that she could blame him.

She had given him her word that she'd leave after a few days if she couldn't turn up anything. Red knew she'd passed that point, which meant she'd gone back on her word. Yet that didn't exactly cover what was occurring between them.

Morgan's uneasiness raked her nerves, leaving her raw and exposed. On more than one occasion, Red had caught him watching her when he thought she wasn't paying attention. The look he gave her was unsettling and his consideration appeared to be intensifying with each passing day.

Red wasn't a fool. She knew what it was, because she felt the sexual tension thrumming through her body, too. It slithered beneath her skin, wrapping its talons around her insides until she could barely breathe. It was only a matter of time before they did something they'd both regret. Or at least she would. Afterward.

Even as the thought entered her mind, Red had to admit that regret wouldn't really factor into sex with Morgan Hunter. But it would cause complications. Ones that until now she'd never had to face.

In the past, sex had always been a physical release from the stress her job brought. She'd never used it to connect emotionally with a man. Not that she had a deep emotional connection to Morgan, but she did *like* him. And that fact alone made the idea of sex with the sheriff extremely dangerous.

Red knew that meant she'd have to be extra vigilant around him and not give into her baser instincts—no matter how badly her body craved his touch. That would mean ignoring the strong line of his lightly stubbled jaw, pretending not to notice his firm lips when they puckered over the mouth of the canteen, and avoiding the heated looks that came from his amber gaze. The warmth from his eyes alone could sear the clothes off her body.

That last thought had Red aching. She squeezed her thighs together and grunted, ignoring her body's steady throb. Damn, she needed to close this case and get out of Nuria fast.

Morgan had watched Gina's sashaying ass until it disappeared inside the share space. He was losing it. There was no doubt in his mind. He'd barely kept his hands to himself today. It was only a matter of time now.

The longer he escorted her around town, the less control he had over his urges. It was as if a veritable army of fire ants had taken up permanent residence under his skin, biting and attempting to gnaw their way out. No amount of scratching could alleviate the itch or ensuing discomfort.

A man shouldn't have to walk around hard as a

pike, which explained his foul mood all day. Sitting in the cab of the vehicle had been downright painful. Morgan needed a woman. Bad. Unfortunately, with Gina's arrival, not just any woman would do.

Damn her tactical team hide!

It didn't help matters that the town was watching them, waiting for him to make his move. How much longer would they be patient? He didn't know. The fact that the full moon would rear its pale head in a few days' time didn't help either. What would he do then? He was barely hanging on as it was. Throw the moon into the mix and he'd never be able to fight the urge to touch her, lick her—and ultimately fuck her.

Morgan's cock grew harder at the mere notion of parting her thighs and partaking of her warmth. For a moment his vision blurred as the wolf tried to slip past him and take control. After several gulps of air and a firm grip on the steering wheel, Morgan managed to calm down.

He knew he should've assigned one of his deputies to accompany Gina, but the thought of another male staring at her lush body, relishing her musky scent, or tasting her moist lips made him slip from sane to murderous in seconds.

He was alpha, damn it. And that meant something, even if Gina didn't know it.

The lights were off in the water exchange and the place appeared to be locked down tight as Red approached. She slipped her palm onto the pad and the door slid silently open, allowing her access.

She was headed for the stairs when mumbles

coming from the exchange area caught her attention. Red paused. She could just make out Jesse's gruff voice.

"She's here about a murder. Asking questions all over town."

There was a pregnant silence.

"I was shocked, too. Rumor has it some woman was found in the dead forest half eaten. Perfect place for one, you know? Can't hear screams in there."

Red listened hard for a reply, but caught nothing.

Jesse spoke again. "My thoughts exactly. We both know what she's looking for. How long has it been since we've seen trouble like this? Twenty years? Fifty? My mind's not what it used to be."

Unintelligible whispers followed.

"The sheriff knows what needs to be done. He'll do what's necessary, once he stops thinking with his cock and starts thinking with his head. I've never seen the man so wound up over a piece of tail. She's a good girl, but she's still IPTT."

There was another pause.

"You're right." Jesse nodded. "It might be time for a change in leadership. We need someone whose priority is the town. We can't have an outsider nosing around in our business. She might find out."

Red ignored the remark about Morgan and willed them to go on. *Keep it coming*. Just a little more and maybe she'd have some answers.

She stepped silently trying to edge closer. Red could just make out Jesse's eye-patched profile. The other person stood behind a pillar blocked from view. A panel under Red's foot squeaked.

The conversation stopped as Jesse swung around,

her one-eyed gaze piercing the darkness. Red sank into the shadows, pressing her body flat against the wall until she all but blended into her surroundings.

"It's not safe to talk here," Jesse said. "The walls have ears." She led whomever she spoke with out a back door.

Red glimpsed the broad shoulders of a man, but she couldn't tell who he was. She'd been unable to hear his voice, which was odd, considering her acute sense of hearing. The urge to follow was overwhelming, but she'd already blown the perfect opportunity to learn something new.

No matter.

Red continued up the stairs to her room, hope blooming inside of her for the first time since her arrival. Something strange was going on in Nuria and she wasn't about to leave until she found out what.

chapter nine

S he is beautiful, in her own unique way. Not like the others. Different. Her red hair glistens like copper in the sunlight. I've seen her here before with the old woman, cooing and fussing, lavishing her love freely. They have the same color eyes. Green. Reminds me of grass, from the pictures I've seen.

I continue to stare, unable to prevent myself as I listen to her breathy voice, whispering endearments. They wash over my body, scoring my skin, leaving wounds of desire behind. How I wish she were speaking to me.

She will.

Soon.

Her breasts jiggle beneath her sweater. The sound of the material scraping over sensitive flesh whispers in the air. I close my eyes as my breath catches in my throat. I imagine my tongue curling around her ripe nipples, teasing her until they engorge with blood, the delicate rosy points stabbing at my mouth, begging for my touch. And my touch only. I can almost taste her.

I open my eyes to gaze upon her loveliness once more, her beauty nearly blinding me.

She hasn't noticed me yet, but she will.

They all do eventually.

I am remarkable.

She's bending over now, palming the floor. Her lush ass raises high in the air as she reaches for something she must have dropped. I lick my lips and feel the flesh between my thighs begin to grow. It's an offer as old as time.

I recognize and accept it.

It calls to me.

She must feel it, too.

She stands and casually glances around. The bauble in her hand flashes blue in the light. She brings it to her dainty ear. Ah, it must be an earring. Not that she needs any adornment. Her beauty is pure.

She's perfect.

That's why I've chosen her to be *my* one.

My only.

I know her first name is Moira. Soon I will know her last. Like a sprite from another world, she flits around the bed, fluffing pillows, comforting the old woman. Why she spends so much time with the soon to be dead and recycled, I do not know.

Can't she smell the stench of decay emanating from the old woman's bones? It nearly chokes me with its putrefaction.

Moira's time would be better spent cradling my body, satisfying my cock, accepting what I long to give to her. What I will give her. Soon. I cannot offer immortality, but she can glimpse the future within my eyes. With her by my side, I can lead my people to their rightful place in society.

I inhale.

The fresh floral scent of clean skin as it mixes with sweet dewy blood wafts in the air. I know it's Moira. No other could expand my lungs and shaft in such a way to create this dazzling euphoria.

She glances over her shoulder and smiles at me. *My what lovely teeth you have.* All the better to bite me with, when I claim you.

How I long to take her here. Now. But I can't. I must wait. The sun is still high in the sky. There are preparations to make and I want to cleanse myself. Like a divine gift from above, the perfect time will present itself.

It always does.

And I am patient.

I return her smile and wave, before moving on to find out more information about her. My excitement builds. It's always like this when I meet someone new. The muscles in my body tense as adrenaline rushes through me. My heart beats wildly in my chest. I have a skip to my step as I anticipate the upcoming event.

Faces pass before my eyes. I answer their questions and they answer mine, yet I barely hear their voices as a steady thrum of *soon* fills my head. At least now I have her last name.

Collins.

The rest of my day is a blur as I gather more information and wait for Moira Collins to leave. She parks behind the building and drives a beat-up hydrogen electric hybrid that looks secondhand. Pity for her, but good for me. The vehicle's condition mixed with the slight modification I decided to provide makes it so easy to follow her home.

Not that she'll ever get there.

I know she won't care because she'll be with me.

She drives unhurriedly past Nuria, leaving the lights and safety of the town behind. I shift my engine to cruise mode and turn off the lights, so she doesn't see me—yet. The road meanders for miles ahead of us. No sign of civilization in either direction. I smile. I can't help it. I'm happy.

I get like that when I'm about to meet the love of my life.

Moira's car sputters, then jerks, coughing out its last gasps of life.

Perfect timing.

She glances into the darkness, her hands gripping the wheel. I can't see her expression, but I imagine she is beginning to experience fear. I don't want her scared, but I suppose it cannot be helped.

I wait for a beat, until she exits the transport, then I turn on my lights. Relief floods her expression. I stop, leaving the comfort of my vehicle behind to approach her. She smiles in recognition as I momentarily come to her rescue. I love this part the best, playing the hero.

"I'm so glad to see you," Moira says.

I wonder how long that glee will last, but I still relish the sentiment. "I'm glad I could be here for you."

My cock is painfully hard, demanding release. I ignore my needs for now and pretend to look at the computerized engine in her craft. I move the cables around for show and furrow my brow. Truth is I already know what's wrong with it.

The missing chip brushes my thigh from inside my pocket. For a second, I consider putting it back in the car, but I know I won't. It's not in my nature.

Moira's smile widens encouragingly. The invitation in her eyes is plan to see.

I accept her enticement.

The smile on her face begins to fade, morphing into terror before my eyes.

The change has begun.

The muscles in my arms and legs feel as if I'm being drawn and quartered. Pain splits my skull, but I refuse to show weakness in front of my lovely Moira. What kind of *man* would I be if I couldn't handle a little pain?

She takes a step back and screams, a second before looking around for escape.

But it's too late.

We both know it.

In a moment, I'll be in my *true* form.

Ah, that's better.

The colors of the world take on deeper intensity. My senses explode with awareness. I understand things on a cellular level. I can smell Moira's fear crisp and intense on the evening breeze. I cherish the musical rhythm of her heart as it slams against her ribs while she labors for breath.

I go to speak, to tell her about all the wonderful sensations, but only a growl comes out. She cowers, clearly missing out on the beauty of this moment. I take a step forward.

Moira runs.

Why do they all run?

Where she thinks she's going, I do not know.

I watch her sprint to my car, frantically searching for a way to start it, but the vehicle will not recognize her palm print. Nor will it recognize mine. She throws herself away from the car and races toward a nearby hill.

There are no homes out here. I know this area like the back of my clawed pad. It's one of my favorite places to run. To chase. To hunt. To kill.

Doesn't she realize she is the chosen one?

She's *perfect*.

I walk after her. There is no reason to sprint. She has nowhere to go. Her screams intensify. The sound makes my cock pulse and the blood gush through my veins. The thrill of the chase begins. I start to lope.

Moira rounds the top of the hill, her muscles straining under the stress of the climb. Her legs fly out from under her as she trips and begins to tumble down the other side. The crunch of bones hitting rocks reaches my ears, along with Moira's cries of pain.

This isn't supposed to happen.

She's ruining my plans.

Moira disappoints me.

I thought she was better than this. I expected her to accept her new position as my mate with grace and beauty. But she's not.

She's like all the others.

Inferior.

Their fear and loathing disgusts me, yet I do not lose interest in the chase.

I know they see superiority when they look upon me. Moira is no exception.

How could they not?

I'm perfection incarnate with my fine pelt, taloned claws, and razor-sharp incisors.

I follow the path Moira took, only to find her lying in a crumpled pile at the bottom of the hill. For a second, she looks like discarded rubble. Her twisted leg points in a strange direction, opposite her body and her eyes are staring skyward at a blanket full of stars.

Oh lovely Moira, what have you done?

Tsk . . . Tsk . . . Tsk.

She whimpers as I come into view.

At least she's still alive. I was about to think this evening had been a total waste. I crouch down beside her and gently stroke her coppery hair with the back of my talons. I'm sure it's downy soft, but I cannot feel it at present.

Moira's whimpers grow in volume and she struggles to gain her feet. I press her back down with no effort whatsoever.

We both know what must be done.

Someone must ease her suffering.

Since I'm the only one here, it'll have to be me.

But first, I strip away her clothing, admiring her breasts, while taking care not to touch her leg. She's trembling now. I'm sure she's as turned on as I am. I run my taloned pad over her skin, leaving a crimson trail of blood behind.

I inhale, my nose inches from her quivering flesh. The sweetness almost sends me over the edge, but I manage to gain control. I must taste her. I stick out my tongue and run it along the oozing path I just created.

Delicious.

Intoxicating.

Perfect.

I lap her flesh again. The rough pad of my tongue rasps her skin, widening the wound I inflicted. She bleeds freely for me now. I try to thank her, but her cries become garbled and my muzzle is wet.

Stay with me, Moira.

I'm not done yet.

My cock has risen higher with my growing need.

I glance down at Moira. Her feminine folds are covered by matching copper curls. I must taste her there. I lick and nuzzle her, savoring her essence. She tries to twist away, but I can still feel the hard nub of her desire.

She wants me.

I knew it.

I yip in excitement, then delve between her thighs with gusto. Laving and nipping, swirling my tongue inside her body. The ambrosia drowns me.

I want more.

I need more.

I will have more.

My body shakes as I continue to taste her lusciousness. It's too much. The sensations. The colors. I can't hold back and I haven't even entered her yet. Oh gods, I'm coming now. I rock my hips, trying to milk my release. Inside my mind, I'm screaming. Outside, I hear only happy growls.

Moira isn't crying anymore.

In fact, I haven't felt her move since *we* reached completion. My hips jerk one last time and I lift my muzzle. It drips with blood. The coppery elixir splats as it hits a growing pool beneath my chin.

I glance down.

Confused.

Moira's abdomen is missing.

For a second I wonder where it went, then I remember. I lick my lips. Moira's essence floods my taste buds, yet leaves me longing for something more. And I think I know what, or more precisely *who*.

I picture the black-haired sorceress who's occupied my fantasies as of late. I've tried to fight our growing attraction, but it's like attempting to stave off the sun.

Gina.

Can you hear me?

I'm calling to you.

I thought the others were perfect, but now I know the truth. They pale in comparison.

You *are* the perfect one.

I close my eyes and imagine Gina Santiago before me. Her long legs bared and her breasts released from their material confines. Her hair would be loose, so I could run my talons through it. I wouldn't waste my seed outside of her body.

No, not with my beautiful Gina.

She's special.

I sensed it.

She would carry my seed inside of her womb. Grow ripe with my spawn, so we could step out of the shadows of hiding and take our rightful place in society.

I know I can convince her. I can be *very* persuasive. But first I must complete my task.

I note the scavengers waiting for me to finish, their squeaks and scurries perk my ears. I do not want to disappoint them, so I gorge myself, devouring Moira's tender flesh, taking her bones into my body. I especially love the crunch of her teeth. They remind me of popcorn kernels. I eat until I can't take another bite.

Come, I urge the creatures of the night.

The scavengers have their niche to fill. And I have mine.

You're next, Gina.

chapter ten

Red awoke with a start, rocketing up in bed. Her body burned and her nipples ached. She wiped her sweating palms on the sheet and tried to calm her raging heartbeat as it pounded painfully. Her gaze darted around the darkened room.

Nothing moved.

She listened, her ears straining, trying to ascertain what had startled her out of a sound sleep. No breathing. No footsteps.

Nothing to explain the sudden rush of adrenaline. Yet it was there, burning beneath her skin like a low-grade fever.

Had she been dreaming? Panic slammed her as she threw back the covers and glanced at her body. Her bedclothes were clean, free of blood. "Oh, thank goodness," she whispered. At least that wasn't the cause of her distress. She bent to retrieve the blanket. The small movement brought awareness flaring to life. Had she been having an erotic dream? Red tried to recall the seconds before waking, but no images came to mind. Yet there was no denying her body's need.

If Morgan were here right now, she'd pounce on him.

Shaken, she stared into the darkness, waiting to calm, but her body was too tense. There was only one way she'd be able to get back to sleep. Red slipped her hand under the covers and into her underpants, while imagining Morgan naked, standing in front of her. She groaned. Moisture met her fingertips as she began to stroke her clit.

Morgan would be hard and erect as he watched her masturbate, his muscles quivering with need. Red's body bowed as she strummed her flesh, her hips rocking against her hand. Her fingers weren't nearly as deft as a man's mouth, but they'd have to do.

Writhing upon the rest pad, she pictured Morgan's dark head buried between her thighs. His golden eyes locked on her face. That was all it took. Her orgasm hit like a shockwave, sending ripples over her body.

"Morgan!" Red cried out his name as she came.

Gasping for air, it took several minutes for the room to come back into focus. By the time it did, she'd finally relaxed. Red fell back onto the rest pad and closed her eyes, replete.

Morgan Hunter stood in the cleansing room unable to move, his mind churning with the knowledge that Gina had actually called out his name while pleasuring herself. For a second, he'd thought she'd realized he was there, hiding like a thief in the night. But she hadn't.

He released a breath he hadn't known he was holding as he watched Gina drop back onto the rest pad and fall fitfully off to sleep. The act had been excruciating to watch, when every fiber of his being demanded that he replace her fingers with his. Mesmerized by the rise and fall of her nipples, he tried to ignore his body's steady ache. It was impossible after witnessing the beauty of her release.

Soon he'd be unable to ignore the craving, even though he had tried for the past three days. If anything, it had become worse.

The physical activity he'd forced upon his body earlier hadn't deterred or dampened his ardor. He wanted Gina more than he wanted his next breath.

Morgan knew he shouldn't be here, that he'd crossed the invisible line from unprofessional to stalker behavior long ago. He was acting like a fool, yet he couldn't help himself. The need was too great and her desire for him wasn't helping.

He scrubbed a hand over his face in disgust. What was wrong with him? He'd never behaved this way around a woman.

He'd stolen into her room. Not sure why or what he expected to happen once he got here. He just needed to see her.

Be near.

He'd been fighting the attraction between them and tonight, he'd lost the battle.

Morgan wanted to feel Gina's skin beneath him, her breasts scraping his chest. Hear her soft cries in his ears as he brought her to peak. He needed to breathe in her scent as he spread her thighs in order to taste her feminine essence. Brand her with his kisses, until she was oblivious to all other males. The urge to fuck her senseless nearly overwhelmed him.

Ashamed and more than a little confused by the possessive feelings coursing through him, Morgan forced himself to move from his hiding place in the cleansing room. He needed to walk toward the door and leave, before he did something they'd both regret—like *act*.

Morgan's muscles ached from standing so still and his cock was hard enough to bore holes through the floor. Each step was excruciating. It took all the self-control he'd cultivated in himself to continue.

He inhaled, taking Gina's lovely sweat-soaked fragrance into his lungs. Morgan swayed, momentarily intoxicated. It wasn't difficult to imagine her in the throes of passion once again.

Morgan bit the inside of his mouth to keep from groaning aloud. He tasted the coppery tang of his own blood as he opened the door and slipped out of the room.

There was no doubt that he'd lost it.

He turned as the door was about to close, needing to catch one more glimpse of the woman he desired before he headed for home.

Gina's form remained still in the darkness, her modest breasts hidden beneath a thin shirt. Morgan could just make out the hard peaks of her nipples as her chest rose evenly. It wasn't difficult to imagine her pearlescent skin, topped with delicious nuggets of rouge-colored flesh. His mouth watered at the thought of tasting her.

He took a ragged breath.

She was *perfect*.

Red listened intently, while keeping her breathing regulated so that it appeared she slept. Slowly she moved her hand until she could grip her pistol beneath the covers.

She was not alone. Someone had been watching her the whole time.

She opened her eyes just enough to allow her to peek out from beneath her lashes and then waited. For what, Red wasn't sure. She was about to give up, when she caught movement in her room.

There.

Her heart nearly stopped in her chest when Morgan stepped out of the cleansing room. Like a shadow dancing in light, he moved silently with a stealth she'd never witnessed in a man.

How in the hell had he gotten in here? And what was he doing?

She hated that her instincts had been right. Red watched him, waiting for him to make a move. He didn't. Instead, Morgan stared at her, his body covered in sweat, muscles tense. His face contorted in what appeared to be a grimace of pain—except it wasn't. Red recognized that expression.

It was *need*.

Desire rolled in waves from his body, battering her, demanding that she notice. And Red did, despite her orgasm earlier. Her senses reacted instantly. The physical response to his nearness hit her like a blow, both frightening and fascinating her.

She wanted him, almost as much as he wanted her. There was no denying it.

Red had known that was the case the second she'd laid eyes on him. She'd just chosen to ignore it. Mutual attraction aside, that didn't change the fact that Morgan had no right to be here.

When she was ready, and only when she was ready, she would invite him onto her rest pad. Not a moment beforehand. Red debated what to do. If she sat up and confronted him, her investigation would hit a dead end, or worse—they'd fuck.

Too bad neither option was acceptable.

Her body screamed at her in protest.

Instead, Red waited. What did Morgan plan to do? The thought sent her senses and imagination into overdrive. What if he walked over and climbed onto the rest pad with her? Would she kick him out? Doubtful. It took effort to keep her breathing steady, but Red managed as her nerves stretched to the breaking point.

If he didn't decide soon, she'd make the decision for him.

Finally, Morgan moved, picking his way toward the door, while his gaze remained locked on her. The panel slid open silently and he stepped out into the hallway. He stared at her for several seconds more and then closed the door.

Red exhaled, her body trembling with the effort it took to remain natural. Morgan's presence posed more questions than it answered. One thing was obvious, they couldn't continue with the investigation any longer. Tonight he'd crossed a line and she'd let him. Red didn't know which was more disturbing, her behavior or his. Tomorrow, like it or not, she'd have to confront Morgan about his midnight foray.

Red did not look forward to that conversation.

* * *

The sun splashed into the room, waking Red from her fitful sleep. Her eyes felt as if someone dumped glass in them during the night, thanks to Morgan's uninvited visit and the erotic dreams that had followed. She swallowed. Her mouth tasted gritty, like she'd been chewing on sand.

Red rose and stumbled to the cleansing room with her eyes closed, debating whether the best course of action was to confront Morgan or proposition him. The latter, though appealing, wasn't really her style.

She relieved herself, then stood to peer into the mirror. Red cracked an eye open and blinked. She froze, her mind refusing to accept what she was seeing. It was like déjà vu.

Not again. Please. Not again.

Dried blood covered the front of her shirt and one cheek. The coppery odor clung to her skin, gagging her. She knew without checking that the blood wasn't hers. Red's stomach rebelled. She threw up what looked like raw chunks of partially digested meat into the waste retrieval system.

Fear sliced through her, leaving her teeth chattering as she recalled Morgan's nocturnal visit. She'd seen him leave and he hadn't come back. Or at least she didn't think he had. What if . . .

Horrified, her eyes bulged. Was it possible she'd harmed him without her knowledge? She barely knew Morgan, but the pain of that thought left her reeling. Red did a quick search of her room, but nothing had been disturbed. Unfortunately, given the last incident, that didn't prove a thing.

She slipped off her shirt, but this time didn't incinerate it. Instead, she bagged the cloth like it was evidence at a crime scene. Hell, for all she knew, it was. She had to find Morgan to make sure he was okay, and then get out of Nuria before this nightmare got any worse.

She stood under the chemical shower for what seemed like an eternity as she waited for her mind to clear and the tears to stop falling. Dressing slowly, Red pulled on her boots as she attempted to recall the events of last night. Surely she'd remember if she'd hurt Morgan, wouldn't she? It didn't bear thinking about.

She slipped Rita onto her wrist, but kept her on standby. The last thing Red needed was for her to run a diagnostic on her. She was scared at what she'd find.

Red swept her hair back off her face and headed out the door. She didn't bother to stop at the instant food dispenser. She doubted her stomach would hold anything. Instead, she walked straight to the sheriff's office and barged in without knocking.

Morgan's assistant sat at her desk, staring at the screen of her compunit.

"Is Morgan here? I need to speak with him." *Please let him be okay.* She sent up the silent prayer without breaking the woman's gaze.

"He's unavailable at the moment. Would you like to leave a message?" She smiled.

"You've seen him this morning?"

The woman frowned. "Yes."

Well at least he was alive. Red released a breath she hadn't known she was holding. "I have to talk to him. It's important." If only to see for herself that he was in one piece. Red didn't wait for a response. She entered Morgan's office. It was empty.

"Hey, you can't do that." The woman called out behind her. "I said he wasn't in."

Red spun around, her gaze bulleting on the woman. "Where in the hell is he?"

"Sheriff Hunter was called out early this morning."

"To where?" Red snapped, not meaning to be rude, but too freaked out to care.

The woman glanced around nervously. "I'm not at liberty to give that information out in the middle of a case."

Red's gaze narrowed. "I've had very little sleep, a shitty morning, and I'm not the most patient person on a normal day. I would appreciate it if you tell me where I can find him. I don't want to have to call headquarters to use the tactical team's tracking system." The threat slammed hard like she'd intended, even though it was a lie. There was no way in hell she'd contact the team. Not until she understood what was going on.

The woman's face flushed with color and she began fumbling through her notes. A moment later Red had the information she needed. She hopped into her hydrogen car, directions in hand, and headed out of town. The road into the desert stretched for miles. Red thought she and Morgan had covered everywhere, yet she knew they'd never come this way. So why did it look so familiar?

Morgan had been having another erotic dream, involving the dark-haired woman. She'd ridden his body hard, her firm thighs gripping his sides as she rotated her hips, grinding her wetness onto his erect shaft. Her nipples were rouge-colored and protruded from her pale flesh like morning blooms at dawn. He'd laved and suckled them until they'd puckered. He could still taste the sweetness on his tongue.

It was only when he'd reached for her to pull her into an embrace that he realized the woman riding him in his dream was Gina Santiago. He should've known she wouldn't leave his dreams alone. Now she was haunting his days and his nights. He'd groaned, unable to hold out any longer. The second his tongue parted her lips the vidcom buzzed, shaking him from his slumber and the best fuck of his life.

That had been forty-five minutes ago. Now here he was standing over Moira Collins' lifeless body. He hadn't even managed to grab a cup of synth-coffee before he'd left.

Morgan glanced around the scene. Moira had suffered like Renee Forrester and at the hands of the same individual. He didn't know how he knew that to be true, but he did. Morgan still didn't understand why he couldn't catch the killer's scent. It was almost as if it had been masked, which was nearly impossible. Not many shifters had the ability, only the ones who'd been around for a while. That narrowed the list of suspects some, but not much.

Morgan knew he needed to get the body back to the dissecting lab before Gina awoke and found out the news. He raised his hand to the comlink in his ear and put another call into Jim Thornton, reminding him once again to hurry.

* * *

Red found Morgan's vehicle parked right where his assistant said he would be. She killed the engine and jumped out. Scanning the area, she didn't immediately spot Morgan. Where was he? She was about to hike down the road when she heard rustling coming from the other side of a nearby hill.

Thank God, she thought. He really was alive.

As she crested the ridge of dirt, the odor of death hit Red in the face, nearly toppling her backward. Her relief plummeted. Red's empty stomach gurgled and her mouth watered. She swallowed hard to keep from vomiting again.

Morgan stood at the bottom of the hill, a woman's body lying at his feet. *There's been another one.* The thought entered her head before Red could stop it. After a couple of deep breaths, she carefully picked her way down the steep incline.

Morgan looked up as she neared. "It didn't take you long to find her," he said, his voice weary.

Red stared at him for a moment. He looked as if he hadn't gotten much sleep either. She should be mad, but all she could feel was grateful. "I wasn't looking for *her*," she said.

Morgan's gut clenched at Gina's words. Even with death staring him in the face, he still wanted her. Like a smoke stick addict, he craved her. He couldn't seem to get enough of her and he hadn't even touched her yet.

He glanced down at the body at his feet. Morgan

had hoped to have the scene cleaned up before Gina arose. He should've known that would never happen. Nothing about this woman came easy, which was probably why he found her so irresistible.

Morgan shifted, trying to catch her scent over the smell of death. He frowned and inhaled again. His heart thudded as the odor of blood hit him. And not just any blood—Moira's blood.

His veins filled with ice, leaving him shaken. There had to be some mistake. Perhaps the body tainted his senses. He sniffed. The scent was more subtle now, but there nonetheless. Morgan stilled, his mind in turmoil.

How had Gina gotten Moira's blood on her?

"Do you know who she is?" Red covered the remaining feet separating her from the body.

Morgan's gold eyes sparked a second before dimming. "Her name is Moira Collins. From the evidence I've gathered it appears she fell down the hill and broke her leg. Unfortunately, for Moira, she couldn't move when the animals closed in to feed."

Red grimaced as she took in the gruesome scene. Blood was scattered for at least fifteen feet. Bite marks of various sizes covered the naked body. The woman's lifeless eyes stared in horror at the sky. "Animals you say?" she asked, circling wide to study the trampled ground.

"Yes, that's what I said," he snapped, drawing her attention away from the body. "When I arrived there were still scavengers feeding upon her. I had to fire a shot to scare them away so I could approach the body."

Red took a deep breath and let it out. Why was he suddenly so mad? She dismissed it and decided to focus on the disturbance around Moira. "If it was a pack of animals, then how come there's only one set of large prints?" She pointed to the ground. "For that matter, why are her teeth missing? Animals tend to like bone that contains a fair amount of marrow. I have never seen one remove teeth."

"You'll eat anything, if you're hungry enough," Morgan barked. "I'm not an expert in animal behavior. We'll know more when we get her back to the dissecting lab."

Red flinched, but didn't back away from the lash of Morgan's temper. Something about Moira and this place seemed familiar. The blood on her shirt came back in a rush. What if? Was it even possible?

She blanched, looking at the prints and then down at her feet. Red felt the color drain from her face a second before her body swayed.

Morgan reached out to steady her, his fingers gently clutching her elbow. His warmth crept into her body despite the clothing between them. "Are you okay?" he asked. "You look . . ." His voice trailed off and he released her suddenly as if he couldn't stand to touch her. "The scene's pretty bad. You don't have to stay."

"I'm fine," she said, except she wasn't. She glanced down at Moira. She didn't know this woman, would swear she'd never seen her before. But some dark place inside of her recognized this scene. She'd been here before, whether she could recall the events or not.

She took a deep breath to calm herself. "Have you called it in?"

Morgan nodded. "Jim Thornton will be here any minute. I suppose you'll call in the tactical team now."

"No." She jerked her head in dissent. "I don't think that will be necessary unless the evidence contradicts your theory." That was the last thing she wanted. They'd strip her of her rank and assign her to desk duty—or worse yet, execute her for murder.

He eyed her cautiously, but Red also noticed the hope he'd been unable to hide, lingering in his gaze. "Does that mean you trust me to find the truth?"

Red nodded. She couldn't explain it, but for some reason she did trust Morgan. On a gut level, Red realized that he was a good man. She refused to acknowledge what else her gut was telling her.

"What do you plan to do, if you don't mind me asking?" he asked softly.

Red knew she couldn't leave now. Not without knowing what really happened, no matter how frightening it turned out to be. She looked at Morgan, meeting his cool amber gaze. She'd have to face what was happening between them, too. No way could she ignore him, if she stayed in town. Her heart picked up a notch at the multitude of possibilities.

"It looks like I'll be extending my leave."

chapter eleven

Jim Thornton arrived ten minutes later dressed in his rumpled gray lab coat. His disheveled red hair poked out in all directions as if he'd just gotten out of bed, which was probably the case. It was still too early for most people to start their day.

He squinted against the bright morning sun and swiped a beefy hand across his damp forehead, leaving a streak of sweat glistening on his skin before glancing their way. The surprise on his face upon seeing Red was quickly masked as he shot a wary glance at Morgan.

Red watched Morgan frown, but he didn't say anything.

"Not exactly what I like to find first thing in the morning," Jim said, pressing a button on the small brown box he carried. There was a ten-second buzz, then a biobag popped out and began to expand like a portable life raft.

Red watched the clear bag grow larger and larger until it equaled the size of the woman sprawled on the ground.

"Looks like an animal attack," Jim said absently as he pulled on thick rubber gloves.

"We thought that was the case, but we're not positive," Red replied, before the sheriff could.

The crease in Morgan's brow deepened. "What took you so long?" he asked. "I had to call twice."

"I got here as soon as I could. I was out doing my normal morning boundary rounds on the other side of the republic, when I received the call. I triggered several speed trackers in my rush to get here. I'm sure your office has already received copies in order to issue the fines." His lips thinned as he peered down at Moira's body. "Sorry I couldn't get here sooner," he said, shooting a glance at Red.

She wasn't sure what Jim was referring to since his presence wouldn't have changed what happened to Moira Collins. Her gut knotted. Did they want to keep her death a secret? The thought didn't sit well with her, even though for now, she wanted the same thing. Red was the last tactical team member anyone would suspect of skirting the law. Other team members considered her hard-nosed, completely unbendable. She may not always listen to orders, but she respected the law. Red laughed to herself at how far she'd fallen from that assessment.

With the biobag fully inflated, Jim hit another button. The bag flipped, encasing Moira's body like a mummy inside a sarcophagus, then with a whoosh of air, slowly began to rise off the ground. "I'll get her back to the lab where I can do a full examination on her. I'm sure I'll find whatever evidence has been left behind."

Red looked at Morgan. He nodded to Jim.

"I'm going to stick around here for a while longer. I haven't finished surveying the scene," Morgan said.

"If you wouldn't mind, I'd like to tag along with Jim. I've heard stories, but I have never seen the work that goes on inside a dissecting lab," she said.

Morgan couldn't hide his surprise. He'd obviously expected her to stay and help. Normally, she would have, but not today.

Jim's, eyes bulged as if his pants had suddenly squeezed his privates. He grabbed a rag from his pocket and wiped his sweaty brow, then glanced at Morgan, silently asking permission. Red thought it was odd, but decided to wait for the sheriff's response.

"I thought you'd want to stick around and investigate the scene further. Make sure that I hadn't missed anything," Morgan said.

Red forced a smile. She needed to get back to the lab and get the blood on her shirt analyzed—not that she wasn't enjoying Morgan's surprise. "I figured you could handle it."

Morgan arched a brow. "That's a first."

"Funny." She smirked.

His eyes sparkled for a moment as he watched her.

"Besides," she continued, "it looks like Jim could use a hand . . . unless you need me to stay."

"I can handle gathering the rest of the evidence. You go with Jim. I'm sure he'll be more than happy to walk you through the finer points of human dissection. It'll only take him an hour or four." He grinned, shaking his head. "You've been warned."

"Don't listen to him," Jim said, his face flushing a dark red that surpassed his hair color. "Some people just don't appreciate the intricate details of human dissection."

"Can't wait." Red reached out to help guide the biobag as she and Jim started to climb up the small hill toward the road. She hadn't decided how she would broach the subject of her bloody clothing yet, but she'd come up with something.

Rocks skittered under their feet, raining down where Moira had lain. The poor woman had suffered greatly after breaking her leg. Red prayed it wasn't at her hands. A twitch at the base of her neck shook her from her morbid thoughts.

Red could feel Morgan's gaze on her back, if the heat scrolling over her shoulder blades was any indication. The sand and pebbles continued to fall, causing her to release the biobag to steady herself. She was unwilling to believe that Morgan's attention had anything to do with her sudden bout of clumsiness.

Red glanced back and caught the speculative expression on Morgan's upturned face. His eyes met hers and the world of death and destruction dropped away. It was only the two of them, and the burning need that incinerated everything else.

Red's body clenched, remembering the scalding heat she'd experienced the night before. His mere presence had fired her blood like nothing on this planet. How could she be thinking about such things at a time like this? Where was her compassion, her professionalism? No matter how wrong she knew it was,

Red couldn't dampen the attraction building between them any more than she could revive poor Moira.

Morgan watched Red's sexy ass as she climbed the hill. His mind was in turmoil, but his body was single-minded—it wanted relief. He had no choice now but to allow her to stay on and help with the investigation, even though it would further complicate matters. It was the only way he'd find out the truth. But he wasn't fool enough to believe that was the sole reason for keeping her around.

He wanted her, plain and simple. This was the first time, since his ex's betrayal with Raphael, that he'd ever wanted anything for himself. Although *want* didn't truly begin to describe the desire rioting through him. He was more like crazed with need—thanks to the moon's pull.

Morgan forced his gaze away from her. He had to focus on this case, this scene—this murder.

Logically, he knew that there was no reason to suspect Gina of the killings. She was down here investigating on her own time, but that didn't explain the blood trace on her body. How had she gotten it? Had she somehow come in contact with the killer? The thought chilled him.

So far he'd been unable to come up with a viable alternative theory. Nothing made sense. Unless she was the murderer. If she was, would he be able to do his duty and eliminate her? The thought of harming Gina left Morgan nauseous. He grasped his abdomen as bile rose in his throat, choking him.

A roar sounded as the engines of the hydrogen

vehicles came alive. He heard tires crunch as they rolled over gravel. Jim and Gina would reach Nuria within thirty minutes, if they didn't stop anywhere along the way.

A warm breeze streaked across the sky, ruffling his hair as he inhaled, trying to dispel the odor of death and to smell Gina once again. It took a moment, but Morgan finally caught her elusive fragrance. He closed his eyes.

The law might be clear in this circumstance, but his emotions and instincts were not. Gina was special to him and not just because she was an unattached female in his territory.

When was the last time a single female from the outside wandered into his territory? He considered the question a second before the obvious answer popped into his head.

Never.

Yet, Gina's nonexistent position in the pack was not what made her distinctive in his eyes. Nor was it her innate courage or confidence. The fact was Gina cared. Any other IPTT officer would've walked away after the case was closed, but not Gina. She demanded justice for those who could no longer speak for themselves.

Morgan ran his hand through his hair, refusing to delve into exactly why that mattered so much. He wasn't prepared to face that particular truth just yet, but he had to face another.

Now that Gina decided to stay there was concern for her physical safety. Morgan knew Gina could take care of herself. She'd been doing so for years on the tactical team, but that didn't change the customs of his people, which clearly stated that any unattached female Other had to be claimed by someone in the pack or run out of the Republic of Arizona. It hadn't been a problem when her plans were to stay a few days, but now that she'd extended her leave, it could cause trouble.

The Nurians established the law long ago in order to protect the pack from outsiders. It also prevented the pack from being torn apart from strife on the inside, since unclaimed females tended to cause fights among the males. The law had been necessary for their survival. Unfortunately, the world had changed little since that time.

Morgan hadn't offered Gina protection because he knew damn well she would have no idea what he was talking about. But the intention was there nonetheless, whether he'd physically claimed her or not. He knew it and so did half the town. That was one of the reasons he'd taken her to dinner the other night. Morgan had hoped to curtail any strife. It had worked thus far, but there was no way of knowing how long it would continue.

If anyone thought to challenge him on his decision to give her free rein, Morgan would be forced to leave the mark of the alpha upon her. He wasn't happy about the prospect, but there was no way in hell he'd allow anyone else to claim her.

Morgan reeled at the turn his wayward thoughts had taken, yet even surprise didn't mask the truth curling around his chest, fluttering his heart. The primal part of Morgan wanted someone to step forward in challenge just so he could bare Gina's neck and mark her.

A growl rumbled out of his throat before he could stop it. No one would dare try to take her away from him. He would kill him if he did.

If he bit her, Gina would carry his mark forever, whether she chose to stay by his side as his mate or return to her life with the IPTT. Morgan understood what the ramifications of that act would mean to him and to the future of his people. If Gina left, he'd never be able to claim another, since the wolf in him wouldn't allow it. Not that he'd want to—but that would mean he'd never have an heir.

He only hoped that it didn't come down to staking a claim. Morgan glanced around the crime scene, remembering the savagery of the attack. With his mark upon her neck, he'd never be able to kill Gina, even if she turned out to be the murderer. In the end, he'd die, too, trying to protect her. Morgan's lips canted. There were worse ways to go.

Red followed Jim Thornton back to the dissecting lab. She hadn't *exactly* been lying when she said that she was interested in the inner workings of his job, but she hadn't told the whole truth. She needed his help.

She considered various ways to subtly approach him about her shirt, but in the end decided to be direct. She watched as he drove his vehicle around the side of the building. He backed the wagon up until its rear nudged a small ramp, and then he stopped, killing the engine.

Red did the same, positioning her hydrogen car beside him. She grabbed the sack containing her shirt, then exited her vehicle. The heat from the sun hit her like a blast furnace. Sweat dotted her brow and soaked her clothes. Thirty minutes ago the temperature had been tolerable, but not any longer.

Jim guided Moira's body up the ramp until he reached the top, stopping at the door. He pressed several numbers on a keypad and a second later a panel opened with a hiss. Cool antiseptic air rushed out to battle the desert warmth, causing waves of heat to flutter before Red's eyes.

She followed Moira's body as it glided into the building on a cushion of air. The room was more spacious than what Red had expected. Steel tables spaced approximately five feet apart dotted the area. Lights hung above each workstation, illuminating dismembered remains. Mulch-gathering drains lined the floor, waiting for human waste. On the far side of the room a white tarp covered a still form.

That was odd, considering everyone else was exposed. Red opened her mouth to ask why, but the ghostly movement of Moira's body distracted her.

The fresh corpse came to rest on the bare table closest to the door as if her destination had been predetermined. The bag encasing Moira disintegrated with a gasp on contact, leaving her tattered remains behind. Bone protruded from her wounds like white twigs jutting out of a branch on a dead tree.

The stench of fear and animal feces lingered on her sparse flesh, accentuating her horrified expression. The fetid odor effectively blotted out the cleaning fluid used in the lab.

An eerie silence swept the room, hushing everything in its wake. Whatever had occurred out in the desert remained permanently etched on Moira's delicate features. Death had not come quickly.

Red's stomach flipped and she swallowed hard. Moira's face branded her mind's eye until she was convinced she'd never be able to extract it from her memory.

Memory, what a joke! She'd always prided herself on her recall ability, but not anymore. Bitterness filled her. Red couldn't remember a thing about a large portion of last night. It was as if someone had come in and removed select images from her mind, leaving only what they wanted her to see behind.

What was happening to her?

Was she physically capable of ripping a woman apart with her bare hands? Red glanced down at her knuckles and noted a few scrapes that she couldn't immediately account for. Her fingernails appeared chipped and jagged. The thud of flesh hitting the waste dispenser this morning when she'd vomited echoed in her mind.

Was she becoming a monster?

If she could do that to Moira and not remember a thing, then what else was she capable of? The thought terrified her. Red pictured Morgan's handsome face and her heart did a free fall to her knees. No one around her would be safe until she found out the truth. It was now or never.

Red faced Jim, her body trembling uncontrollably. "Mr. Thornton, could you do me a favor before you get started on your examination?"

He turned and smiled, until he noted her condition. Concern immediately replaced his jovial expression. "Are you okay?" he asked, removing the gloves he'd worn on the scene. He dropped them into an evidence bag, then donned a new pair with a smack.

"I'm fine, just cold." Her teeth chattered as if on cue. The sound was followed by another tremor wracking her body.

"It takes awhile to get used to the temperature change from outside to in here. I don't even notice it anymore." He pointed to a cabinet on the other side of the room. "I have extra lab coats in there, if you want one."

"That won't be necessary, but thanks."

"Suit yourself." He nodded.

"About the favor," Red said, reminding him.

"Yes, of course, what did you need?" he asked, shoving a finger between each digit to ensure the gloves were in place.

"I have something I'd like you to take a look at." She clenched the clear bag one last time, then held it out for him to inspect.

"What's this?" He frowned, bushy brows enveloping the tops of his glasses. "Is that blood?" he asked.

"Yes."

Jim's face paled.

Red took a deep breath and let it out slowly. "I'd like you to analyze this for me. I need to know whose blood this is."

His bushy brows furrowed, turning his eyes into tiny gleaming pinpricks. "Where did you find that? It wasn't at the scene, was it? Morgan didn't mention finding any clothing." His voice rose with the level of his concern.

"No, I didn't find the shirt with Moira's body." Red's throat closed, nearly choking off her words.

She'd never remove evidence from a scene. Why would he think such a thing?

Because you're acting suspicious, the little voice in her head said.

"Then where did you get it? I'll need to know for my reports." *And my own curiosity* was left unspoken. He reached for the bag.

Red drew it away from his grasp, suddenly unsure of her decision. She knew she was being ridiculous, but for the first time in her life she was actually scared. The feeling was alien and decidedly unwelcome. Red straightened, throwing her shoulders back and lifting her chin. She was no coward. She'd face the truth head on as she faced life. Red forced her muscles forward, releasing the bag and its contents reluctantly into his care.

"I'd appreciate it if you'd keep this out of the official reports for the time being. I'd prefer that it remain between us," she said.

He grimaced. "I'd need to know why you're asking this of me before I complied. It would also help to know who you're after. I don't want to get in trouble with the tactical team for suppressing evidence. They would pull my license and imprison me."

"This doesn't have anything to do with IPTT and I'm not after anyone specific. I'll take full responsibility for your actions. You have my word."

"Why would you do that?" Jim looked uneasy. "Have you mentioned this to Morgan?"

"No."

Red knew he didn't believe her. He probably suspected a setup and she couldn't really blame him. The tactical team hadn't always been a respected law-enforcement agency. There was a time when they'd savaged the continent in lawless abandon. Many had died for no reason.

That had been years ago, long before her grandfather had taken over leadership. Hell, he hadn't even been born when the massacres occurred, but some people never forgot the team's sordid past. And it looked as if Jim was one of them.

"I'm asking for your help. I rarely, if ever, do that."

Compassion filled his face, but the resolve in his voice remained steady. "Gina, whose shirt is this?" he asked, lifting the bag to take another look at the bloody contents.

"Mine," she said softly.

chapter twelve

Who does Roark Montgomery think he is, snapping at me like an angry mongrel dog? I don't take orders from him. I take orders from no man. He should know that by now, but he obviously needs a reminder.

I thought we had an understanding, but I was wrong. My fist rockets into a nearby wall, crumbling the plaster. It tumbles onto the floor, leaving a pile of rubble behind. Pain reverberates up my arm and blood covers my knuckles.

My eyes pinch shut to relish the sensation. It passes too quickly and I find myself slowly lapping the signs of injury away. The coppery taste of my essence tickles my tongue, while at the same time scorches my throat. Yet even that small pleasure does little to diminish my anger.

The beast struggles against my mental bindings, threatening to rise, forcing me to tamp it down. It wouldn't do to show my true self at present. For now I have the role of protector to play. I cannot give in, no matter how tempting. The goal of living out in the open is near.

Our heated conversation keeps repeating in my mind like a stuck vidreel. I told Roark that I'd take care of Gina Santiago. And I will . . . just not the way he expects. My word is not to be questioned.

I have more honor in one claw than he has in his entire body. He won't even do his own dirty work. A sign of weakness if there ever was one. He prefers someone with superior intelligence to act in his stead.

Sniveling useless excuse for a human. I cannot wait until I can feast upon his entrails. Sadly, they'll probably be bitter like the man. I can no longer worry about him. He's taken far too much of my time as it is. My thoughts should be on more pleasurable pursuits.

Ah, Gina . . .

My lovely Gina.

I long to touch you.

The other women were pale imitations compared to you, dearest mate. Your strength makes you perfect for ruling at my side. I don't think it will take much to convince you. All you need to hear is the truth, then you'll be more than willing to take your rightful place. I can sense these things.

Why do you hole up in the room with death surrounding you? Does the stench of dissection not sicken you? No matter. Soon you'll return to the place you consider safe. That's when I'll make my move.

I have the cloth bag to slip over your lovely head. I made sure it was downy soft and I promise I won't tie it *too* tight around your slender throat. I want you alive when I'm fucking you. Then you will know what it feels like to have a real man between your thighs.

And oh, what lovely thighs they are.

I can't wait to have your long legs clasped behind my back, squeezing my sides. I close my eyes and can almost see your lips parted in passion, your dark head thrown back in preparation for my mark.

If I flicked my tongue, I feel as if I could taste the salt upon your pale skin.

Inhaling, I try to capture your luscious fragrance, only to meet with sterilized putridity. Opening my eyes, I recall where I am and what surrounds me. The disappointment is intense and immediate. People pass, giving me friendly nods and smiles as if they're unaware of how revolted I am to be here.

Straightening my clothing, I respond in kind, then quickly get back to work.

I must bide my time. There is still much to be done. People expect me to solve their problems. No one suspects how tired I am of them looking to me for support. If they aren't strong enough to survive on their own, then they should consider death preferable.

The time passes slowly. I make a show of everything that I do for I want people to remember seeing me. It'll be difficult to slip away undetected, but I'll manage somehow. The sun begins its gradual descent. My anticipation grows with the length of each shadow.

Gina should be back at the share space by now.

I continue to work, waiting for an opportune moment to take my leave. It comes during shift change. I'm finally free to do what needs to be done to ensure the survival of my people.

Excitement burns through my body as I look forward to our joining. The drive seems to take forever as I weave through traffic, when I know it's only been minutes. I pull around the back. The last thing I need is for someone to notice my car.

The warm desert air welcomes me like an old friend as I leave the vehicle. I don't bother to lock it. I'll need to depart quickly. I gaze at the sky. The moon is nearly full. Soon Gina and I will share the night together, worshiping the moon while sating our bodies on the flesh of the weak.

Glancing around once more to ensure no one has noticed my presence, I enter the building. It isn't hard. I helped set up the security system. I have access to half the homes in this town and no one is the wiser.

Insulated water barrels line the bare wall, waiting to be purchased by customers. Each drum is numbered in the order that it was received, not that water ever has a chance to go stale.

Jesse's attention to detail might be the death of her someday. The smell of chemical purifiers saturates the tiny room. I wiggle my nose to clear it. It wouldn't do to sneeze. I listen, but hear no sounds beyond the air filtration system.

The share space is empty. I don't sense Jesse or Gina around. Disappointing, but not doom worthy. There's still time. I settle into the oncoming darkness, fully prepared to wait for as long as it takes. I'm nothing if not patient.

An hour passes and I begin to pace. Where could she be? Glancing at my watch, I calculate how much time I have left. Not much. I must return soon before

I'm missed. The walls seem to close in around me. I gasp in an attempt to breathe, then tug at my shirt, loosening the collar.

A few minutes more tick by and I must be willing to face the facts. Someone has delayed my beloved's arrival. My hands curl into fists in a move that I hope will suppress my disappointment. It doesn't work. I have an inkling of where Gina is and who she's with. It doesn't bode well for his future.

I turn to depart the same way I arrived when the front door opens and bangs shut. Her delicious aroma greets me a second before I see her. Destiny comes to my aid.

I watch as Gina bounces through the door, her long black hair slipping carelessly out of its bindings. The urge to run my fingers through its silken mass is strong. Then her scent hits me again, this time stronger and on a primitive level. Like the desert after a rainstorm, her musk permeates the air.

My canines begin to grow without the help of the change. Strange, but it's just another sign that she's the one. I welcome the pain for it reassures me that this moment is real. I have waited a lifetime for a woman like her. I will not let this opportunity slip past me.

Gina glances around wide-eyed, but I move behind a thick pillar before she can see me. Her senses are keen, but mine are better. My steps are silent as I maneuver into place and wait for her to pass. She's getting closer. I can almost taste her now. I lick my fangs in exhilaration.

Her body is tense. I can see it in her shoulders. She practically thrums. I know how to make her relax. My palms itch and my cock twitches at the thought.

The bag slips through my fingertips as I open it wide in preparation. It should easily slide over her head. I must time this perfectly. Goodness knows I don't want to ruin the surprise.

I expect her to fight back. I'd be disappointed if she did not. A true mating can't take place without a bit of violence and blood to seal the union. Will her nails rake my flesh? Will she bite? I certainly hope so. It'll only add to my excitement.

I need to steady my breathing or she'll hear me. I feel like a pup when it first catches whiff of a female in heat. It doesn't really know what to do, but it never forgets.

Gina's round hips sway as she walks toward the bar, drawing my attention to her apple-shaped bottom, which plumps her pants enticingly. Drool floods my mouth. The urge to take her from behind is strong.

Too strong for me to resist any longer.

I step out from my hiding place. From here I can almost touch her. I force my hands down and fist the corners of the bag. Just a few more inches and it'll slip over her head. The ropes will do the rest.

Afterward, I won't have to worry about her cries. Not that I'm concerned. I'll kill anyone who tries to take away what's rightfully mine. The thought of squeezing the life out of someone brings a smile to my face and instantly relaxes me.

I move forward, careful to keep my body downwind. I'm close now. Oh so close. I'm surprised she can't sense my presence or feel my hot breath on her skin. She must be distracted.

I take another step and something creaks beneath

my feet. That's unexpected. I curse a blue streak under my breath, but it's too late. She's discovered me.

Gina's head snaps up. Alert. "Jesse is that you?"

She starts to look around, but I can't allow that to happen. There is no time to waste. My muscles bunch and quiver, then I lunge for her. We collide and my body weight carries us forward, throwing her into the bar. Gina's breath escapes on a gasp and she crumples beneath me. The sensation is exquisite. So soft. So sweet. So wonderful. I follow her down, allowing my length to blanket her.

She's mine now.

chapter thirteen

Red heard a creak and glanced around the share space. Her skin prickled. "Jesse, is that you?" she called out.

The small sound was the only warning she had of the impending attack. Red hit the bar with enough force to make her think she'd been playing chicken with a hydrogen bus and lost.

The air whooshed out of her lungs and her ribs strained to keep from cracking. She gasped repeatedly, but couldn't seem to catch her breath. Her knees crumpled beneath the weight behind her, taking her to the hard floor.

Red couldn't see who had hit her, but she could feel him. His cock was erect and nestled between her butt cheeks. He shifted, deliberately allowing his hard ridge to caress her. This could not be happening. Didn't this idiot know rape was punishable by death?

She strained to look over her shoulder and caught a glimpse of dark wavy hair before he pressed her face down, grinding it into the floor. There were a lot of dark-haired men in town. It could be just about

anyone, but she couldn't shake the feeling of famil-
iarity.

He pushed harder. Red cried out. Her cheek and
nose scraped and her eyes began to water. She tried
to hit her navcom's distress button, but he held her
arm, preventing her from calling for help. She should
never have placed Rita on standby. Red had been so
worried about what her navcom would find or say
that she forgot there was a possibility that she would
really need her.

"Release me now and I'll let you live." She struggled wildly, her fists pounding the floor as she tried
to squirm out from under him.

He didn't answer, only rocked his hips once more
to let her know what he had planned.

"Fine! Have it your way," she ground out between
clenched teeth. "I am going to kill you when I get out
of here. Do you hear me? You're dead."

Something soft slipped over her head cutting off
her threat. A second later the lights winked out.

"No!" she screamed, but the material absorbed her
cries. Red reached for her pistol, fingertips straining
to find the gun stock, but her attacker was one step
ahead of her, knocking it out of her grasp.

"Shh . . ." he soothed as if that would get her to relax. His lips and teeth brushed the side of her neck at
the slope of her shoulder.

Alarm bells went off in Red's head. For some unknown reason, she didn't want him anywhere near
that spot on her body. Panicked, she fought harder,
her fingernails curling into the floor as she tried to
rise.

The strings around her neck tightened, choking

her. Red gasped. She didn't know what this bastard's game was, but she wasn't going to make it easy for him. Lungs burning from lack of oxygen, she struggled to stay conscious.

Whoever had her was stronger than anyone she'd ever encountered. Her head swam and she kicked back, connecting with the man's shin. She heard a grunt, but he didn't say anything to betray his identity. Smart. That realization sent fear trickling down her spine, its icy fingers stroking each vertebra.

"Get off me you son of a bitch!" She coughed, attempting to break his grasp, but it only made him squeeze harder. Red gurgled.

"Mine," he whispered, but the sound was muffled from the blood roaring in her ears and she couldn't make out his voice.

Stars burst behind her eyes and her limbs began to tingle. Red felt herself being lifted into the air like a bludgeoned cloud floating on a sky of crimson. The fight left her body.

She couldn't seem to focus her thoughts. Was this what death felt like? It wasn't so bad.

"What in the hell is going on here?" Jesse Lindley's voice boomed, shattering the serenity.

Red opened her mouth to answer, but no words came out. She felt herself falling a second before her shoulder collided with the ground. Pain splintered through her body, dampening the sound of the struggle happening around her.

Jesse screamed or let out a war cry. Red couldn't tell which. Furniture crashed and banged. Something or someone bumped her leg, but she was too out of it to move. The last thing she remembered was feeling a warm, sticky liquid coating her fingers. Then there was silence.

Red awoke to Morgan standing over her.

"Are you all right?" he asked, his voice cracking as he smoothed her tangled hair away from her face. He clutched a black bag, his knuckles white from holding it so tight. The same bag someone shoved over her head earlier.

"What happened?" she asked, her voice straining from the effort.

"I was hoping you could tell me." His brow furrowed and he dropped the bag so that he could help her sit up. His thumb brushed against her throat and she winced. "Sorry," he said, grimacing.

"Where's Jesse?" Red croaked, blinking in an attempt to get her eyes to focus. "I heard her yell. I think she saved my life."

"She's hurt pretty bad." Morgan's jaw clenched and his gaze shot across the room. "Kane is tending to her now. He had to sedate her after she tried to attack him. She was out of her mind with fright."

Red tried to stand and gasped, clutching her side. Her ribs hurt, along with the rest of her body. "I need to go to her. She might have seen who attacked me."

Morgan's golden eyes flared. "She's pretty drugged up and won't be able to talk for a while. She has a lot of internal injuries. Some serious. And her jaw was broken in the struggle."

"Shit," she muttered. Red sent a silent prayer to the universe. Jesse had to recover. She refused to have her death on her conscience. "Who found us?"

"A farmer who'd come in late for his shipment of water. He heard the struggle, but by the time we got

the door open whoever had attacked you was gone."
Morgan touched her cheek with the back of his knuckles. "You're going to have a few bruises. I want Kane
to check you out again. He only managed to clean up a
few of your scrapes before we discovered Jesse behind
the bar."

"I'm fine." Red swayed as she got to her feet.
"Pissed off, but fine."

Morgan reached out and grabbed Gina's arm. "If it's
all the same to you, I want to hear from the expert."

Morgan's heart pounded in his chest. The attack on
Gina had been too close for his peace of mind. If Jesse
hadn't arrived, they might very well have found Gina's
body in the desert like Renee's and Moira's. He shuddered. It didn't bear thinking about. His muscles tightened as every protective instinct in his body surged to
life and demanded that he mark her.

Whoever was out there hunting women didn't care
if he brought attention to their people. It was almost
as if he courted it. Morgan couldn't imagine anyone
being so stupid—or insane, but there was no denying
the facts.

Kane approached a few minutes later, concern shadowing his features. "I have Jesse stabilized, but I have
to get her to the emergency care facility. How are you
doing?" he asked, reaching out to examine her scalp.
"You're lucky that I was driving by when the farmer
rushed outside. Another few minutes and you might
have had more than a lump to contend with."

"I'm fine." Her breath hissed out of her lungs when
he pressed down.

Kane's expression clouded with concern. "I hate to contradict a lady, but you have quite a lump on your forehead that isn't supposed to be there." He shined a light in her eyes. "I don't think you have a concussion, but I'd like to take you in for observation overnight."

"I appreciate the concern, but I've had worse injuries, believe me. I'll have Rita check me out."

"Is she a doctor?" Kane asked.

"Not exactly." Gina grinned and hit a button on her wrist. Nothing happened. "Hopefully she didn't get damaged in the fight." She shook her wrist, then pressed the button again and her navcom came to life.

"Gina, what has happened? I am detecting injuries all over your body. Should I notify the nearest medical facility?"

"No, Rita, that won't be necessary. The doctor is here." Gina glanced at Kane. "I have something else I want you to do instead."

"Are you certain?" Rita asked.

"Yes. I need you to do a body scan for me. Let me know if there's anything I need to be worried about," Gina said. "Also, scan my skin for foreign DNA. Pay special attention to my neck and right shoulder."

"Scanning now," Rita said.

Morgan looked at Kane's creased forehead, then back at Gina. "Your attacker touched your neck." It wasn't a question. Morgan felt his color drain as he reached out and moved Gina's collar aside. "Where did he touch you?" he asked, trying to choke down the panic clogging his throat. What would he do if she'd been marked by another? He'd kill him. The answer sent a shiver through him.

"He kissed me right where you're looking," she said. Gina's eyes widened when she glanced at Morgan's face. "What's wrong? Is something there?"

Morgan didn't immediately answer. Instead, he searched the skin around her neck and shoulders. "Nothing is wrong," he said finally, releasing a heavy breath. "I just wanted to make sure that he hadn't . . . injured you."

"Scan complete," Rita announced, racheting the tension surrounding them. "Gina, I've found several bruises on your arms, legs, knees, ribs, and throat, a couple of minor muscle tears, and a knot on your forehead, but nothing life threatening. Do you want me to call for backup now?" Rita asked.

Morgan and Kane tensed.

"That won't be necessary. I have backup. The sheriff is here. What about foreign DNA?" Gina asked.

"Negative, but I did detect antibiotic wipe residue."

"You were pretty banged up, so I told Kane to clean your scratches so we could see how bad you were hurt," Morgan said.

"I understand," Gina said, the disappointment in her voice ringing clear. "You can go back to sleep now."

"I could be of more assistance to you if I remain alert."

"I know." Gina smiled. "Thanks anyway. I'll call you if I need you."

"As you wish." The screen dimmed and the voice disappeared.

"That's handy," Kane said. "But I'd still like to take you in."

Gina looked at Morgan, indecision clearly on her scratched face. He reached out and gently touched the line of her throat where the rope from the bag had dug into her skin. Anger pulsed thick and heavy through him and his nostrils flared. He hadn't been here in time to protect her, but he was here now.

Morgan wasn't about to let Gina out of his sight. He'd failed her once already. There would not be a second time. Anything could happen at the emergency care center. Even if he posted guards, there were too many people to watch. Hell, he didn't even know who they should be looking for. It was like trying to track a ghost in a cemetery full of them. He needed to take her where he could see the attack coming.

"I think it's best if I take her home with me," Morgan said.

Gina's and Kane's heads whipped around. Any other time it would've been comical, but the effect was ruined when Gina winced. "I want her someplace I can keep an eye on her," Morgan said. "Someplace safe."

"Morgan, I'll be fine here. Really," she said, glancing around warily.

"You have a knot on your head. You keep swaying with the slightest breeze. I'm not asking, Gina."

"Cousin, I think she'd be better off at the center," Kane stepped closer, crowding them.

Morgan's gaze snapped to his and a rumbled warning reverberated from his chest. He covered it with a cough. "And I think she'll be safer with me. Whoever attacked her wouldn't dare come after her at *my* home. It would be suicide."

Kane slipped an easy smile upon his face. "Whatever you say, cousin. Whatever you say."

Two orderlies entered the share space and placed Jesse on an air-cushioned transport cart. They carefully guided her out of the building.

"Is she going to be okay?" Gina asked, her lower lip trembling.

Kane reached out and touched her hand. "She'll be fine. She's stable and tougher than half the people in this town."

Gina laughed, but she didn't look assured.

Morgan tipped her chin, until he could see into her eyes. "Kane won't let anything happen to her. Trust me. He's the best."

Morgan led Gina outside to his transport. After he settled her, he went back inside to review the crime scene. There'd been one hell of a fight, mainly between Jesse and the assailant. She hadn't been much help when Morgan arrived, her body already in shock from the brutal attack.

The farmer who had discovered Jesse and Gina found Kane first, then called the sheriff's station. If he hadn't, they might very well be dead.

Unfortunately, he hadn't seen a thing. No one witnessed the attacker fleeing—only heard it. The hair on the back of Morgan's neck bristled. Was it possible he was still here? He took a deep breath, then slowly exhaled.

Too many people frequented the water exchange. It was impossible to distinguish their scents. The only strong odors belonged to Jesse, Kane, the farmer, and Gina, which was no help at all.

Morgan climbed the stairs and entered Gina's

room. He quickly gathered her clothes and belongings because she wouldn't be coming back here, if he had anything to say about it.

His fingers closed over her shirts. For a second, he brought the material to his face and breathed in. Her scent filled his nostrils and his eyes closed. He'd come close to losing her tonight. The thought nearly unmanned him. His jaw clenched and he shoved the shirt into her bag, then sealed it along with the other items.

He took the stairs two at a time. Gina's eyes were closed and she rested her head against the door frame. They sprang open upon his approach. For some reason, it comforted him to know that even injured she was alert and prepared for battle. She wouldn't be taken down easily again. He smiled as a sudden bout of pride swelled inside him.

She truly was perfect.

Morgan drove back to his place, taking care not to hit too many bumps along the way. Dust plumed behind them obscuring the view of Nuria as they drove out of town. Gina dozed fitfully, her head bobbing with the uneven terrain. A bandage covered the lump on her forehead, but he could still see the shadow from the newly forming bruise on her cheek.

His grip tightened on the wheel until his knuckles cracked. Impotent rage stormed his senses, leaving him feeling battered and weary. How dare a rogue wolf come into his town, his territory, and threaten all those under his protection?

Morgan's body spasmed, throwing him back against

the seat with a smack. Pain sliced through his skull as the beast tried to claw its way out. The rogue was not only trying to bring danger to the town, but he was also challenging Morgan's pack status. No one would take over leadership of Nuria without a fight. Morgan took a deep breath and released it slowly. He repeated the action twice more until his precarious control slipped back into place.

Gina had been through enough already. She didn't need him frightening her. She wasn't prepared to face the truth—he wasn't sure she'd ever be.

He reached out and touched a wisp of her hair. The silken strands slid through his fingertips. It was silly, but Morgan needed to feel her to prove to himself that she was really okay. He inhaled her delicious scent into his lungs. Her fragrance calmed the beast's bloodlust, but did little to slake his anger.

Morgan pulled into the drive leading to his home. Gravel crunched under his tires. He glanced at Gina, but she was still asleep. He hated to wake her, but she'd be far more comfortable in his rest pad.

The thought of Gina twisting in his sheets naked brought his erotic dream crashing to the forefront. He'd never get the scent of her off his rest pad. Morgan nearly groaned as he parked the vehicle and shut down the motor. He reached over to touch her, but at the last second hesitated.

What would she think of his home? Would the modest size bother her? Would she hate the sparsely decorated space? Suddenly the nerves in his stomach erupted. He shook his head at his own foolishness. It wasn't as if she'd be staying in Nuria, so he had no need for concern. Yet the fluttering in his abdomen continued as he brushed the side of Gina's neck with a fingertip.

She jerked awake. Her eyes were wild and unfocused as she took in the interior of the cab. "Get off me," she cried, her fists flailing.

Morgan faced her so he could control her movements. He didn't want her to hurt herself. "Gina, it's okay. It's me, Morgan," he said softly. "I woke you to let you know that we're here." He nodded in the direction of his house.

It took Red's mind a second to register Morgan's words. Hell, for a moment she'd glimpsed his dark wavy hair and thought her attacker had returned.

"I'm sorry," she said, brushing the hair out of her face. Her ponytail had come loose during the struggle and she hadn't bothered to retie it. She looked out the windshield and spotted a tidy little sand-colored home that appeared well cared for. "It's lovely. Let's go inside."

Morgan's home was sparsely decorated, the furnishing kept to a bare minimum based on need of use. Yet it held a warmth within its light brown walls and tan ceilings that her unit had never achieved.

"Can I get you something to eat?" he asked, moving into the kitchen. He pressed a button on his food and beverage dispenser and a synth-beer popped out. He twisted the lid and tipped it back, taking a big swallow.

"I could use one of those." Red eyed the beer with longing. "My throat's too sore to do justice to anything solid."

His lips thinned and he nodded. Another beer dropped down. He opened the container and handed it to her. "Have you remembered anything else?" he asked, taking another swig of the frothy brew.

Red shook her head. "I've told you everything I know. It happened so fast. I barely heard him coming and by the time I had, it was too late. He had to have been waiting for me. That's the only explanation that makes any sense. And if that's the case, then he has to know his way around town." She sipped her beer, the cold feeling good against her raw throat. "But why me? Why now? How did he know I'd be there?"

Morgan ran his hand through his hair, leaving it standing on end. "I don't know. He must have been watching you for a while. Waiting for the perfect opportunity to strike."

She shivered at the thought. "Do you think I was getting too close to something?"

His jaw tightened and he drained the contents of his beer in one gulp. "You can take the rest pad."

Red glanced through the open archway at the unmade rest pad beyond. It wasn't hard to picture Morgan's naked body sprawled beneath the bedding. His flat muscled chest, trailing down into lean hips and a big—

Her gaze dropped to the front of his pants and heat flooded her face. She cleared her throat. "Where are you going to sleep?" she asked, not sure what answer she wanted to hear.

Morgan followed her gaze, then looked into her eyes. Desire flashed between them, crackling the air like static electricity. His lips quirked. "I think you've had enough excitement for one night. I'll take the chair. It's comfortable enough. I don't plan to sleep anyway."

"You can't do that," she protested. "I don't need someone to stand guard over me. He may have gotten the jump on me once, but it won't happen again."

He stared at her hard, his expression stony, daring her to continue. Red nodded and picked up her bag. Morgan showed her where the cleansing room was and then left her to go call Kane.

Red cleaned herself up the best she could, cringing at her reflection in the mirror. She knew it could be worse, but she'd probably have a shiner in the morning. She finished up quickly and exited in time to hear Morgan ask Kane about Jesse.

"How is she doing? Has she settled down enough to give you a description?" He paused. "I see."

She took a step forward, not wanting to eavesdrop, but desperate for news on Jesse's condition.

"Right." Morgan let out a frustrated breath. "Can I question her tomorrow?"

Red edged closer.

Morgan spotted her and waved her forward. "Okay, I understand. I'll catch up with you tomorrow. What was that?" He glanced at her. "She seems to be doing fine. Standing in front of me right now, waiting for me to disconnect. Yeah, got to go. Bye." He severed the connection.

"How is Jesse doing?" Red asked, bracing for his answer.

Morgan looked at her, his amber eyes glistening with unexpressed emotion. "She's stable for now. Got out of surgery thirty minutes ago. Kane's done everything he can for her. All we can do now is wait."

"I feel so useless standing around here. I couldn't help her back at the share space. I couldn't even save myself." She growled in frustration.

Morgan reached for her hands and gently uncurled her fingers. His rough pads brushed the fleshy part of her palm and heat radiated up her arms and through her chest.

"Right now, the best thing you can do for Jesse is to get some rest and heal. She wouldn't want you pushing yourself after what you've both been through."

Red reluctantly pulled her hands out of Morgan's grasp. His touch was distracting enough without the dollop of caring lavished on top. She'd never seen this side of him. It was disconcerting—and wonderful. It would be so easy to let go and fall into his embrace. He offered strength and safety with no strings attached.

That shocked her more than anything. He really wanted to take care of her. When had anyone outside of her family ever offered to care for her? Never, whispered over her skin, leaving gooseflesh in its wake.

It was going to be a very, very long night.

Morgan sat vigil, watching Gina sleep. Her chest rose and fell in gentle intervals. She'd sworn she had been too wound up to rest, but had passed out within seconds. He grinned at the memory. Her raven hair was spread across his pale pillows and she'd tossed her arm over her forehead.

The last time he'd seen her like this desire had

been coursing through his body, riding him hard. It still simmered like a stew under the surface, but the urgency had been replaced by the need to protect.

He smiled as she made murmuring noises, her nose snuffling as she turned onto her side. She truly was the most beautiful woman he'd ever laid eyes on. He couldn't believe how unaware she was of the power she held. Instead of wielding that potent feminine weapon, she hid it, like she was ashamed. Something in her hazel gaze seemed lost and alone. He longed to wipe that trace of uncertainty away.

Morgan scratched his stubbly chin. He'd researched her background, but had found little beyond the official records. Her parents had been killed, one in a car accident, the other by the hands of a murderer. Her sister had died with her mother, leaving Gina an orphan.

Shortly thereafter, she had moved in with her grandfather, Robert Santiago. He'd changed her last name, probably to protect her from the tragedy surrounding her.

He'd tried to research her parents, but found nothing beyond the fact that her mother was a pureblood and Robert Santiago's only daughter. Her father's records had been purged of all pertinent information, leaving only his name. There'd been no listing of his birth parents.

Morgan had found no record of him being raised in a labor farm. Officially, he didn't exist. Only someone with the highest security clearance could expunge that kind of information.

Someone like *Robert Santiago*.

He stilled. No wonder Gina knew so little about herself. She was an anomaly that shouldn't exist. His mind reeled as the ramifications of what this meant for him and his people sunk in. Her history had been erased to protect her and to hide her. Morgan knew it was for the best given where she grew up and what she did for a living, but it still angered him. What was so bad about being different? He sighed, his gaze landing once more upon Gina.

How many other people like her existed out there? Was she the only one?

She flopped over, then twisted violently. A whimper escaped past her full lips. Sweat beaded her body. Morgan sat up and leaned closer. Her arms flailed in an attempt to fight off an invisible attacker. She was having a nightmare. Morgan reached out to touch her, to wake her before she injured herself.

Gina lurched forward, nearly toppling out of the bed, and screamed. Her eyes flew open a second before the tears fell. Morgan jumped out of his seat and caught her. He pulled her into his chest. She fought for a moment, until her mind registered whose arms enclosed her.

"It's okay. I've got you," he soothed, rocking her gently.

Gina clawed at his arm as if he were the only life vest in the middle of a roiling sea. "I had a dream," she gasped, crying harder.

"I know," he said, brushing the hair away from her face. Morgan pressed his lips to her moist forehead, taking care to avoid the knot.

She snuggled in closer. As much as he wanted to, Morgan couldn't resist kissing her again. He trailed his lips down the side of her face, following her delicate jaw line. When he neared her mouth, she turned, meeting him.

Morgan groaned as the kiss deepened. Her tongue darted out, tentatively, teasing his lips, luring 'him closer. How many nights had he dreamed about the feel of her mouth upon him? It seemed like an eternity. She was as sweet as he'd imagined and more.

His hand fisted in her shirt as he drew her closer. The urge to strip her bare was strong, but Morgan's common sense was stronger. She'd been through a hell of an ordeal. No matter how bad he wanted to fuck her, this was not the time. He wanted her whole and willing when he took her. Not scared and injured.

Morgan's body ached, demanding that he finish what he'd started. He forced his hands to release her, then he pulled back. The loss of warmth from her lips left him bereft. He took a shaky breath. Gina's chest rose and fell deeply. Her eyes were glazed when she looked at him.

"Why did you stop?" she asked, breathless.

"Not because I wanted to," he grit out between clenched teeth, his erection throbbing. "But you're hurt," he reminded them both.

She nodded, but didn't look happy about the situation. "Will you at least stay? I don't want to be alone."

"I haven't moved. I'll be right there." Morgan pointed to the chair he'd positioned near the rest pad.

Gina shook her head. "No, here with me." She patted the spot beside her.

Morgan closed his eyes. She was killing him. The thought of sliding into the rest pad beside her had the blood roaring into his ears and other parts of his already hard body. But he couldn't deny her, not in this.

"Sure," he said through the tightness in his throat. Morgan took his shirt and shoes off, then crawled in beside her. He lay on the rest pad, his muscles tense. Gina curled up next to him, her warmth tempting his senses, daring him to hold her. Morgan fought to remain impassive, but lost the battle quickly. He turned, dragging Gina into his arms until her back rested against his chest.

She stiffened when his erection brushed her bottom, but then relaxed. He was grateful because he didn't want to fight with her and he certainly wasn't going to apologize for his condition. A few moments later, he heard the telltale signs of sleep. Morgan closed his eyes, resting his chin on the top of her head, while her soft hair tickled his nose.

She felt so good lying next to him, better than he'd imagined. He could easily get used to this, but knew he shouldn't. Gina would be gone the second the murderer was found. Logically, he knew that, but his heart wasn't listening.

He was just about to doze off when the vidcom chirped. He pressed a button to lower the volume before it woke Gina, then hit another to answer the call. Morgan prayed it wasn't Jim Thornton with news of a body. He didn't know how much more he could take.

The screen brightened and Morgan released the breath he hadn't known he'd been holding. Kane's smiling face appeared before him. "How's Jesse doing?" Morgan asked, his voice a whisper.

"She's as well as can be expected. The healing has begun, so I think she'll survive. How's my other patient?" Kane asked.

"She's fine. A few nightmares, but nothing serious." Morgan shifted Gina until he could look directly into the vidcom.

Kane's gaze followed his movements. A second later, his smile dropped. "Yeah, I can see that," he said, no longer looking at Morgan.

Morgan glanced down and swore under his breath. Gina's erect nipples were visible through her thin T-shirt. He moved fast, tucking her back under the covers. For some reason, he didn't want Kane or any other man looking at her that way. "It's not what you think," he said.

Kane's expression hardened. "Are you in the rest pad with her?" he asked, his voice low and oddly strained.

"Yes, but—"

Kane cut him off. "Then it is *exactly* what I think."

chapter fourteen

Anger roils through me, surging until I can barely breathe. The odor of disinfectant fills my nostrils as I dispose of my bloody clothes, destroying the last remnants of Gina's lovely fragrance with them. My fist clenches until the bone cracks. I release it and grab the old mic, bringing it slowly to my mouth. A second later, I murmur a command into it.

I've barely had time to hang up the mic when a page blasts over the antiquated intercom system, calling all nurses on duty to room 308. I slip into a nearby room before the stampede begins, cracking the door so I can watch the people rush by.

It will take them awhile to reattach all the life-support tubes I disconnected, while they wait for the on-call physician to arrive. Unfortunately, that won't save the patient. Peterson may not have died peacefully, but at least he left this planet for a worthy cause. After all, true love doesn't occur everyday.

The last of the staff rushes by.

It seems my little diversion has served its purpose. They are completely unaware of my presence.

My shoes squeak as I make my way down the dimly lit hall. I never heard that sound before, but I guess it's always been there. I suppose I've been too focused to notice until now. Strange how it's the little things that you miss.

They put Jesse Lindley into room 104. It's at the far end of the opposite hall from room 308. Funny how that worked out. She should still be sedated for the pain, but awake enough to realize who's come to visit.

I'm sure when she opens her eyes she'll be as excited to see me as I am to see her. Too bad she doesn't have the capacity to scream. It would make our time together all the more pleasurable.

Glancing up and down the empty hall, I take a moment to listen to the sounds around me. No footsteps herald a nurse's approach, but I hear a frantic commotion as they fight to save Peterson. I smile and slip into Jesse's room.

Her eyes are closed and her jaw is bound, preventing movement. Pale skin showcases the blue bruises forming on her cheeks and around her eyes. I slide a chair in front of the door. It won't bar anyone from entering, but it will slow their progress and give me time to escape. Not that I'll need to. They don't ever see me, not even when I'm standing right in front of them. You could say that while I'm here I am invisible.

I lean over Jesse and inhale. Blood fills my nostrils and my arm begins to throb where her canines ripped through my skin, tearing muscle. Subconsciously, I rub the spot, fighting the feelings of revulsion and betrayal. I jerk my sleeve up and glare at my arm. The angry wound will heal, but not quickly.

Wolf bites rarely heal fast.

I would have gladly welcomed Jesse into the pack when I became leader. All she would've had to do is promise loyalty and obedience, but now that moment has passed. She lost her chance when she attacked.

It's her fault that the sheriff has my woman ensconced in his home. He's probably marked her by now, which means only death will break their bond. How could this have happened? I was so close. A growl of pain and frustration rips from my throat as I glance down at the old woman lying before me. Who knew the bitch was so strong?

I take several deep breaths. I must calm down. What's done is done. If I close my eyes, I can still feel Gina wrapped lovingly in my arms, pressed against my body, her ass snuggling my cock. If it wasn't for this one-eyed bitch, she'd still be there. She ruined everything. My anger rises once more like lava erupting from a volcano.

How dare she attack me?

Me of all people.

Her disrespect will cost her dearly.

I step closer and extend my hands, curling them around her bandaged throat. The gauze scratches my sensitive palms. It takes little effort to apply force. All I have to do is squeeze.

Jesse's face begins to turn a delicate shade of red. It's a pretty color I'd like to see more of. She still hasn't moved, which tells me the drugs are working in my favor as I'd hoped.

A gurgle escapes as her lips turn blue. I smile. The sound is music to my wolfen ears. This is such a delightful game that I don't know why I haven't played it until now. Cocking my head to get a better look at Jesse's face, I decide I must try it again soon.

Just a few more seconds and it'll be all over. I release my hold to draw out the moment. I don't want the pleasure to end so quickly. I realize when I start to choke her again that I'll have to take care of the sheriff next. It pains me to do so, but he sealed his fate when he took Gina away. Besides, like Jesse, he's done enough damage already.

The door behind me bangs as it hits the chair. The screech of metal gliding over the floor fills the room. I only have a moment to release Jesse and smoothly run my fingers along her throat. She gasps, air filling her starved lungs as the nurse appears by my side.

"How is she doing?"

I glance her way and grin. The nurse's features relax and soften in invitation. *Maybe later,* I try to convey with my gaze, before answering. "She seems to be fine now. A moment ago she was having trouble breathing, but the obstruction appears to have lifted. I'd say she's one lucky lady. If I didn't know any better, I'd swear she was a cat with nine lives."

The nurse laughed, showing genuine relief in her amber eyes. "I doubt Jesse would appreciate that observation. She's a dog person all the way." She walked around the rest pad to smooth out the linens.

"What brings you here tonight?" I ask, careful to keep my expression benign.

"The sheriff asked me to call him when she stabilizes." She tilted her watch to check the time. "It's late, but he said he wanted to know the second it occurred."

"I don't think he wants to be disturbed right now." My voice hardens before I can stop it.

She frowns in confusion. "But he was quite insistent."

"You know Morgan, he just wants to be kept in the loop." I slip my mask of civility back on. "Don't worry, the world won't end if you notify him tomorrow."

"Are you sure? I really don't mind, since my shift ended a few minutes ago. I just wanted to check on my patients once more after that weird incident in the other wing before I contacted him."

I feign ignorance. "What happened?"

"Didn't you hear the announcement?" she asked.

"No, I must've missed it. I've been wrapped up in my own thoughts."

She nodded in understanding. "It's probably nothing." She waved it off. "Everyone's been jumpy since they brought Jesse in."

"That's understandable." I display a measured amount of concern until she feels she can confide in me.

"It looks like someone disconnected Carl Peterson's life support. He flatlined before we could reach him."

"Oh no."

"It's horrible. We found his tubes removed and lying on the floor. The staff speculates that he was dead before it happened." She glanced around the room as if suddenly afraid to be overheard.

I furrow my brow. "How odd. Who would do such a thing?"

"I know. It's crazy." She shook her head unable to comprehend the larger picture.

I pull her close and hug her in a faux attempt to comfort her. "I'm sure there'll be a rational explanation for it in the end. I doubt very much that a lunatic is on the loose in the emergency care center."

She nodded in agreement, then stepped out of my embrace. "You're probably right, but I won't feel better until I find out what it is."

"Me either. I daresay I probably won't sleep a wink after what I've witnessed this evening."

"Are you sure about the sheriff?" she asked, glancing at Jesse. Concern marred her expression.

"Positive." My gaze trails from her head down to her toes and back again. "It'll wait until morning."

I gently brush the hair away from Jesse's face. The nurse beside me smiles at the display of tenderness. I decide to make a show of it. I blink rapidly as if trying to fight back the tears. "How could someone do this to a woman so beloved?" I ask.

She grasps my arm, her eyes filling with unshed moisture. "She'll be okay. I know she will."

I squeeze her hand, then lean down until my nose touches Jesse's ear. The move is intimate. "Can you give us a moment?" I ask in order to ensure our privacy.

"Yes, of course." The nurse walks over to the door and steps into the hall. I wait for her to close it behind her. A soft snick pierces the silence and joy fills my heart.

"Next time," I whisper, so Jesse can hear me.

A lone tear slides down her cheek. I reach out and catch it with the tip of my finger before it hits the pillow and bring it to my lips. It's salty, much like her personality. Too bad she's become a liability.

I pull away and call out to the nurse.

She enters the room expectantly. "Is there anything else I can do?"

So obedient, so enthusiastic, she will make a perfect addition to my pack. It's unfortunate she's already marked. Luckily, there are ways around such things. "Make sure Jesse's not disturbed. We wouldn't want anything to happen to our only witness."

chapter fifteen

Mike Travers stared at the synth-document in his hands and blinked, unable to believe what he'd just read. The cooling system hummed in the background as it attempted to pump air into the antiquated building. It failed.

He loosened his tie. Mike glanced around the room to ensure his privacy, then reread it, his eyes greedy for the information stored on the forbidden pages.

Shock spread through him once again. It wasn't the news that the IPTT agent in Nuria was Gina Santiago, or that her grandfather was the commander, Robert Santiago, that held him spellbound. No, it was what he'd found when he hacked into the sealed records at IPTT itself.

For years rumors existed that an Other and a pure-blood human had successfully bred, producing a hybrid offspring. He'd dismissed the information like everyone else after the government warned of potential health hazards accompanying such unions.

Back then, when you showed too much interest in the Others, it was grounds for imprisonment. The governing body could hold you for as long as they liked and no one could do a thing about it.

Luckily, those barbaric days had ended, but the hate still remained, hidden stealthily out of the way in wait of the unsuspecting.

He read the report again, his fingers shaking with the effort to remain calm. Her father, Marcus, had been killed in a car accident. He'd died of a broken neck, according to the public report, when she was young.

After further digging, Mike found evidence that investigators suspected homicide, but no one had been willing to put his career on the line to prove it. An all too common practice after the war.

Gina's sister and mother hadn't been so fortunate. Whoever murdered them hadn't bothered to hide it. The scene resembled a slaughterhouse. The women had been killed and dismembered like chattel. The people behind the hit probably thought they'd eliminated the threat. Little did they know.

Robert Santiago and his granddaughter, Gina, had discovered the scene. He'd taken her away shortly thereafter and changed her last name to match his own. Mike shook his head in amazement. The old man had managed to protect her all these years without a single soul catching on.

Elation filled him until he glanced at the screen's blinking cursor. Deflated, Mike sat back. Roark Montgomery was expecting a full report from him. If he presented too little information, the bastard would become suspicious. If he gave him a full report, then he wouldn't have any ammunition for later. That just wouldn't do.

Mike knew all about government secrets firsthand. Secrets had changed his life, had his entire family annihilated, cost him everything he held dear. Yes, he knew all about the secrets that men kept, but this one would be his and his alone. He'd add it to his personal list and pray that in the end it didn't cost him his life.

Damn, he needed a drink. Bad.

He glanced around his small office at digital filing cabinets and the bare walls until he spotted his canteen. Mike sighed with relief. At least he wasn't going to have to slip out of the building to his car for a quick fix.

He bobbed back in his chair and stared across the room. He didn't feel like getting up from behind his desk in order to retrieve it, so instead, he raised a finger and concentrated on bringing the object to him.

The canteen rose, floating through the air on invisible hands, or in this case, his thoughts. A simple enough task that even a child could perform. He should know, he'd been doing it since he was five. His psychic ability was the main reason he'd been recruited during the war. The canteen dropped onto the desk in front of him with a small thud.

"That's better," he said, opening it to take a swig. The aroma stung his nostrils, causing his eyes to water. This was going to be a very good year. He could tell without even tasting it.

He lifted the container. The second his lips parted, the hot blood rushed down his throat, bringing all his senses crackling to life. His heart sped and his skin flushed under the onslaught.

Mike didn't realize how thirsty he'd become. His

ability to go days without feeding had saved his life on more than one occasion. So had being able to face the sun, a feat almost unheard of in lab vamps.

Almost . . .

Today was different though. Mike was thirsty.

He was sitting upon a gold mine of information and he knew it. The crinkled document in his hand could change the face of the world, if it leaked to the right sources. It would also in equal measure fuel and destroy Roark Montgomery's campaign.

Mike grinned, tipping the canteen again, filling his mouth. He held the coppery substance on his tongue, savoring the peppery flavor a second before swallowing with a smack of his lips.

"Ahh . . ."

He sealed the canteen, then turned back to the comp-unit on his desk and began to type at a furious pace. The tap, tap, tap of the keys effectively broke the silence. The doctored report he presented to Roark would be detailed and thorough, but would not include Gina Santiago's little secret.

For now, her secret was safe with him.

Roark Montgomery sat behind his desk, staring out at the great expanse that made up the Republic of Missouri. The woods were all gone, along with the rivers and lakes. The only thing left were the vast fields that used to grow crops.

If all went well, he'd soon be sitting in a luxurious office on the East Coast executing his plan to unite what used to be the United States, Canada, Asia, Africa, South America, and Europe. He swung away from the window and stared at the documents before him. All of them could wait.

Right now he was only interested in one document. His brows drew down. What was taking Travers so long? He should've been able to dig up information on the IPTT agent in Nuria by now.

Roark hit a button on his desk. "Travers, I'm still waiting for that report."

There was a pause. "I have it now, sir. I'll be right in."

Roark pressed the button again and disconnected the call. He glanced at the map on the wall, which held all the republics around the globe. A smile formed on his lips as he leaned back and steepled his fingers under his chin.

Soon they will all be mine.

It had been Roark's lifelong dream to rebuild the world in its former image. He'd grown up hearing stories about patriots and heroes from his father and grandfather. They'd both served in what used to be the military.

That was why when he was old enough Roark joined the IPTT. He'd excelled in the rigorous environment. It had made a man out of him, which was why it goaded Roark to no end that Commander Robert Santiago refused to back his campaign. With IPTT backing, he'd win by a landslide.

Stubborn old bastard.

The door opened a moment later and Mike Travers entered with a fist full of documents. "Here are the reports you asked for, sir," he said, handing them to Roark, then glancing away.

Roark's eyes narrowed. What was he up to? First

insubordination, now evasion. He didn't like this sudden turnaround in his assistant. Roark let it go for now and looked down at the reports in his hands.

He scanned the documents quickly. His gaze shot to Travers when it reached the name of the agent in Nuria.

"Is this correct?" he asked, excitement filling his voice. "Is it really Robert Santiago's granddaughter down there poking around?" *Could he be that lucky?*

"Yes, sir."

"Is it an IPTT-sanctioned visit?"

Travers shook his head. "No, sir. From what I could ascertain, she is there in an unofficial capacity."

"Is she checking out the boundary fence?"

Travers frowned. "No, she seems to be following up on an animal attack."

Roark smiled to himself. This was perfect. Exactly what he needed to gain the IPTT's support.

"How long is she planning to stay?" he asked, watching Travers' expression closely.

"That's the odd part. According to the documents I was able to uncover, she should've been back by now."

Roark did grin then. "I wonder what's keeping her." Had his man gotten to her already? If so, that was quick. Not that he cared. She simply was a pawn to be used and discarded. He needed to get in touch with his contact in Nuria to find out what was going on. His patience was wearing thin. Roark no longer wanted her managed. That would've been fine for a lone female team member, but not Robert Santiago's granddaughter. No, Gina Santiago deserved special treatment.

Her death would bring the IPTT into line faster than anything else Roark could come up with. She was young enough to cause outrage. He could blame her demise on the Others and kill two birds with one stone as the ancient saying went. His election would be a foregone conclusion.

Roark glanced up from his thoughts and spied Travers. He'd completely forgotten about the man's presence. He supposed he should compliment him for a job well done, but he didn't want to give Mike any misguided hope that he had a future with him.

"That will be all, Travers. Next time don't take so long."

Mike gave a slight bow. "Yes, sir. It won't happen again." He turned on his heel and exited, leaving Roark with his thoughts.

He glanced at the private comdevice. His contact had been furious the last time he'd called, but it had been an emergency, much like now. He'd have to risk his wrath, not that Roark was concerned since he planned on having Travers execute the man once the election was ensured.

He had to call. Roark needed to give the man new orders. Only then, would he breathe easier. He picked up the comlink and slipped it onto his ear and began to enter a sequence of numbers.

The line crackled, then slowly cleared. Roark waited, his heart pounding in his ears. His stomach twisted as he realized what he was about to do. The connection snapped into place with a pop.

"Yes!"

Roark took a deep breath and let it out slowly, reminding himself once again why he was doing this.

It's for the good of the people. They meant everything to him. It was his destiny to unite them. He believed that with all the fiber of his being.

"I have a job for you to do," he said, not sure what response to expect.

"I thought I made it clear the last time that you called and broke protocol that I didn't want to hear from you again unless it was an emergency."

"You did," Roark said.

"Has the war started?"

Roark frowned. "No."

"Has someone discovered our plans?"

"Not that I know of."

"What do you mean, not that you know of?" The man cursed loudly.

Roark shot up in his seat, his back rigid against the chair. "I mean no." He shook his head even though the man couldn't see him.

"Then I'm going to disconnect."

"Wait!" Roark gripped the arms of his chair in tight fists, then forced himself to release the synthetic leather. "I have important intel for you. The IPTT agent that you have nosing around down there is Gina Santiago. She's the granddaughter of Robert Santiago, the commander of IPTT."

Silence met him, so he continued. "If something should befall her, I'm sure the IPTT would do anything and everything in its power to find out the truth."

"That does change things slightly," the voice on the other end of the connection said.

"Slightly? Her lineage changes everything. With her out of the picture, IPTT will fall into place, granting me instant backing for whatever tactic I choose to take. You and your *people* will have your own area to live in. Isn't that what you wanted?"

Roark felt the color rising in his face as anger spread through his body. He didn't need this right now. He wouldn't tolerate defiance, especially when the defiance came from an animal.

"So you want me to kill her?"

Roark could hear the sudden tension in the man's voice. He didn't like the idea of killing a woman. Correction, he thought. He didn't like the idea of killing *this* woman.

"Is that going to be a problem?" Roark asked.

"I want to hear you give the order."

Roark groaned. "I already have."

"No!" the man said. "You've alluded to what you'd like me to do. It's not the same as giving a direct order."

Sweat broke out on Roark's forehead. Something wasn't right. Was the man recording their conversation? Surely not. To do so would be implicating himself . . . unless he was truly mad. Shards of fear skittered over his skin, leaving gooseflesh in its wake.

Roark couldn't afford to go down that mental road. It was far too dangerous—and frightening. He brushed it aside. He needed this man for a while longer. If that meant obliging him, then so be it.

They were too close to turn back now. The loss would be devastating and unrecoverable. He closed his eyes and counted to calm himself. If the man wanted a direct order, then Roark would give him one.

"Okay, have it your way. I'm ordering you to kill Gina Santiago." Roark grit out. He longed to reach through the comlink and punch him in the throat. Wipe what he knew would be a smug expression off his face.

"I'm afraid that will not be possible," the man said, after several seconds.

"Excuse me?" Roark balked. Surely he hadn't heard him correctly.

"I said, that won't be possible."

Fury filled Roark. He slammed his fist onto his desk, knocking over a nearby water canteen as he struggled to get his temper into check. "Do you want to tell me why the hell not?"

A small mocking laugh echoed in his ear. "Because I have other plans for her."

"Listen," Roark spat. "I'm not asking here. I am giving you a direct order. Kill the girl."

"Hmm . . . as I recall, I don't take orders from you. I believe we agreed this was a partnership, not a dictatorship. Or have you forgotten? I could arrange to have the contract sent to you, if you need a reminder."

Roark snarled. "I haven't forgotten a thing, but in order to make a partnership work, there has to be cooperation. That's all I'm asking for here."

"No, you're not," he snapped. "You're ordering me to kill Gina."

The intimacy used to say her name momentarily shocked Roark, then he lost control. "You asked me to give you an order you crazy son of a bitch!" he shouted in frustration.

"Watch your tone," he warned.

"What makes her so special? You never had a problem killing women before, or have you forgotten?"

"They were different."

"Different?" Suddenly, the hair on Roark's arms rose. He was missing something. He scanned the report, but nothing obvious leapt out at him.

"It's not important that you understand. All that you need to be aware of is that in this instance I disagree with the course of action you've chosen."

Roark's vision narrowed to a red haze. "If you don't do this for me, I'll be forced to send in someone who will. You aren't the only person available for the job."

Another silence met his ears. This time Roark could almost feel the chill emanating from the connection. The air froze in his lungs.

"That would be a huge mistake on your part. I will not tolerate interference."

"How ironic, neither will I. You have forty-eight hours to get the job done. I'll await confirmation." Roark hit the disconnect button before the man could respond. He knew he was playing with fire, but he had no choice. His hand had been forced.

I have other plans for her. What was he talking about? What other plans? Roark realized he probably should've asked, but he'd been too angry to think.

He didn't know what was going on between the man and Gina. His imagination took flight and a myriad of possibilities crossed his mind. Oh good God! A shudder racked his body at the thought of a pureblood woman being intimate with an Other. Did she even know? Or had he forced himself upon her like a mongrel in rut?

He supposed it didn't matter now. Hell, she'd likely welcome death if she found out the truth. Goodness knows he would. He pictured the beast straddling the woman, fucking her into submission. It was a fate worse than death.

Roark nodded as understanding dawned. He was doing her a favor. No self-respecting woman would want to continue after finding out she'd given herself to an animal. The filth would remain with her for the rest of her life. She'd be a social pariah.

Yes, yes, he'd definitely made the right decision. All doubts evaporated in the dry lemon-scented air that filtered restlessly through his office. He glanced once more at the report on his desk.

The man would just have to understand that Gina Santiago's death was for her own good, and the good of the people.

chapter sixteen

Red awoke encased in soothing warmth. She'd been having the most delicious dream that involved wet and wonderful kisses. She snuggled deeper, wiggling her butt until she slotted against the hard mass behind her. Her eyes flew open, when she heard a groan. She tried to move, but a strong masculine arm shot out, stilling her progress.

"Morgan?"

"Who else would it be?" The playful tone in his voice surprised her.

"I—uh . . ."

"Don't make any sudden moves. You don't want to rip the bandages." Something tickled the back of her neck. She quivered. Red realized it was his hot breath a second before his hand stroked over her stomach, sending heat radiating out until her fingers and toes tingled with the excess.

Red swallowed hard, attempting to ignore her response to his nearness and the erection nudging her. Impossible to do, given its size. The growing awareness stretched between them. Her nipples puckered and moisture seeped between her thighs.

Morgan inhaled deeply, then froze. His fingers bunched in her shirt, but he didn't try to remove it. Every muscle in his body grew rigid as if he fought some invisible demon. He fisted her clothes one last time, then released them, but kept his arm over her body. His iron restraint brought her relief and frustration in equal measures. What was he waiting for?

Red realized that some part of her wanted him to rip her clothes off and have his way with her. She wanted him to lay bare what had been building between them, so that they could both move on when she returned home. The ache between her legs told Red exactly how bad the need had become.

She had to leave. Now. Before she did something torturously stupid like beg. "You should probably let me up," she suggested, even though the last thing she wanted to do was get out of the rest pad.

Morgan bucked his hips and she gasped, her body threatening to melt.

"Morgan, I—"

"I know," he said, releasing her reluctantly. "You're hurt."

"Actually, I'm feeling much better." She rose to her feet and pain shot through her body. The attack came back in a flash and Red swayed. Morgan was up and out of the rest pad in seconds, pulling her against his bare chest.

"Are you okay?" he asked, tilting her chin until he could look into her eyes. Concern and something else etched his sleep-weary features.

Meeting his gaze had been a mistake. Red found herself falling into the honey-rich pools. She swayed into him. It had nothing to do with her injuries from last night, but obviously Morgan thought it did. He steadied her.

"How are you feeling this morning?" he asked, his hands soothing her skin as if he needed the contact as much as she did.

"I'm fine, just a little shaky. I have to get to the emergency care center and check on Jesse."

He wrapped her in his embrace, careful to avoid her bruises. "I understand," he said, brushing his lips over her forehead.

Red wasn't sure what to make of this "new" caring version of Morgan. Somehow the attack had destroyed whatever internal barriers had separated them. He no longer hid his emotions, even though she clung desperately to her shields. He didn't notice, and if he did, Morgan didn't seem to care.

"I'd say you could take the cleansing room first, but I'm afraid to let you go in there by yourself. You still aren't steady on your feet," he said, glancing in the direction of the room.

Red turned fully in his arms. "What exactly are you suggesting?" Her eyes widened when she glimpsed the fire in his amber gaze. "I think I'll be all right."

Morgan shook his head. "I'm not willing to take that chance."

"But—"

"You're used to public cleansing rooms." It was a statement of fact, since everyone alive on the planet had used a public cleansing room to bathe at one time or another.

"Yes."

His expression turned speculative. "You're not

modest, are you?" He laughed at his own question. He knew just like she did that modesty went out of fashion over a hundred years ago.

Red glared. "No."

"So then this isn't going to be a problem."

Red knew logically that bathing with an audience shouldn't be a problem—and it wasn't . . . normally. She'd done it so many times before that she wasn't even aware of the people around her.

And that was the crux of her problem: she was overly aware of Morgan. She'd never showered in front of a man like him. Hell, she'd never met a man like him before coming to Nuria. It was as if he was a different species and she couldn't keep her eyes off him.

For the first time since she could remember, Red actually felt uncomfortable. Her stomach flopped, and then did a double flip at thought of him staring at her nude form. She swallowed hard.

"I probably don't need a shower today," she said, sounding lame to her own ears.

Morgan laughed. "You have dried blood in your hair and, no offense, but you stink."

"Thanks."

"You don't want to show up at Jesse's bedside looking like you just left the water exchange. She's been through enough already."

He was right, of course, but that didn't make her decision any easier. She was in no way ashamed of her body, never had been. She liked the muscles in her legs and arms, and the concave dip in her stomach. Red even liked her wide hips, but that didn't mean she wanted Morgan inspecting them while she did her best to pretend that he wasn't there.

Red rolled her shoulders. She was being ridiculous. This was just a shower. She'd make it quick, then get dressed and head to town.

Morgan leaned in until his mouth brushed her ear. "To save time, I will take one with you."

The breath left Red's lungs in a whoosh. Her gaze automatically strayed down to the front of Morgan's pants. The ridge of his erection was still clearly visible in the loose clothing. Her eyes shot back to his face in time to see him wipe away a wicked smile.

"I didn't mean to kiss you last night." Red blurted out the lie before she could stop herself.

He shrugged, seemingly unaffected. "You may not have meant to, but I'm sure glad you did. I doubt I could've waited much longer." His gaze locked on her mouth and he ran his thumb along the unmarred part of her jaw line.

Red quaked, despite her resolve, then shook her head. She had to think clearly and Morgan touching her wasn't helping. "I mean it was wrong after everything that had happened."

Morgan's teasing expression faded and he reached down to grasp her upper arm. "Sometimes when we've been through a traumatic event we need physical contact to ensure we're still alive."

"I don't need physical contact," she denied.

His gaze softened. "We all need human contact, Gina, even those of us who deny it. I'm not about to apologize for that kiss. I've wanted to do that ever since I laid eyes on you and you can't tell me that you haven't felt the same." He stepped back, daring her to refute his words.

Red's mouth open and closed a few times, then she glanced away. She couldn't lie to him again, no matter how badly she wanted to. "Fine, have it your way. We can shower together," she said, stomping off to the cleansing room without a backward glance.

Morgan watched Gina walk away. He'd angered her, but he wasn't about to let her deny what was happening between them, even if he didn't understand it all yet.

He followed her into the cleansing room, trying not to gape as she stripped off her clothes. Her rosy nipples peaked under his gaze. Looking down, he caught a glimpse of a shaved mons. He swallowed, to keep from drooling. The urge to drop to his knees and bury his face in her sex rode him hard.

Naked, she was even more beautiful than he'd imagined. It had been sheer hell, trying not to touch her all night. Now, he could barely breathe. Every movement was agony. His shaft rose to full mast as he unbuttoned his pants with trembling fingers. At this rate, he'd never survive the shower.

Gina leaned over and turned on the chemical spray. The white globes of her bottom jiggled enticingly and Morgan bit the inside of his mouth to keep from groaning. It would be so easy to sink into her from behind. The beast within him wanted that and more.

Morgan's body shuddered as he took a step back, so she was out of reach. Gina didn't bother to wait for him to finish undressing before she stepped under the spray, which was probably for the best since it gave him a few moments to pull himself together.

By the time Morgan mustered the courage to drop his pants she'd finished. Gina glanced down at his cock and arched a brow. "I guess it's a good thing I went first. I don't think we would've all fit in there together," she said, grinning, then grabbed a towel and exited the cleansing room.

Morgan stood there riveted in place, his mind replaying every word and every step he'd made. Finally, a smile twisted his lips and he laughed, before stepping into the shower. She hadn't been completely unaffected by his nudity after all.

He'd seen the curiosity and the hunger burning in her eyes, even though she'd masked it with humor. Gina wasn't about to make it easy on him, but that didn't matter, because like all wolves, he loved a good chase.

Red and Morgan drove to the emergency care center. The halls were fairly quiet when they arrived with only a few visitors and on-call staff around. Jesse Lindley's eyes were closed as they entered her room and her breath rattled in her chest. Red frowned, and so did Morgan.

"I don't understand," she whispered, not wanting to disturb the old woman. "I thought she'd show improvement today."

"She should have," he said evasively.

"She doesn't look any better to me. What do you think?" Red asked, concern causing her voice to quaver.

Morgan glanced back at Jesse. "Her color has improved a little, but I expected her to be awake."

Red's brows drew together. She'd hoped Jesse would be awake by now, too. Partly because she needed answers, but mainly because it would let her know Jesse was going to be okay. Instead, it looked as if she were barely clinging to life.

"There has to be something we can do," she said, wringing her hands.

Morgan nodded. "I'll be right back."

"Where are you going?"

"To find Kane and get some answers."

Red glanced at Jesse. "I'm going to wait here just in case she wakes up."

Morgan squeezed Red's fingers in reassurance, then left. The second the door closed behind him, Jesse's eyes flew open. Red gasped and rushed forward.

"How are you feeling? Are you in pain? What can I do?" The questions slurred together in her haste.

Jesse tried to open her jaw and speak. She winced at the effort.

"They had to seal your jaw shut because it was broken in the struggle," Red said.

Jesse held up her bandaged hand and pretended to write.

"Of course." Red began searching the drawers in a nearby cabinet in hopes of finding synth-paper and a pen. Jesse couldn't speak, but she could communicate. Red found the items and returned to Jesse's side.

Putting the pen in her hand, Red held the paper steady. Jesse had just put the tip of the pen onto the paper, when the door flew open. Her eyes widened and she quickly scribbled something that Red couldn't make out, then pushed the paper aside in disgust.

"What is this? I don't understand," Red murmured, trying to decipher what she'd written. Her gaze followed Jesse's line of sight. Morgan and Kane stood in the doorway.

She looked back at Jesse and saw the fright etched upon her features. Red crumpled the page, shoving it into her pocket, before turning to face the men. Why would Jesse be afraid of Morgan and Kane? Was she expecting someone else? Did she think the killer had returned? Red reached down to hold Jesse's hand.

The old woman moved fast, clutching Red's forearm in a death grip. Her gaze went back to the two men and her hand tightened to the point of pain. Red's muscles coiled and gooseflesh dotted her skin. Jesse was trying to warn her. She had no doubt in her mind. The question was, about whom? Red nodded in understanding and she released her. Jesse seemed to visibly relax.

"It's nice to see that you're finally awake," Kane said, stepping forward.

Morgan followed.

"Gina, you're looking better. Did you *sleep* well?" His expression took on a lascivious cast.

Red stiffened and her gaze shot to Morgan, but his attention was locked on Jesse. Had he told Kane about the shower this morning? It didn't seem like Morgan to do something like that, but then again, she didn't know him well. In truth, she didn't know either man.

"How is she doing?" Red asked instead of answering Kane's question.

"She's okay. Still in a lot of pain. I'll have to give her something to take care of it."

Jesse shook her head violently.

Morgan turned to his cousin. "I don't think she wants the medication. It might be best to allow her to heal naturally."

Kane smiled. "I think I know what's best for my patient, Sheriff." He reached out and touched Jesse.

She flinched.

"See, I told you she was in pain."

Jesse's eyes filled with tears as Kane brought an inoculator to her arm.

"It'll be okay. Soon your troubles will be over," he said, pushing it through her skin and releasing the plunger.

Her eyes swam a second, then drooped.

"She'll be out for several hours," Kane said. "You're welcome to stay, but I don't think there's much point."

Morgan glanced at Red. He didn't look happy, if the tick in his jaw was any indication. "I have some reports to file at the office. It shouldn't take long. Do you want to come with me?"

"No." Red shook her head. "I'm going to head over to the dissecting lab. I have to speak with Jim Thornton about something." She gazed at Jesse a moment longer, fear still beating at her. The warning was clear, even if her method was not.

Kane grabbed her hand, tearing her away from her thoughts. Morgan's gaze bulleted to their joined fingers and he stepped forward.

"I'd like to check you out before you leave in case that machine of yours missed something," Kane said, releasing her when he noticed Morgan's reaction.

"Fine, but you're wasting your time." She shrugged. "Rita's never wrong."

"If it's all the same to you, I'd like to see for myself," he said, tightening his grip.

"Make it fast," she said.

Morgan's body remained tense.

"I thought you were going to your office, cousin." Kane prodded with a smile.

Morgan returned his grin, but it didn't reach his eyes. "I've changed my mind. I'd rather make sure Gina is okay first."

"I promise I won't let anything happen to her."

"I know, but I'd feel better if I were there all the same," Morgan said.

"Suit yourself," Kane replied, guiding Red out of the room.

The examination only lasted a couple of minutes. Kane rushed through it with Morgan looking over his shoulder. Normally, Red would've been annoyed by Morgan's behavior, but since it helped her get out of there sooner, she let it slide.

"Are you sure you're going to be okay on your own?" Morgan asked as they reached his office.

"I'll be fine. I don't plan to go anywhere else besides the dissecting lab."

He frowned.

"I swear," she added.

Morgan didn't look convinced by her sincerity, but he nodded anyway. "I will give Jim a call and let him know that you're on your way. I'll be over as soon as I finish my reports. If I have to step out, Maggie will know how to find me. Don't go anywhere other than the dissecting lab without letting me know."

Red's temper flared. "I don't need your permission, Sheriff."

Morgan's lips thinned. "If you can't listen to orders, then I'll just have to assign one of my deputies to stand guard over you."

Her eyes widened. "You wouldn't dare."

"Wouldn't I?" He cocked his head in challenge.

"I do not need a babysitter," Red hissed. "I'm perfectly capable of taking care of myself."

"I beg to differ," he said, stepping forward to crowd her.

Red's body came to life at his nearness, softening despite the anger coursing through her veins. What the hell was happening? Her breath left her lungs.

"Morgan, I—" She cleared her throat to remove the unexpected rasp.

"I've given you a choice," he said gently, his gaze latching onto her mouth.

Red licked her lips. "I'll stay with Jim."

"Good idea," he said, flashing a victorious smile.

Jim Thornton stood in the dissecting lab hosing down the empty tables with sanitizing spray. Protective clothing covered his body and a filtered mask concealed his mouth. Red stepped into the room and gagged as the noxious odor bludgeoned her nostrils. Her eyes began to water and Jim's image blurred.

"Sorry, my dear. I didn't notice you standing there. It's good to see you up and about," Jim said, voice muffled. Shutting off the valve, he gazed at her, while Red wiped her eyes. "Stinks doesn't it?"

She coughed, unable to answer.

"It's gotten so that I barely notice it myself."

Red cleared her throat. "I don't know how you could miss it."

Jim shrugged and smiled. "Thirty years of doing this job and your olfactory senses are permanently fried."

Red laughed. "I'm sure that's a defense mechanism."

Jim's eyes twinkled. "Now I know you haven't come down here to talk about my job and the various odors associated with it."

"No." Red straightened and breathed through her mouth. "I've come about that shirt I gave you the other day." Her stomach soured at the thought of what would be revealed.

"Yes, of course. Let me just get the results of the tests that I ran. I'll be right back."

Red watched Jim head toward his office then began to pace. She glanced around the dissecting lab at the various tables that now sparkled from the cleaning. The bodies were long gone. She was about to turn back, when she spotted the white tarp in the corner. Red stopped, frowning.

That one had been here the last time she'd spent time in the lab. Jim had told Red all bodies must be disposed of quickly in order to recycle the parts. So why was the one under the tarp still here? Maybe it wasn't even a body. Perhaps it was an animal that Jim had brought back to dissect.

Curiosity got the better of her. Investigating gave

her mind something to do while she waited. Red glanced toward the door, but saw no sign of Jim. She listened for footsteps. Nothing. The sound of the air filtration system droned in the background. She glanced at the tarp once more.

"Screw it," she said, walking across the room to the lone table. Red looked over her shoulder one last time before lifting a corner of the tarp. She shrieked and stumbled back. The gruesome figure of a woman stared up at her.

Flashes of Lisa Solomon's shredded body spilled into her mind. The similarities were too close to ignore. Whatever had killed Lisa and Moira Collins had also attacked this woman.

She took a couple of deep breaths, then stepped forward to examine the body. The woman had been dead awhile—quite awhile. Red was no dissecting lab director, but she'd seen enough death to recognize its stages. This woman clearly predated Moira and Lisa.

Morgan had lied from the very beginning. He knew something was killing women. Had known all along.

Red dropped the tarp and clutched her stomach as pain that rivaled the attack ripped through her. Damn him. She'd trusted him with her life. Her mouth began to water as she fought down the urge to vomit. She recalled Jesse's battered face. Was that why she looked so scared when Morgan and Kane entered her room? Did she think that one of them was behind the killings?

Red pulled out the crumpled piece of paper in her pocket and stared at it. Why would Jesse scribble nonsense on the page? She turned the synth-paper on its side and looked again. "Oh no," she gasped, slapping a hand over her mouth. It looked like an *H. Hunter.*

Rage shook Red's body violently. She'd come so close to sleeping with Morgan last night. What if he truly was the enemy?

Footsteps echoed in the hall. Red rushed across the room to stand near the door. Jim Thornton was obviously involved in the cover-up. She'd trusted these people, and she didn't trust anyone. This incident drove home the reason. How could Morgan do this to her?

Jim walked into the room holding synth-documents in his hand. He was so preoccupied with them that he nearly walked into the door. He glanced up at the last second and stopped in front of her.

His brow furrowed. "Are you okay, Gina? You look a little green."

"I'm fine," she bit out. He didn't seem to notice.

"Did you touch anything at Moira's crime scene?" he asked absently, flicking through the pages.

The question temporarily deflated Red's anger. "No, why?"

"I'm sure it's a mistake in my testing. I'm going to run the shirt again."

Red brushed the loose strands of her hair away from her face. "Jim, what do you mean by mistake?"

"It's nothing."

Red reached out and grasped his hand. "Please tell me what you found."

Jim's face flushed. "There are minute traces of Moira's DNA mixed in with your blood on the shirt."

"How's that possible? Up until last night, I didn't have any injuries."

He shifted, his gaze darting around the room as if he were searching for means of escape. "I'm not sure. Like I said, the tests must be off."

Red's stomach sank. She couldn't seem to catch her breath. Jim was lying. She knew it. And it wasn't just paranoia over discovering the woman's body. Had she killed Moira during the night? What if she'd killed the other women, too? Was it even possible? And worse still, had Jim lied out of fear? But that didn't explain the attack on her and Jesse.

Her thoughts beckoned to the hysteria waiting at the edges of her mind. Fear threatened to crush her, but Red knocked it aside, focusing instead on her building anger toward Morgan.

She rushed past Jim, nearly toppling him. Red had to get to Morgan. She needed to hear an explanation for the lies. If he'd lied about this, what else had he lied about? Had he been lying to her this morning, when he pretended to care?

Pumping her arms, Red ran harder, paying no heed to the dizziness threatening to overwhelm her. She needed to know the truth and with all that had transpired in the past few days, she was itching for a good fight.

Red flew to the sheriff's station, ignoring the curious glances as she sprinted down the sidewalk. More than one person looked behind her to ensure no one was giving chase. She didn't care what they thought. The only thing that mattered was finding Morgan.

Red kicked herself for kissing him. How could she be so naïve? He'd played her from the start. The mere fact that she'd been attracted to him should've been all the warning she needed. Somehow being around Nuria had made her soft.

Well no longer. The bitch was back and Morgan wouldn't know what hit him. Her lungs heaved as she rounded the block. The sheriff's office lay ahead. She didn't break stride, thundering over the threshold.

"Where is he?" She gasped, pressing her hand against the stitch in her side.

Maggie's eyes widened. "What's wrong?" She looked past Red as if she were searching for the hounds of hell.

"Where?" Red asked, marching forward. She threw the door to Morgan's office open and strode in, but he wasn't there. This was beginning to be a habit with him.

Red's head whipped around. "He's not here," she said, stating the obvious.

Maggie stood and backed away. "He had to run home for a couple of minutes. He forgot something. Said to tell you he'd be right back."

"Did Morgan drop my car off here?" she asked, scanning the office. She was in no mood to wait for his return. His house would be a far better place to confront him.

Maggie pointed outside. "It's around back. He had one of the deputies pick it up. Do you want to tell me what happened so that I can notify the sheriff?"

"No!" Red strode toward the door. "That won't be necessary. I'll fill him in when I get there. All I need from you are directions to his home."

Red watched Maggie tap the comlink in her ear.

Morgan would know she was on her way in a matter of seconds. She didn't care because he had no idea what she'd found at the dissecting lab and neither did Jim Thornton.

The drive took a little longer than she'd remembered. She was so focused on her anger that Red didn't notice the car that had stopped down the road. She jumped out of her vehicle and raced inside, leaving the door open.

"Hey," he said, in way of greeting. "Maggie called and said that you were upset. What happened?"

Red's fists balled and she swung, catching Morgan off guard. His head snapped back, but he made no effort to stop her. "You lying son of a bitch. I can't believe that I bought into your bullshit."

Morgan licked the trickle of blood off his lip. "What are you talking about?"

Red's voice trumpeted. "I'm talking about the body under the white tarp in the dissecting lab. You've known all along that women were being murdered. I bet you could hardly contain your laughter. The jokes on IPTT, right?"

Morgan's cheeks colored.

"What else have you been concealing? How many more bodies are there?"

Morgan's gaze narrowed. "Calm down."

"I will not calm down." Red rounded on him, her hands moving to her hips. She glanced at the rest pad and noted the fresh linens and candles nearby, but was too far gone to consider their meaning. "I can't believe that I almost slept with you."

Morgan jerked as if he'd been slapped. "As I recall, you *did* sleep with me."

She growled in frustration. "You know what I mean."

Morgan walked over and shut the door, locking it, before advancing on her. "I received an interesting call from Jim Thornton. Seems like I'm not the only one keeping secrets."

Red gasped. She wasn't keeping secrets. Well, maybe a few, but that was different. She hadn't remained silent to deceive anyone. "That has nothing to do with this."

"It could have everything to do with this situation and you know it," he snapped.

"Are you accusing me of something, Sheriff?" Red asked, stepping into his space. "If so, why not arrest me?" She held her hands out in front of her with her wrists together in preparation for the energy binds.

"Don't be ridiculous." He snarled. "I base my findings on facts, not assumptions . . . unlike some tactical team members I know."

Red hauled her fist back and swung again. This time Morgan was ready and caught it easily. His amber eyes flared. Whether in warning or in promise, she didn't know.

"I let you hit me once. That was enough foreplay." He flashed her an unholy smile, then pulled her into his body. His hard cock pressed into her stomach and he rolled his hips. "Fuck now, fight later," he growled a second before his lips crushed down upon hers.

There was no time to protest. Not that she could think of anything to say. Her thoughts scattered under the press of his mouth. Red struggled, but her body was already surrendering.

"Stop fighting me, I don't want to lose control," he pleaded, deepening the kiss.

"Never."

Morgan's lips were insistent, demanding her submission. He fed upon her mouth, devouring her like a man dying of thirst.

"Gina, your heart rate is going up dangerously high," Rita came out of standby mode and chimed.

The sensations were too much. He was too much. She pulled back, determined to stop him, but he leaned forward and nipped her bottom lip. The tactic worked.

"Damn you." Red hissed at the sting of pleasure-pain, then closed the gap between them once more.

Red's hands reached for the front of his outer shirt and began to unfasten it. She needed to feel his hot skin beneath her fingertips. Before she could get it open his thumbs brushed her nipples, sending heat searing through her body. She gasped, but he swallowed the sound.

His hands seemed to be everywhere at once, scouring her skin, while stroking her need. He didn't give her time to think or breathe as he mounted his assault on her senses. The anger only fueled their passion.

Red reached beneath his shirt, feeling the crisp hairs that trailed deliciously into his pants. She followed the velvet path down until he flinched. She smiled against his lips. Apparently, the sheriff was ticklish.

He didn't give her time to explore any further. His hands whipped out, manacling her wrists. "I won't last long if you touch me right now." He circled her arm until he reached her navcom, then hit the release switch. "You won't need this. I don't want Rita telling me what your body's reactions are. I want to find out for myself." He dropped the navcom onto a nearby table.

"Gina, I can't help you when you remove me," Rita said.

"It's okay," she gasped. "Go to sleep. I'll check in later."

Red tried to touch him again, but found herself backed into the wall. Morgan raised her arms over her head. "Stay," he said, nipping her shoulder.

Flames devoured Red. Her sex wept in anticipation. He didn't make her wait long. Morgan stripped her pants and boots from her body, then lifted her with one hand. The man was stronger than he looked. The fingers of his free hand found her clit and began circling it, teasing her flesh until she was fully prepared to grovel. Red didn't have to.

Morgan found the tiny nub and pressed down. Red's head dropped back against the wall and she cried out, her hips jerking as she reached a lightning-fast completion. Her mind was still whirling when she heard Morgan shuffling clothes. A second later he lifted her and his cock snuggled against her tight entrance.

He growled what sounded like "mine" under his breath, then slipped an inch inside. Red mewed. He was so big, so hot, and intoxicatingly hard. Morgan's hips rocked and he sank even further. His breathing deepened and sweat dotted his forehead.

"You're going to be the death of me," he choked out.

Red knew all he had to do was drop her and she'd

be impaled, but he didn't. He was taking his time, savoring the moment. Her heart pattered at the thought. Damn him for making her care.

Morgan couldn't think of anything but the warm, wet spot he was sinking into. Not her anger, not his deception, nothing but the woman he'd wanted since day one. Gina felt better than any nocturnal musings he could create. She was so blessedly tight and soft beneath his hands that it took effort not to thrust for all he was worth. Somehow he managed to leash the beast, or at least he'd thought he had until Gina's inner muscles squeezed him.

Morgan closed his eyes, riding a wave of desire. She was like a molten fist, encircling his cock. "If you do that again, I can't be held responsible."

She laughed softly. "Do what?" she asked, her body squeezing him again. "This?"

Morgan let out a pained cry of defeat. He'd planned to draw out their first joining, worshiping her body the way she deserved, feasting upon the wetness between her thighs, but she'd taken the decision out of his hands. He reached between their bodies and stroked her clit, taking care to rake it gently with his nails. She bucked against him as her need began to build once more.

"Like that, do you?" He smiled and did it again, while at the same time thrusting up. He sank to the balls into her, his legs shaking with the effort to remain standing. She wasn't heavy, but his blood had been diverted somewhere else. Somewhere infinitely more important at the moment.

Gina yelped, then moaned as he ground his cock into her. He pressed down, then strummed her clit faster and faster. Gina came apart again in his arms, her body milking him.

The beast surged, breaking free. Morgan lost all sense of his surroundings. He rode her hard, thrusting and gliding. She wrapped her legs around his waist. Their flesh slapped together, the suction they created pulling him deeper. He kissed his way over her cheek, before nibbling on her ear. The salt of her skin tickled his tongue.

One of Gina's hands sunk into his hair, while the other clutched his ass, her nails leaving tiny darts of pleasure imbedded in his skin. The sensation only spurred him on to take the ultimate step. The one that would change both their lives forever.

Morgan jerked, releasing her ear long enough to trail his lips along her exposed neck. She tilted her chin, giving him greater access. Telling him without words that she was his. Morgan felt the canines in his mouth lengthen and there wasn't a damn thing he could do to stop them. The urge to mark was too strong. The wolf knew he'd found his mate.

He bellowed, then bit down where her nape met her delicate shoulder. Her blood filled his mouth, drowning his senses in the heady aroma. He needed more. Had to have more. He sucked harder, drawing her coppery essence down his throat, while his tongue lapped voraciously.

Gina mewed, but didn't ask him to let go, her body too busy riding out another fluttering orgasm.

Morgan drove in deep, his body expanding and convulsing as he did so. He emptied himself inside of her pulsing warmth, feeling a sense of peace settle over him. He laved Gina's neck tenderly to soothe the sting, while continuing his shallow thrusts. His knees shook from the effort to remain upright. After she'd milked every last drop of fluid from him, Morgan slowly released her so she could stand.

"That," he murmured, nuzzling against her neck, "was incredible." He kissed the spot he'd marked. "Remind me again what we were fighting about."

chapter seventeen

Gina's angry. Her black hair is pulled tight and her lovely face is flushed with the volatile emotion as she enters Morgan's home. Her strange hazel eyes spark as she pulls her tiny fist back and lets it fly, connecting hard. Morgan's head snaps back. I didn't expect her to strike him, but I can't deny the pleasure the physical blow brings me.

This is better than I'd hoped. I can now be there for her to help pick up the pieces. She's too smart to waste another moment with him. Her voice raises and I hear her mention a body. No wonder she's angry.

So they did find my first kill. I was beginning to wonder. Morgan kept his silence well, but he obviously had help. Probably in the form of Jim Thornton. I should've dealt with him long ago, but I needed him. He was the only one who made regular sweeps of the desert. Without Jim, no one would've discovered the women I'd chosen.

Gina, my love. The others meant nothing to me. They were pale comparisons to you and your beauty. We are destined to be together.

The fight escalates, but I can no longer hear them

now that Morgan has closed the door. Tension flows out of the home and into the desert around me. It warms my heart and I can't keep the smile from forming on my face. Pride fills me as I watch the angry she-wolf hold her ground.

Perhaps I should knock on the door and intervene. Now would probably be as good a time as any. Straightening the front of my clothes, I start to turn away. Morgan's next move stops me cold. My muscles lock as I realize something in the atmosphere has changed.

Morgan's grabbed Gina and pulled her against his body. The alpha in him has been provoked into action. No! I scream inside my mind. This cannot be happening, but I know it's true. His head descends rapidly and I know what he's going to do before he does it.

Why isn't she struggling harder? Gina fight. Now is your only chance to escape him. If he touches her, he will not let her go.

A second later, his lips capture hers. The fight in her body is ineffectual, almost as if she's not really trying to break away from him. She twists her wrists, but her mouth remains attached to his, hungry, searching.

That's when I see it. The subtle softening of her body that tells me she's surrendered.

No! No! No! Get away from him, Gina. Tell Morgan that you are mine.

The alpha doesn't waste any time. He swiftly moves her across the room and backs her into the wall. Morgan's still kissing her, but the urgency has changed. He's going to take her right there in front of me.

I want to burst through the window, but I know his home has been reinforced. Everyone who lives away from the safety of town adds thickness to their walls and windows for additional protection. Not even I can enter by force.

Damn it! He's baring her breasts. The breasts that should've been mine. Her pink nipples peak as they scrape his chest. My mouth waters as I long for a taste of her tender flesh, but there is nothing I can do besides watch. The rest of her clothing follows swiftly.

She's shaven between her thighs, leaving her nether lips glistening. Her body wants him, even though she'd claimed otherwise. Morgan inhales, taking her fragrance into his lungs. He doesn't waste any time removing his clothing. He's erect and ready as he seeks out her moist entrance.

Their nakedness burns into my retinas, permanently scarring them with their image.

I rip at the wall, trying to gain entry. My claws leave deep furrows, but are otherwise useless. Let me in! She's mine. Get the hell away from her.

My mind splinters as I watch Morgan lift her and thrust his cock into my bitch. He's fucking Gina like I should be, taking her against the wall like a beast in rut. He'd probably planned this all along. I should've known that his disinterest was feigned.

I watch helplessly as he thrusts into her again and again, driving her body up the wall with each upward movement. His face is flushed and covered in sweat, but he doesn't slow his movements. Gina's breasts bounce at the force of his taking. Her eyes remain at half mast as her short nails dig into his skin, scoring him in the way of our people.

It only seems to spur Morgan on.

My mind's in turmoil. I don't know what to do. I

have to stop them, before it's too late. The moment is still salvageable. It may take several fucks to get his scent off her body, but I'll do it. I will do whatever it takes to erase Morgan's memory from her mind.

Then I see it, the subtle movement that dashes the last of my hope. She's baring her neck to him as a moan spills from her parted lips. Perhaps he's too far gone to notice. She tilts back even further and flexes her fingertips.

No! Gina no!

Morgan glances up, his gaze latching onto her exposed neck. I see the red haze cover his eyes as blood lust takes over.

The roar in my ears is near deafening as I watch his canines lengthen. His eyes have returned to gold now and they're glazed with mating fever. He's going to mark her. Claim her for himself. Why now after all these years does he decide to take a mate? And why Gina, when Morgan could have any other? Doesn't he understand that she's mine?

Maybe he does. The insidious thought filters through what's left of my human mind. Pain tears through me as the beast tries to break out to stop him. Mine, it screams, flailing outside the window.

I watch in horror as Morgan's teeth sink into the crook of Gina's creamy white neck. I catch a flash of blood rimming his mouth as he greedily sucks and swallows her essence with the lap of his rough tongue.

For a second, he glances my way. I swear I see his smile mocking me, but then it's gone.

The window sill crumbles beneath my razor sharp claws as I watch his eyes close in ecstasy. He's taking what should be mine. I can almost smell the coppery odor and the musk from their sex wafting in the air. It sickens me.

Gina will pay for her betrayal with the loss of someone she holds dear. I thought to spare him, but now I realize that was naïve. He is beyond redemption and must suffer the ultimate price. Marking Gina will cost Morgan his life.

I had to wait for the sun to set before I could sneak into the hospital. There were too many people coming and going to enter undetected. The room I'm in is quiet and smells like the antiseptic used to cleanse the fixtures. The stench sickens me, but still I wait.

The nurse making rounds should be finished in a few minutes. Once she passes, then I'll be free to slip down the hall and fulfill my promise to Gina. I told her she would pay for her infidelity. She must learn that actions have consequences.

I will not be denied my right to claim her as my mate. Morgan's death will invalidate his mark, but first I have to punish her. I don't want to. It hurts me to be put in this position. She had a choice. Instead of choosing wisely, she lowered herself to lay with swine.

Ah well . . .

What's done is done.

Footsteps in the hall herald the nurse's arrival. I step behind the door a second before she opens it and looks inside. There are no patients in this room, now that I've disposed of the old man in the cleansing room. His pain and suffering are over. My care will be rewarded in the end.

The woman slips back out of the room after spotting the light under the door of the cleansing room. She won't check on him again until long after I'm gone. I wait and listen as her footsteps grow fainter. Cracking the door, I peek out. The lights in the hall have been dimmed, leaving shadows clinging to the corners and ceiling. Perfect for concealing my approach.

I leave the room, giving one last glance over my shoulder. I can smell the old man's blood over the cleaning fluid. It's dank and musty like rest of him. I wasn't even tempted to take a sip. It doesn't take long to reach Jesse Lindley's room. She's at the end of the hall. The nurse will have already been by on her rounds. I have at least an hour to play.

And play I will.

The room is dark. Much darker than the hall as I enter. A slip of light slices the shadows long enough for me to see Jesse's quick intake of breath. I close the door behind me, knowing she's awake.

"There's no need to pretend," I say, walking toward her.

Hatred spills from her eyes, letting me know without words what she thinks of me. The feeling is mutual.

"I want you to know that I'm here because Gina reneged on our agreement."

Jesse frowned in confusion.

"She spread her legs for our alpha and let him place his mark upon her. Now you must pay."

The old one-eyed bitch had the audacity to smile at me.

"You think that's amusing?"

She nods.

Before her head finishes the movement, I backhand her. Jesse groans. "I am in no mood to be trifled with and angering me won't help your situation."

She reaches for the call button, but I yank it out of the wall before she can press it. There will be no rescue from emergency care personnel. No one can help her now. She just doesn't realize it yet, but she will.

My fingers reach around her neck and begin to squeeze the life out of her. She struggles, pounding at my wrists with her bandaged hands. It's ineffectual and we both know it. Her throat feels good beneath my grip. When her eyes roll back in her head, I shake her until she regains consciousness.

I don't want our game to end too quickly. I want her to suffer. I need her to suffer as I have. It's the only way to punish Gina for her betrayal.

My nails score her skin and the wolf inside me catches its first whiff of blood. Jesse's essence isn't near as aged as the old man's. Familiar pain engulfs me. I stare down at my hands and watch my fingers reshape into large handlike paws. Talons sprout from my nail beds, burning as they unsheath. Jesse's struggles increase as she tries to shift into her true form.

I cannot let her.

There's a chance she could get away. My grip intensifies until all that's left are a few gurgles and kicks from her feet. Jesse's eye remains wide with fright and acceptance. She understands that a sacrifice was needed. It was part of her duty to be an example of what happens when you betray me.

When Gina arrives at the hospital, she'll recognize the truth and beauty in Jesse's death. She'll accept the punishment I've seen fit to dole out. The steady pierce of the flatline from her heart monitor finally reaches me. I only have a moment to react. My body contorts painfully to return to its *alien* form. The emergency staff enters the room as I start chest compressions. Must make a show of trying to save her life.

"What happened?" Glenda, the night nurse, asks as she approaches.

"I have no idea. I stopped in to pay my respects and she seized on me," I say, continuing to pump her chest like it will actually do some good. It won't. I made sure of that. Nothing will bring her back.

If by chance she did return, I'd be forced to kill everyone in the room. Let's hope it doesn't come to that.

Nurses come and go, carrying inoculators full of various medications. I stay close for five more minutes before I slowly back away from the bed. Don't want to leave too soon or they might become suspect.

"It's too late," I say. "She's gone. Her heart must have given out."

Glenda steps forward with tears in her eyes. I reach out and clasp her shoulder. "Should we notify the sheriff?" she asks.

I glance at my watch and furrow my forehead as if I'm actually giving it some thought. "No, let him rest tonight. No sense ruining his evening. Get Jesse's body prepped for the dissecting lab."

"But shouldn't Sheriff Hunter view the body first?"

I force a smile, when all I want to do is rip her throat out. "Why should he? It's obvious she died of natural causes."

chapter eighteen

Morgan pulled Gina onto her knees, leaving her open for his penetration. He'd been fucking her for hours, partly to avoid the upcoming conversation he knew they needed to have, but mainly because he couldn't seem to get enough of her. She made him insatiable. And he liked it. Liked it so much that he never wanted it to end.

He kissed his way down her back. She was healing fast thanks to her heritage. The bruises from the attack were barely visible. Morgan continued his carnal exploration, pausing to nip the globes of her bottom before nudging her legs wider apart.

A delicious fragrance engulfed him as he dipped his head between her legs, pressing his tongue into her wetness until she shuddered. He loved making her do that. He wiped his mouth as drool threatened to escape. So far Morgan had found five different places on her body that produced quivers and he was determined to find more.

Her spicy taste exploded in his mouth as he lapped at her entry. She dripped in readiness. Had he ever been with anyone so responsive? Morgan didn't realize he was growling until Gina started to giggle.

"You enjoying yourself back there?" she asked, glancing over her shoulder.

He grinned. "You know I am. Aren't you?" A swipe of his tongue followed the question. This time he plunged in, exploring her depths more thoroughly.

Gina's knees shook, threatening to give out.

"Oh no you don't," he said, hoisting her up with one arm from behind. "I haven't nearly gotten my fill yet. You taste incredible. I could feast on you for days." He cocked his head. "Hmm, that doesn't sound like a half-bad idea."

Gina's eyes narrowed. "We still have to talk," she reminded him.

"I mustn't be doing my job very well if you're still able to form coherent thoughts. I suppose I'll have to try harder." Morgan nibbled the backs of her thighs until he reached her knees.

She flinched. "I had no idea that biting could be so erotic," she said as he made his way back up.

"You haven't seen anything yet," he said, positioning his shaft at her ripe entrance. Morgan thrust forward at the same time his mouth came down upon her shoulder. The double penetration sent Gina into an unexpected orgasm. She whimpered. He tongued the spot, matching his thrusts.

She was everything he'd ever imagined and more. And best of all, she was his. Gina may not know it yet. He'd still have to figure out a way to tell her, but it was only a matter of timing. The wolf in her ran deep. He could taste it in her sweet blood. It called to him on a gut level, demanding the alpha in him answer. And he had, by claiming her.

Morgan knew Gina felt it, too, even if she didn't realize that's what it was. That's why she'd surrendered, offering him her body and baring her throat, after he'd proven his dominance. Some part of her recognized him as her mate, just as he'd recognized her.

He'd never grow tired of Gina and he'd gladly spend the rest of his long life trying to please her. Now all Morgan had to do was convince her to stay.

Red's body was humming. Each thrust from Morgan brought her closer to oblivion. She'd had sex before, enough times to know it had never been like this. Sometime over the last several hours, she and Morgan had connected. It wasn't a frivolous kind of bond that came from simple attraction, but a soul-deep melding that let her know she would not be walking away unscathed.

That strange connection didn't excuse his lies or the deception, but she was capable of separating her job from physical gratification. Or at least she had been until now. Her emotions were in a jumble. She couldn't seem to focus with Morgan's heated body wrapped around her like a blanket.

Red felt the steady build of desire as he fucked her from behind. It coiled deep in her belly, winding tighter and tighter until she could barely breathe.

"Harder," she murmured, throwing her hips back to meet him.

Morgan's rumbling growl vibrated his chest, sending gooseflesh dancing over her arms. His hips slammed forward as he sped up. He seemed to like the change of pace as much as she did.

The wet slap of skin on skin and labored breathing filled the quiet of the room. Red closed her eyes, relishing the feel of his cock filling her. With each rolling thrust it seemed to thicken, expanding to the point of discomfort, only to send her soaring higher.

Red cried out as her orgasm tore through her like a blast from a laser pistol. Her nipples stabbed the rest pad as her arms gave out and she dropped face first onto the pillow. Morgan supported the lower half of her body, keeping it raised, driving deep . . . and deeper still until she could almost feel him in the back of her throat.

He ground into her one last time, sinking his fingers into her hip bones, then with a groan he jerked as his body found release. He collapsed next to her, pulling her into his arms a second before sleep overcame them.

Red awoke shortly before dawn to find Morgan staring at her with a strange expression on his face.

"What?" she asked, brushing at her mouth and eyes self-consciously.

"You are beautiful," he said, touching her cheek with the back of his finger. "I can't get over that you're mine." He pressed his lips to her forehead, then drew back.

"Yours?" she asked, confused. The words had a nice ring to them, but seemed a little premature. They hadn't known each other long enough to make any kind of commitment. At least that's what she told herself as her heart jumped for joy. "Morgan, I—"

"For as long as you're here in Nuria," he added hastily.

Somehow it sounded better before the addition. Her heart stumbled, then fell. Surely she wasn't disappointed. That would mean she actually cared. It was probably just the sex talking. So what if it had been phenomenal. She could find someone else just as good. *Yeah, sure you can.* The little voice in her head popped off, sounding more than a little like Rita.

Red shook her head. Now she was hearing her navcom without wearing it. That didn't say much for her state of mind. She needed to end this line of thought or it would lead to a mandatory mental health check once she put Rita back on. Red still couldn't believe she'd allowed Morgan to remove her. It was a testament to how far gone she'd been. She slipped the navcom on.

Rita sprang to life. "Gina, where have you been?"

"Here," she replied, shaking off the mental cobwebs.

"Where is here? You've never taken me off this long unless I needed repairs. Which is often I might add."

"I'm at Sheriff Hunter's home." Guilt assailed Red for a moment before she recalled whom she was speaking with and what she'd been doing. "Some things need to remain private," she added, glancing in time to see Morgan smile.

"I do not understand," Rita said.

"And I don't have time to explain." It was time she and Morgan had that little talk. "Do me a favor and power down."

"But you just placed me on your wrist."

"That's an order, Rita."

"Very well. Going to standby."

"Why did you lie?" she asked Morgan, cutting to the chase.

He stiffened beside her. "I see it's back to business."

"Just answer the question."

"I didn't think it was necessary to mention Renee Forrester's death since I'd already attributed it to an animal attack."

"Do you still believe that?" Her gaze bore into him, but Morgan didn't flinch.

"Yes, I do."

She searched for any sign of deception, but found none. "I don't understand why you didn't mention her, when I asked specifically about bodies."

His face pinched with discomfort. "You came to Nuria expecting a cover-up. I wasn't about to add fuel to your suspicions."

Her gaze dropped to his stubbled chin. The short dark hairs only accented his lush mouth. She could still feel his kisses on her throat, the sting of his teeth upon her skin, and the glide of his tongue as he tasted her. Heat spread through her body and Red swallowed.

Morgan's eyes crinkled and his mouth twitched.

"You aren't helping," she said, looking away.

"With what?"

She huffed. "With my line of questioning."

He tilted his head until he was staring into her eyes. "I thought I'd answered everything you'd asked."

Red met his gaze. "No, there's one thing you haven't responded to yet."

He sighed heavily. "What is that?"

She took a deep breath and released it. "Why did you suspect me of Moira's murder?"

It was Morgan's turn to look uncomfortable. "I didn't. At least not at first. It wasn't until Moira's DNA was found on your shirt that I suspected."

"Jim told you."

"Yes, he contacted me before giving you the results, and then again, after you left the lab in such a hurry. This is my town, remember?"

"How could I forget?" She stared, watching his expression carefully as she phrased her next question. "Do you still suspect me?" Red asked, steadying herself for his answer. She knew it was hypocritical of her to ask, since she'd suspected him. Hell, she did suspect him. Red just didn't know exactly how far he'd crossed the line.

"I'm not sure a crime has been committed," he said, avoiding her question. Morgan held up his hand when she opened her mouth to speak. "The deaths are tragic. You'll get no argument from me. If I believed for a second that we were hunting a human being, I'd be the first to call in the tactical team. But I know we're after an animal . . . possibly several." He glanced away, unable to meet her eyes. "I don't know how Moira's blood got on your clothing, but I promise I'll help you find out."

Red listened to Morgan's words, attempting to

read between the lines. He knew more than what he was saying, whether to cover up his investigation or to protect her, she wasn't sure.

The thought that he might risk his career for her only brought on more confusion. He'd known her just a short while. What might he do for someone he'd known a lifetime? She opened her mouth to ask when the vidcom buzzed.

Morgan reached over and pressed a button to answer the call. Red only had a second to cover herself before Jim Thornton popped onto the screen.

His eyes widened and his face flushed until his ears were beet red. "Excuse me," he said, coughing and glancing away. "I didn't mean to interrupt, Morgan, but I thought you'd like to know that the emergency care center just dropped Jesse Lindley's body off at the lab.

Pain sliced Red as the news fell from Jim's lips. Tears stung the backs of her eyes, but she refused to let them fall. Jesse dead? How? She couldn't seem to breathe. Her chest hurt too much. She sprung out of the bed, ignoring her nudity, and began to pace. Morgan swung the viewer away so that Jim only caught a glimpse of her.

"What the hell happened?" he shouted, before slowly lowering his voice. "I'm sorry, Jim."

"It's okay. I understand." He cleared his throat. "The report says natural causes. Heart, maybe? I'll know more once I finish my preliminary. Kane was in attendance when she died. He pronounced. There were several nurses on scene, too."

Red's head jerked at Jim's last statement. Poor Jesse. She'd survived the attack, leaving her with a wired jaw and bandaged hands, only to die of a heart attack. The synth-paper with the letter *H* came into her mind and her stomach soured.

Was it possible? Had Kane had a hand in killing Jesse? Had he been the one to attack them? It didn't make any sense. Why would he, when there was no reason to target her? He was a respected member of Nurian society. Yet Morgan hadn't left her side all night, so there was no way he'd gone to the care center. She glanced at him. Worry drained his features. Was it concern for Jesse—or his cousin? He could always be covering for Kane.

Red's muscles clenched, squeezing her heart until she could barely breathe. Had she misjudged him so thoroughly?

Would he cover up murder for a family member? He certainly seemed loyal enough. *You don't even know if it is murder yet.*

Morgan stared at the viewer. "What aren't you telling me?" he asked, his voice held no inflection.

"Something's not right with the body," Jim said.

He stilled. "What do you mean?" He glanced toward her and sat up straighter.

Red stared at Morgan. Tension crackled between them. She wasn't about to leave the room and miss what Jim had to say.

"I haven't opened her up yet, but there's hemorrhaging in the eyes. That only happens in strangulation deaths. I've gone over the charts twice and no obstructed airway was mentioned."

Morgan ran his hand through his hair. "Maybe her throat got crushed during treatment," he suggested, but he didn't sound convinced.

"I'm sure you're right." Jim coughed. "Like I said, I'll know more when I open her up."

"Let me know what you find." Morgan hit the disconnect, severing the call.

Red could hear the desperation in Morgan's voice and it pained her that she could do nothing to ease it. And she certainly couldn't tell him about her suspicions, not without proof. He'd never believe her. Hell, she wouldn't believe herself, not with Moira's DNA hanging over her head. Red didn't even know if she was on the right track, but Jesse had tried to warn her about something and it had cost her. Her life. She'd have to keep her investigation quiet until she finished. She couldn't take the chance that Morgan might find out and tip his cousin off.

Kane was family—the closest family Morgan had in town. He wouldn't accept her findings easily. Goodness knows, she wouldn't either if someone told her that Robert Santiago was a murderer. Red prayed that somehow she was wrong about this, but her gut was screaming. She wouldn't turn her back on the old woman now that she was dead. She owed Jesse, her life.

"I can't help but feel this is all my fault," Red said, running her hands over her arms and pacing.

"Why would you think that?" Morgan asked distractedly.

She stopped and looked at him. "If Jesse hadn't come in during the attack, she'd be fine right now."

"You don't know that."

"Yes," she nodded, "I do. Jesse paid the ultimate price for her interference. You know it and I know it," Red said, blinking back fresh tears.

Morgan rose off the rest pad and grabbed her, pulling her into his embrace. "Listen to me," he said, his lips brushing the side of her head. "You did nothing to deserve that attack and neither did Jesse. I will find the individual responsible. You have my word." He rocked her from side to side, the warmth of his body seeping into her, soothing. She wanted so badly to believe him, but what if it turned out to be Kane? Would he still feel the same?

Red tilted her chin to meet his gaze. There was no mistaking the depth of emotions swimming in Morgan's amber eyes. She couldn't let him do it. Red cared too much to let him risk his life for her. There was no way in hell she'd lose Morgan, too. Her resolve hardened and she pulled out of his embrace, steeling herself for what she needed to do. "I can't let you go after him."

Morgan blinked as if he wasn't sure he'd heard her correctly. "What do you mean?"

"For some unknown reason, he's after me. I won't allow anyone else to get hurt trying to protect me."

"Gina."

"No." She took a step back, when he reached for her. "Jesse died because of me, Morgan."

"No, she didn't."

Her jaw clenched. "Yes, she did. I'm not going to be responsible for your death, too."

Something warmed in his expression and Red realized she'd just admitted she cared. Well, it didn't matter. Morgan knowing her true feelings didn't change anything between them. She was a highly trained tactical team member. Her attacker had gotten lucky the first time. He wouldn't get a second chance.

Morgan advanced on her. "Gina, I don't want to argue. I know this area far better than you do. No one can hide in my territory for long without me finding them."

Red's lip quivered. She wished more than anything that were true, but Morgan wasn't looking for a stranger. He wouldn't expect it to be anyone close. If she was right, the news would break his heart. Red swallowed past the sudden lump in her throat. *Emotions sucked.*

"Let me handle this, Morgan."

"Gina, please listen to reason. I've been on the job a long time and have had to do a lot of distasteful things over the years to keep Nuria and my people safe. I won't let whoever did this get away with it. Jesse meant a lot to me. I take her death personally. There is more at stake here than you realize. I swear, I will find him."

She shook her head and retreated farther away, holding out her hands to keep him back. "Not if I find him first."

chapter nineteen

I gave you a chance and you blew it," Roark said. "You were supposed to kill her."

"I never agreed to that. In fact, I told you specifically that I had other plans for Gina. That hasn't changed, only been delayed."

"I don't care what you had planned. I gave you a direct order and you ignored me. I won't put up with this kind of insubordination."

A growl rumbled over the connection, hurting his eardrum. "I thought I explained what you could do with your orders. Obviously, I need to go over it again."

Roark bristled at the undisguised threat. "Don't you growl at me. I am done playing with you. Do you hear? Done. Her death is the only way to hit the tactical team where it hurts. You know that as well as I do. Don't you want them brought in?"

"You know I do, but there are other ways to do it that don't involve killing her."

"I thought you wanted to obtain leadership among your people?" Roark sat back, surprised at the man's resolve. What was it about this woman that made her so special? She was attractive, but not overly so. Maybe they'd had sex as he'd first suspected. Roark was repulsed by the thought.

"It won't take killing her to obtain power. All I need to do is remove the alpha. She'll become mine by proxy."

"I don't care about your little internal power struggles. I don't care if she's the best lay to come down the pike in a century. I'm not about to blow this election because you've developed a conscience about this particular piece of ass. Understand?"

"She isn't just *any* woman."

"What is that supposed to mean?" Roark asked, frustration riding him hard. "I've read the file. She's nothing other than the perfect victim from what I can see."

He snorted. "You are only human. You wouldn't understand."

"You're probably right. I don't speak animal," he snapped, letting his temper get the better of him.

"Watch yourself, Roark. You forget your place."

Roark scowled. "It's you who've forgotten *your* place. You seem to have forgotten everything and that includes all of our plans for the future. I really thought we understood each other."

"Oh, I have no doubt that we do," he rumbled. "I'll say it again. Slow enough for even you to understand. I will not kill Gina Santiago. She's mine. Do not interfere."

Roark laughed, the maniacal sound tearing from deep in his gut. "No can do. I'm sending someone in to take care of the job. Someone who doesn't have a problem following orders."

He rocked back in his chair, a satisfied smile on his face. Roark wished he could see his expression at the news, but he supposed he'd have to settle for imagining it.

"What have you done?" There was an edge of panic in his voice that Roark had never heard before. This woman had definitely shaken the beast up.

"I warned you before and I don't make a habit of repeating myself. My man will be there by tonight."

"I wouldn't do that if I were you," he said. "You are making a colossal mistake."

Roark tapped his desk with his fingertips. "Then I guess it's a good thing you're not me." He hit the button to disconnect and glanced out his office window at the clear blue sky.

It was always a risk sending Mike Travers in for cleanup duty, not that the man hadn't done it dozens of times before. Still, there was always a chance that he could get caught. It was remote of course, but there, lingering in the back of his mind.

If for some reason that happened, Roark would have to deny all knowledge, but the taint would remain as it did for the human supporters of equal rights for Others. Those people were outcasts now, having to scrounge to survive.

Roark refused to be put in that position, but he would if Travers got caught. People wouldn't forget. *Voters* wouldn't forget. He needed to ensure that Mike didn't get caught. And if he did, that he didn't get a chance to talk.

He reached into his desk drawer and pulled out synth-alcohol, tipping the contents down his parched throat. It burned like liquid fire and caused his eyes to water. It wasn't as good as the real stuff, but few bottles of that remained and only in the hands of serious collectors.

Roark took a deep breath and exhaled, rolling his neck to ease the tension building there. His bones cracked like toppled dominos. When he'd finished, he hit the page button to summon Travers.

Mike entered a short time later, carrying a wad of synth-papers. "You called me, sir."

"Yes," Roark said, shoving the empty alcohol container into the recycling bin. "I have a job for you to do."

Mike stilled and didn't say anything.

"I need you to go to Nuria."

"Does this have something to do with Gina Santiago?" Mike asked, fingers trembling.

"Yes."

"What would you like me to do?" Resolve filled his voice along with what sounded like weary acceptance.

"I want you to do what you do best," Roark stated, glancing out the window again at the glorious day. "I expect a call when it's done."

"Yes, sir."

Mike slipped from the room, his thoughts in turmoil. How was he supposed to kill the *missing link*? How could he not? Roark would send someone else to do the job if he refused. He'd also dispose of him at his earliest convenience. Mike shivered, suddenly cold in the sweltering heat.

He didn't fear death. Over the years Mike had

come to know the reaper fairly well. No, he feared the method. Not all killers cared about the means used to take out their prey. Mike prided himself on giving the target a quick death. But then, he wasn't sadistic.

There'd only been one exception, and that had been for the man who'd annihilated his family. It had taken extra planning to draw out his death in the most painful manner imaginable.

Mike had sent his energy inside the man and allowed it to expand until all his orifices bled. This continued for days in the desert until the madness of not knowing when the end would come overtook the man and he ran himself into the boundary fence.

Mike could still hear the sizzle as the man's skin hit the fence. The smell of burnt flesh wafted in the air on a plume of charcoal-gray smoke. It was one of the happiest moments of his life . . . until afterward. Mike had realized that his tormentor's death didn't bring his family back or ease the survivor's guilt he lived with daily.

He didn't look forward to killing Gina Santiago. He didn't look forward to killing, period. But like most things in life, he had little choice. He'd return to his home and pack a few items needed for his trip to Nuria. He'd make sure her death was swift and maybe while he was there Mike would find Roark's connection and take care of him, too . . . just in case he proved to be his replacement.

Mike Travers arrived in Nuria at sunset. He parked on the outskirts of town, hiding his vehicle among rubble, taking only the equipment he would need for the job. He'd have to hurry once he was finished. People in small towns noticed strangers. He wouldn't be able to slip out undetected.

He made his way through the desert, keeping an eye peeled on the road. Mike didn't want anyone driving by and finding his car. At least not yet. It took thirty minutes to reach the fringe of the town. The buildings here were vacant, their windows covered with synth-wood to deter trespassers.

He broke the window in what looked to be an old auto sales lot office. From the dust and cobwebs, it was apparent no one had been there for a long, long time. Mike pulled out a rag from his bag and began to wipe the place down. He may be here for a while until he located Gina and he'd rather not spend it in filth.

Filth reminded him too much of the cell he'd spent ten years in. For a second, he couldn't seem to breathe and panic savaged him. The cage they'd kept him in was cramped like this place, but without the windows.

He'd been so naïve to volunteer for the experiments. At the time, men and women like him were touted as heroes. Patriotic soldiers, who were their country's last defense. He'd believed in what the effort stood for. Trusted the men who'd told him that he'd still be the same man, when the treatments were over. In the end, Mike allowed the scientists to change him.

In return for his sacrifice, they'd turned him into something that nightmares couldn't even recognize.

They manipulated his DNA until food no longer

replenished him and blood was the only thing that kept him alive. They'd tweaked his brain until he could project his thoughts and move larger objects with his mind. He rarely slept more than a few hours a week. He'd been told these changes were a temporary side effect—much like the halt in his aging.

And still he'd believed them . . . right up to the point when they locked him up and made plans to exterminate him.

In those bleak days, Mike had imagined what the outside world looked like. The dreams had kept him sane, when his life had become an endless series of tests and torture. And they'd continued until the lab's ultimate destruction.

No one knew exactly how the explosion happened. Many thought sabotage. In the end, Mike didn't care. All that mattered was escape. It was only later that he'd discovered that what the scientists running the lab had done to him was permanent.

The telekinesis he'd been born with had been modified, strengthened. It was a gift that proved invaluable over the years, while the need for blood turned out to be a curse. He could walk in the sun unlike some of the scientists' other experiments, who had blown up on contact with ultraviolet rays, but the thirst never went away.

In fact, it grew with every passing year. It was only his will that kept him from madness. His will, and the urge to find the last of the men responsible for his family's death.

He let out a long breath and continued to clean. An hour later, the place was presentable enough for him to call it home base. It was time to find Gina.

Roark had ordered someone to break into her home at IPTT while Mike had researched her background. Whoever had done the job stole some of her dirty clothes, which was exactly what Mike needed now.

He pulled out one of Gina's T-shirts and brought it to his nose, inhaling her scent into his lungs. He should be able to find her if she was within a hundred-mile radius.

Mike dropped the shirt and slipped his laser pistol into the inside pocket of his jacket. A minisword ran the length of one sleeve. It would inhibit his movement, but the position put the deadly blade at hand's reach.

Night embraced him as he stepped into the twilight. The stars shown from above, twinkling merrily around the nearly full moon. In the distance, a coyote howled. The sound was cut short by a deep rumbling snarl, then there was silence.

Mike shivered, staring into the darkness. There were predators here, human and animal alike. Some just as dangerous as he. Mike would have to stay alert if he wanted to survive this mission.

Raphael Vega inhaled the sweet night air deep into his lungs. He'd had a good rest and now needed nourishment. There were a few women in town that he could go to, but he wasn't looking for company tonight, only food. They didn't like it when he ate and ran.

He glanced out over the shadowed horizon, relishing the night sounds as the nocturnal creatures scurried out of their hiding places. His footsteps were silent as he made his way into Nuria. Raphael would heed the sheriff's thinly veiled warning to leave town some other time. He'd missed being around others who considered his unique traits normal. That's why he'd returned. It was why he'd always return here.

. He continued into town, scenting the air as he went. Perhaps he'd make a stop at the hospital and pick up a pint or two of O negative. He was in the mood for something spicy.

Raphael took another deep breath and stilled. A strange fragrance wafted in the air. He frowned and inhaled again. The odor was still there, but stronger now. He tilted his head, turning slowly in a circle. The scent reminded him of something.

He thought back, but memory eluded him. *It was probably nothing*, he thought. But for some reason Raphael couldn't make himself let it go. When he'd turned south, the scent grew stronger. This time something niggled at the back of his mind.

Something about the fragrance was familiar. He'd smelled it before in his youth. It made him think of family. Raphael's heart hit his ribs as his brother's memory flooded his mind.

It wasn't possible. His family had been dead for years. He breathed in again. Whatever was causing the odor was coming closer. Had he finally lost his sanity? He'd been expecting that to happen for the last hundred years.

Without conscious thought his feet moved to intercept the elusive odor. There was probably a perfectly logical explanation for the sudden sense memory, but for the life of Raphael he couldn't think of what it might be.

He rounded the corner of Spruce St. Whatever he was tracking had moved, but it was easy enough to follow.

The individual was heading out of town. Raphael frowned when his quarry made a sudden left after four miles. The only person who lived in this direction was the sheriff. His gut tightened and he picked up his pace as a sudden urgency pressed upon him.

There weren't many places to hide around the sheriff's home—a few sand dunes and a couple of dead cacti were about it. Raphael circled wide, keeping himself downwind. He didn't want the person with the elusive scent to know he was here until he got a good look at him. Sand sifted under his feet as he scanned the area.

For a moment he saw nothing in the darkness but the endless desert. He was just about to turn around and return to town when a slight movement caught his eye. Someone was crouching behind the dune closest to the sheriff's side window. Raphael glanced through the window and saw Gina Santiago hunched over a compunit at a desk and Morgan wandering in and out of the kitchen. They were the epitome of domestic bliss. He would've smiled at that thought if the sense of danger wasn't so great.

He looked back at the huddled figure. The outline of a weapon rose from the shadows. Raphael moved without formulating any kind of plan. He didn't know whom the target of this assassin was, but he knew he had to stop him.

The person took aim.

Raphael stepped out of the darkness. From this distance he could tell it was a man, like he'd suspected, but he couldn't see his face. The scent was overpowering now, nearly drowning him.

"I wouldn't do that if I were you," he said.

The man swung around, his eyes wide with fright. The pistol came with him until it was leveled on Raphael's chest.

"It can't be," the man gasped.

Raphael took a step closer, unable to believe his eyes. "Michael?"

"Raph?"

He couldn't seem to breathe. His eyes had to be playing tricks. Somehow loneliness had conjured the image of his brother. His dead brother. Raphael took a step back as emotion overwhelmed him.

"It's not possible," he said. "You're dead."

"I could say the same about you," Raphael replied, fighting back the hysteria threatening his mind.

"But how? I saw you die." Mike blinked repeatedly, trying to disperse the years of unshed tears. He replayed the last moments before hell rained down upon them in the lab. Raphael had been moved to isolation for more tests—the same area that had exploded.

As if reading his thoughts, Raphael answered. "When the explosion hit, the wall to my cell crumbled. I glimpsed daylight and made a dash for it."

"But the sun?"

"Burned like hell, but as you can see, I didn't explode. It was no more painful than what they'd been doing to us for years with the experiments. I suppose I should be grateful to have mixed blood. The vampires who weren't psychic didn't fare so well. I tried to go back and find you after my wounds had healed, but by then, everything was gone. Our parents, the cells, you, everything."

Michael couldn't seem to swallow the lump in his throat. All the anger and years of despair poured over him in violent torrents. He shook and the earth around him began to part. Raphael barely acknowledged the tremor.

"All the years, all the grieving, the separation, it was for nothing. You've been alive this whole time."

"I'm sorry to disappoint you." Raphael gave him a sad smile. "I cannot deny the loss of time, but that's over now that we've found each other."

Mike shook his head and the air thickened from the movement. "You don't understand. We can't go back. I can't go back."

Raphael stepped forward and clutched his brother's shoulder. "No one is asking you to."

He let out a strangled wounded cry. "You don't know what I've done. What I've become."

Raphael glanced at the weapon in his hand and then at the house beyond. "I have a pretty good idea. If you are looking for someone to play judge, you will not find him in me. We have both done things in order to survive. Things I for one am not particularly proud of." He looked back at his brother. "I do have one question, though."

"What's that?"

"Why?"

Mike blinked. "You don't want to know who?"

Raphael shook his head. "No. Only why?"

"You're not going to like it."

"Perhaps, not. But I would still like to know."

"Very well, then help me up and I'll tell you everything." Mike held out his hand. Raphael didn't hesitate. He reached out and plucked him off the ground and pulled him into his arms. The embrace was heartfelt. It was several seconds before Mike was willing to release him. He was afraid if he did that Raphael would somehow disappear.

"It's good to have you back, brother."

Mike smiled, feeling joy for the first time in centuries. "It's good to be back."

chapter twenty

Red stared at the green screen of the compunit on her desk until her eyes blurred. She'd hoped she would have more success today than last night at Morgan's home. Red had grabbed an unoccupied desk at the sheriff's office and had been working for hours with no luck in finding a connection between the three women. She couldn't seem to get Jesse Lindley's horrified expression out of her mind from her visit to the dissecting lab yesterday.

Her eyes filled with tears and she quickly wiped them away before anyone noticed. It wouldn't do to fall apart now. Morgan had been in and out of the office all day, taking care to check on her each time. His concern for her well-being only made the situation worse.

She glanced at the screen once again, scanning medical backgrounds and employment. None of the women worked in or near the emergency care center. They all had different hobbies, which kept them miles apart. She had to be missing something.

Red dug deeper, scanning their immediate family. Nothing leapt out. With a frustrated sigh, she reached to turn off the machine. A second before her hand hit

the button Red's gaze landed on a mention of the
elder care center. She'd seen that before in Moira's
file. She flipped to another screen and began to scan.
It only took a minute to find. That made two for two.
If Renee had a grandmother in elder care, then Red
had found the connection.

Sure enough, Renee Forrester had a grandmother
who'd passed away at the facility. Something about the
deaths jarred her memory. Red hit a button to bring up
the files that held the images of two of the victims.
One's eyes were missing, while the other's ears were
gone. What was that story her grandfather used to tell
her when she was little about a girl with a red coat or
cape?

She tried to recall the story, since Red knew it
somehow involved grandmothers. Wasn't there a wolf
in that tale? Why would Kane follow a child's story?
He wouldn't. She was tired and grasping at wisps of
smoke. Red woke Rita.

"Take a reminder," she said.

"What is it you'd like me to remember?"

"I need to look up a story about a wolf that terror-
ized a girl dressed in red."

There was a pause.

Red glanced at her navcom and frowned. "Rita,
did you get that?"

"I received the message, but it does not compute.
Wolves have not existed in this area for over seventy
years."

Red chewed on her bottom lip. Hadn't Nancy told
her that she'd spotted wolves? She'd said it had been
awhile since she'd last seen them, but that was certainly less than seventy years ago. Nancy didn't look

a day over thirty. "Don't worry about it, Rita. This isn't about a real wolf."

"Affirmative, then your message has been saved."

"Thank you."

The connection crackled. "You're welcome. Is there anything else you'd like me to do?"

"No."

"Commander Santiago has been trying to reach you on your private line. Should I contact him now?"

Red's stomach fluttered. "No, not yet. I'll do it later. You can power down." She'd purposely avoided contacting her grandfather because she didn't want him to worry. She also wasn't sure how to begin to explain her visit to Nuria. If he found out about the attack, he'd send in the entire tactical team and the killer might slip away.

She put her head down on the desk.

"Are you okay?" Morgan asked, touching her shoulder.

Red had been so preoccupied with her own thoughts that she hadn't heard him approach. "I'm fine. Just tired."

"Why don't you rest in my office? I can work out here."

She stood and stretched her arms over her head. "I think I just need some fresh air to clear my head. I've been staring at the compunit for hours."

Red also needed time to go to the emergency care center to see if her suspicions panned out. She had no intention of confronting Kane. If he was behind the murder, then he was far more dangerous than she'd ever imagined. He'd killed Jesse and possibly three other women.

Morgan watched her, his amber eyes growing liquid with concern. "I know you're feeling better, but you are still not 100 percent. Until you are, I'd appreciate it if you'd take it a little easy."

Red smiled. She couldn't do otherwise. Ever since they'd slept together and then had that long talk, he'd hovered over her. Hell, he'd started beforehand and it had only gotten worse. She'd never had anyone other than her grandfather show this much concern about her well-being. She'd be a liar if she didn't admit that it affected her deeply.

"I swear I won't do anything overly strenuous." She met his gaze. "And I promise I'll be back within an hour."

Morgan hesitated. He looked as if he might protest, but suddenly thought better of it. Red wanted to reach out and hug him for trying so hard not to push her right now. He hadn't asked for anything other than what they'd shared, but she could see the fire banked in his eyes. Morgan might not admit it, but he wanted more.

And Red was beginning to think that she did, too.

The emergency care center was bustling when she arrived. Red kept an eye out for Kane, but hadn't spotted him yet. With luck, it would stay that way. She strode toward the nurse's station. Two unfamiliar faces stood behind the low counter, but they both greeted her with a smile.

"May we help you?" they asked in unison.

"Is Dr. Hunter here?"

The nurse with the blond hair turned to the brunette

for assistance. "I haven't seen him, but that doesn't mean anything. Would you like me to page him?"

"No, thank you. Could you direct me to the elder care center?" Red asked, addressing the brunette.

"Just head straight down the hall and make a left. You'll see a set of double doors at the end of the ward. Pass through them and you've entered the elder care center." ·

"Thanks!" Red strolled down the hall, keeping her eyes peeled for Kane. Doctors and nurses passed her, a few pausing to give her curious stares, while others nodded in her direction, showing a strange deference.

Red nearly laughed as she glanced down at the front of her clothes. Nothing appeared to be out of place. Maybe they recognized her from her visits to Jesse, but that didn't make sense either. She hadn't seen half these people when she'd come to visit. Surely they hadn't heard about her and Morgan. As if to confirm her fears, two nurses passed her and broke into giggles. Red blushed. Horrified. Morgan was right about little towns knowing everyone's business. She'd figure out a way to deal with them later. The only important thing was to find out the truth for Jesse Lindley, who was lying in the dissecting lab because she'd stepped in to help.

Red ignored the medical staff members bustling around her and picked up her pace. She made a left and headed to the end of the hall. A huge sign hung over the double doors of the elder care center demarcating the entrance.

She pushed them open and stepped through. The smell of urine and antiseptic cleanser burned her nose and eyes. She could almost taste the ammonia. Red choked and swallowed rapidly as her stomach pitched. How could anyone stand to be in this area? Her gaze darted, taking in the elderly patients in their rooms and the ones gathered in a large common area. Their sad, downtrodden expressions told her without words that they were very well aware of the conditions around them.

Sadness welled within her as she imagined the three women who'd visited their grandmothers here. How could anyone take away the one bright moment in their lives? She continued until she reached the nurse's station.

A woman twice as wide as she was tall stared into a vidscreen giggling. She didn't bother to look up as Red approached. "May I help you?" she asked, watching the entertainment with rapt attention.

Red stood in front of her, but didn't say a word. She placed her hands on the waist-high counter and began to drum her fingers.

After a minute the woman glanced at her hand and then arched a disapproving brow. "I asked if you needed any help," the woman repeated. "There's no need to be rude."

Red blinked. How could this woman think she was being rude, when she'd barely acknowledged her presence? She resisted the urge to reach over the counter and shake the stuffing out of the woman. "I didn't want to interrupt," she explained.

The woman scowled.

"Is Dr. Hunter in today?"

The woman's expression changed to dreamy delight before she answered. "No, he was so distraught over losing Jesse Lindley that he called in today. It's so sad. Poor man blames himself for her heart attack. Can you believe that?"

Yeah, I can, Red thought, since it was looking more and more like Jesse had help.

"It's too bad he's not here though, since he always gives the ladies something to look at besides these white walls. Even a skinny little thing like you would find him attractive."

Red ignored the woman's dig. "How well do you know him?"

The woman grinned and winked. "Not as well as I'd like. He's a serious piece of man flesh."

"Yeah, even I would find him attractive, I get it. Do you mind if I ask you a few more questions?" Red asked.

The woman shrugged. "I suppose that would be okay. You have," she glanced at her watch, "five minutes before I begin my rounds."

"It won't take long," Red said, noting her stain-covered uniform. "Do you know Renee Forrester?"

"Yes, lovely woman. She comes in for a visit every week and spends about two hours with her grandmother, Maureen Jennings." The woman frowned. "Strange, I haven't seen her lately."

And she wouldn't ever again, Red thought in disgust.

"Do you mind if I have a word with Maureen?"

The woman's eyes narrowed in suspicion. "You better not upset her," she warned.

"I wouldn't dream of it." Red wasn't about to tell the elderly woman that her granddaughter was dead. She'd leave that to the sheriff's office. It was cowardly, but she just couldn't bring herself to break the woman's heart.

You don't have any problem stomping on Morgan's, the little voice in her head whispered.

With him, she had no choice. A killer was on the loose and she wouldn't allow anyone else to get hurt if there was any way in her power to stop him. The only thing that kept her going was the realization that Morgan would do the same thing.

She followed the nurse down the urine-smelling hallways to room 112. Maureen Jennings sat in a rocker next to the window, knitting what looked to be a scarf. Gold-rimmed glasses rested upon her classic nose, while silver ringlets haloed her small head. She glanced up from her task when they entered her room.

"Oh dear, for a moment I thought you were Renee," she said, glancing at Red.

Red's heart dropped. "Sorry, not today."

"Gladys, aren't you going to introduce us?" Maureen stared at the nurse expectantly.

The woman turned crimson when she realized she hadn't bothered to catch her name. Red let her squirm for a few seconds, then stepped forward and clasped Maureen's weathered hand.

"My name is Gina Santiago. It's a pleasure to meet you. That's a lovely scarf you're making."

Maureen beamed. "It's a surprise for Renee. Are you a friend of hers?" she asked.

Red glanced at their pressed palms and slowly released the woman. "No ma'am. I can't say that I had the pleasure."

The woman frowned and looked at Gladys.

"Well I guess I'll leave you two," the nurse said, beating a hasty retreat.

Red watched her go, then turned back. "Do you mind if I take a seat?"

"Of course not." She moved her synth-wool out of the unoccupied seat and then patted the chair for her to sit.

"Thanks," Red said, regretting every second of what she was about to do. "Can you tell me when you last saw Renee?"

Maureen's storm-gray brows furrowed. "Hmm . . . no, I can't rightly recall. The days all blend together here."

"I can imagine. I'd appreciate it if you'd at least try."

She screwed her face, pursing her lips in concentration, then suddenly released a frustrated breath. "I just don't know. Why don't you contact Renee and ask?"

"She's hard to reach."

"That's strange. I've never had a problem getting ahold of her. Do you want me to try?" She reached for the comdevice on the table, but Red stilled her hand.

"That won't be necessary."

The woman released the device and peered into Red's face. "There's something you're not telling me. I can tell when you lie."

Red's face flushed and she stood. "I don't know what you're talking about. Thank you for your time. I'm sorry I bothered you." She walked to the doorway and stopped, glancing over her shoulder at Maureen, who was watching her expectantly. "One last question."

Maureen nodded, sadness dulling her features. She grasped the scarf she'd been making, wadded it, and then tossed it into the recycling bin. Red followed the fabric, listening to the soft thud as it hit the bottom of the unit. She blinked back tears as comprehension dawned.

She sniffled and her lower lip began to tremble. "Did Dr. Hunter ever come around when Renee visited?"

Maureen blinked in surprise. "He's dropped in on occasion. After speaking with him, I thought he and Renee might make a good pairing. I tried to play matchmaker, but Dr. Hunter didn't seem too interested in my granddaughter. Pity, really. He'd make a good addition to the family. Why do you ask?"

Not interested? Red's surprise must have shown in her expression.

"That wasn't what you were expecting, was it?"

Red shook her head. "No, ma'am."

"You want to tell me what happened to my granddaughter?"

Red closed her eyes against the pressure building in her temples. She looked around the bleak room with its white walls and mobile rest pad. The only bright spot this room had ever seen was now lying in the dissecting lab on a steel slab, waiting to be dismembered.

Lies burned like acid on her tongue as she opened her mouth to speak. Instead of offering reassurance, she blurted, "I'll find the man responsible. I promise." Red took off down the hall before Maureen could respond. She needed to find the other woman and get out of here.

A visit with the other victim's grandmother turned up much the same information. Kane showed no interest in any of the women, going so far as to ignore them, which made no sense. Why ignore the women you plan to attack? Unless it was to distract everyone.

Red supposed anything was possible. But that didn't explain how he'd done it and why. There had to be something lurking in Kane's past that drove him to this point. She'd dig deeper until she found it.

So far her quiet little investigation had yielded a decent amount of circumstantial evidence. Kane knew all the women through his connection to the elder care center. He was lead medic and could easily slip in and out of this place without anyone seeing him. Red shuddered at how easy it would be.

Kane, along with everyone else in town, was familiar with the layout of Jesse Lindley's share space and could have lain in wait. All these things together might be enough to get a warrant, but it was doubtful that it would lead to an arrest.

Red could find no motive for the attacks and there'd been absolutely no trace evidence left behind at the scenes. Morgan hadn't even found usable DNA after her attack. Well, he did, but there was no way to determine when it got there.

No one was that good at killing. No one. Every murder provided evidence. All you had to do was look in the right place. Yet there'd been none that she could tie to Kane or anyone else for that matter.

She had scoured the crime scenes and the photos, finding nothing for her efforts. It was impossible. It was as if a ghost had killed the women. Kane may be a lot of things, but he wasn't a phantom. She had to keep looking.

Red ran a hand through her hair, tugging out her ponytail. She rubbed her scalp, trying to sooth the tension building steadily behind her eyes. Red couldn't take suspicions and speculations to Morgan. He'd laugh her out of his office or worse yet, run her out of town. And who could blame him?

By the way, Morgan, I think your cousin is the lunatic behind the murders. Proof? What's that?

She strode down the hall, her body trembling to keep her emotions in check. Red hadn't come right out and told the women that their granddaughters were dead, but she might as well have.

She'd always been a terrible liar. Why had she thought she could waltz in here, ask a few questions, then leave untouched? It was naïve at best, unprofessional at worst. Red swiped a hand over her face and rushed toward the exit.

She threw open the door, relishing the feel of the dry heat as it greeted her. The sun hung low in the sky, but it hadn't quite breached the horizon. Sweat immediately broke out over her skin, dotting her forehead and trickling between her shoulder blades. She walked a few steps away from the building, needing more space.

A breeze wafted over her, leaving a thin sheen of grit and sand behind. There was no use trying to wipe it away, another would only replace it. Taking several deep breaths, she managed to expel the urine scent from her nostrils, but nothing could remove the pain.

She bent at the waist, her hands resting on her

knees, and wept for all the senseless destruction of human life, all the families that had been torn apart, never to mend, and all the wasted futures that no longer existed. She pictured her mom, dad, and little sister, imagining what they would've done given more time. Such a waste. Sobs racked her body.

The violence never ended. She might manage to capture Kane, but there'd be another to quickly take his place. More deaths, more loss. Morgan flashed into her mind, bringing instant comfort, followed closely by another wave of sadness. She continued to weep, this time over the impending loss of the only man Red could ever see herself loving.

chapter twenty-one

Morgan looked up from what he was doing as Gina entered his office. Her hazel eyes were swollen and rimmed with red, her normally clear complexion blotchy. She sniffled, glancing around in search of something. Morgan opened his desk and pulled out a tissue, handing it to her as he came around his desk.

"What happened?" he asked, running his arms over her body. She didn't appear to have any injuries.

"I'm fine," she said, taking a step away from him. She didn't meet his gaze.

Morgan's gut clenched. "Then why have you been crying?"

Gina sniffed again and turned her back on him. "I haven't. It's from the dust."

She was lying, but he didn't press. All Morgan wanted to do was pull her into his arms and comfort her. Yet she didn't seem to want him to. His apprehension rose.

"Where have you been? You said you weren't going to be gone long." He didn't want to admit how worried he'd been or that he'd actually sent a deputy out to find her. When the man had returned empty-handed, Morgan had panicked and thought about calling in the tactical team for assistance. He was glad now that he hadn't, but it was a testament to how far under his skin she'd managed to burrow.

Gina stood in silence so long that he began to fear she wasn't going to respond. Morgan reached out, stopping short of touching her.

"I needed to follow up on some information I found in the files of the three murdered women." She turned and met his gaze.

Morgan dropped his hand away. "Where exactly did you go?"

"I went to the elder care center. Do you remember a children's story that contained a wolf, a grandmother, and a girl dressed in red?"

He could feel the blood drain from his face as his gaze shifted to the wall. Morgan knew the book she was referring to. It was his and Kane's favorite story when they were kids and the reason they'd chosen wolf DNA in order to aid their country during the war. A tattered yellow paperback copy currently sat in his safe next to Jesse's death chip recording, which documented her time and cause of death and noted her personal belongings. He rarely got the book out to read because it was so fragile. It was the only personal belonging that managed to survive from his previous life. "You're talking about 'Little Red Riding Hood,'" he said finally.

"Yes, that's it." She nodded. "I couldn't remember the name. Something about the photos reminded me of that story, so I checked outside immediate families and found a connection. All three women had grandmothers staying at one time or another at the elder care center. Kane's linked to all the patients."

"That could be a coincidence. There are a lot of elderly people living there," he said, not liking the direction she was headed. "Besides, he works there. Kane's checked on every patient in that facility. There have been times when he's been the only doctor working there. Without him, a lot of people would've died."

"He could also get access to Jesse's room without anyone seeing him," she pressed on. "Who better than a doctor who knows the care center in and out?"

Morgan's stomach knotted. "I don't see how this has anything to do with a child's story," he lied. How many times had Uncle Robert read that story to him and Kane? More times than he could remember. That's why he'd hung onto the book. Morgan had always hoped that he and Kane would read it to their kids some day.

"I noticed something else about the victims. One had her eyes missing, while another had her ears removed. The third had no teeth. Couple that with three grandmothers in the elder center. Sound familiar?"

"Sounds insane." Morgan forced himself to breathe. "I suppose you think Kane is the Big Bad Wolf." He was . . . but he prayed that Gina didn't know that.

Gina snorted. "Of course not. There's no such thing."

He flinched. "So then why suspect Kane? What motive would he have for killing these women or attacking you? Assuming you think he is behind your attack."

Her expression dropped. "I haven't been able to

figure that out yet, but I will. I wanted to come to you first before I approached the team. I believe I have enough circumstantial evidence to get a warrant issued."

Panic engulfed Morgan. "Did you find DNA? Prints? Anything concrete?"

She hesitated. "No, not exactly."

"No? Or not exactly? Which is it?" he asked.

"No, I haven't yet."

"Then you have nothing," he said. "You don't want to drag Kane's name through the mud with suppositions and gut feelings. This town depends on him. The whole damn republic counts on him to keep the place running."

"He's the only one who connects to all the victims, including me," she said. "I wouldn't have broached the subject, if I wasn't sure."

"But you're not sure. You said so yourself." Morgan began to pace, his mind in a riot. If Gina called in the tactical team, then their secret would be discovered. He couldn't let them run a DNA test on Kane. He had to think of something. Come up with some way to stop her. Change her mind.

"Let me look into it," he offered, not believing for a second that Kane was involved. Yet the seed of doubt had been planted, rooting itself in his own suspicions. Gina had gathered enough information to give him pause.

"Like you looked into Renee Forrester's death?" she tossed out. He tensed and slowly turned to face her. She believed he'd covered up the murders. Hell, he had been covering them up, but not for the reasons she suspected.

"Morgan, I'm sorry, but I have to do this."

"Save it." He shook his head. "You don't have to do anything."

"These women deserve justice."

"And they'll get it. All I'm asking is that you trust me on this."

She crossed her arms over her chest. "You're asking me to turn my back."

"No," he pleaded, "I'm not. I am asking you to leave this case to me. Let me handle it in my own way."

"Which is?"

Morgan stopped and faced her. "Quietly. Without the eyes of the world looking in."

Gina glanced away. "I don't think I can do that."

Pain lanced Morgan's chest, shredding his heart. Why had he expected anything less? She didn't trust him or believe that he'd do the right thing. How in the hell had he thought they could somehow work things out and stay together? He'd been a fool. A fool who'd marked and mated with Gina. And now she was going to destroy his world and his people unless he gave her a good reason not to.

There was only one thing Morgan could think to do. He walked past her and shut the door, locking it with a soft click of a button. She still hadn't stirred, but was watching his every move.

"I'm going to share something with you that I've never shared with any other outsider," he said, unbuttoning his shirt.

"What are you doing?"

"There is something that you need to know about me. I should've told you a long time ago, but I didn't know how. Now you've left me no choice."

"Morgan?" She frowned. "I don't understand. What are you talking about? Why are you undressing?" She took a step back. "I don't think this is the time or the place for that."

"I'm about to trust you with my life," he said, continuing to strip.

Red watched Morgan drop his pants. Her gaze strayed to the front of his underclothing, but he wasn't aroused. Instead, he remained tense, almost agitated as he strolled behind the desk.

"Whatever happens, I need you to remain calm and not run away," he gasped and clutched his chest. "Promise me, Gina."

Welts rose from beneath his skin.

"Morgan?"

"Promise," he barked, an almost gutteral sound coming from his throat.

Red jumped. "I promise." She couldn't seem to look away as he contorted in pain.

Sweat ran down his body in rivulets and he dropped to his knees with his head thrown back. A howl shattered the space, ringing out so loudly that Red had to cover her ears. Bones popped and blood splattered the wall. She stared in horror as hair covered Morgan's body. Talons sprung from his fingertips and his amber eyes turned golden. His sensuous lips peeled back to reveal jagged canines. Red took a step back, her hand reaching for her gun—the gun she'd left at Morgan's home. She didn't dare take her eyes off him for fear he'd attack.

What had Morgan told her? She dropped the

thoughts as quickly as she grasped them. Survival kicked in and she searched the room for a weapon. He took a step toward her, his claws clacking on the concrete floor. Red matched his steps until her back hit the wall. Heavy musk filled the air, battling the odor of blood for supremacy.

Morgan advanced on her, drool dripping from his mouth, pooling on the floor. Gone was the man. In his place stood a two-legged, feral beast. He stopped within a foot or so, then sniffed. All the stories she'd heard, all the articles she'd read, nothing came close to describing what it was like to face an Other in the flesh.

It was horrible. He was horrible. That thought brought Red up short. This was Morgan. The same man who'd nursed her back to health. Cared enough to make sure that she ate. Protected her when she couldn't protect herself. Made love to her.

Oh God, she'd slept with him. Red clutched her abdomen as panic threatened to rise again. Morgan tilted his head, watching her. He leaned forward to nuzzle her and she flinched.

"Don't touch me," she said reflexively.

Morgan dropped his head and slowly backed away. It took several seconds for him to shift into human form. The process appeared to be as painful as the initial change. When he finally returned to normal, he was lying on the floor naked and shivering.

Red couldn't bring herself to move. She could barely breathe. Her heart thundered in her ears, blocking all sound but the blood rushing through her veins. Part of her wanted to believe what she'd just witnessed was a hoax of some sort, an illusion that only Morgan could perform. The rational side of her knew the truth.

The man she'd slept with, the man she cared about, the man she respected almost as much as her grandfather, wasn't a man at all. He was a creature. An abomination that didn't exist except in the imaginations of children and a few paranoid adults like Roark Montgomery.

Morgan staggered to his feet and began to dress.

She forced her voice past the lump of fear in her throat. "You weren't going to tell me, were you?"

He didn't look at her or even acknowledge that she'd spoken. Morgan pulled on his pants and reached for his shirt.

"Aren't you going to say anything?"

He stopped in the middle of lacing up his boots. "What's left to say? You've clearly made up your mind about me."

Red pushed away from the wall; so many emotions swirling, so much confusion. "What the hell did you expect? Your blood is dripping down the wall for goodness sake." She pointed at the newly formed pools of crimson. A fat drop took that moment to swan dive into the center of the larger puddle with a *ker-plop*.

"I needed you to understand the facts before you rushed off to IPTT headquarters and put in an order for a warrant." He ran a hand over his face. Lines that hadn't been there moments ago, etched the corners of his mouth. The change had obviously taken a lot out of him.

"You're asking too much from me," she said, turning away to gather her thoughts.

"Am I?"

Red spun. "Yes, you are. I believe that Kane is a murderer and you're asking me to ignore my hunch."

Morgan stood and strode across the room toward her. "No, that's not what I'm asking." He reached out and grasped her forearms, but Red jerked away. He laughed, a pained sound that plucked at her heart.

"What's so funny?" she asked.

"I was just thinking about last night, and how you couldn't get enough of my touch. Now, you can barely stand the sight of me."

She frowned. "And that's funny to you?"

Morgan sobered. "No, it's not. But it is reality," he said bitterly.

"I'm sorry, but this"—Red swirled her hand—"is too much. It's my duty to report this kind of thing to IPTT."

"Your duty, eh?" He shook his head. "And what about mine? It's my job to protect the people of Nuria, human and Other alike. I can't do that if the world finds out the truth."

"Is the whole town made up of Others?" She stepped forward. "Was Jesse?"

Morgan watched her, his amber eyes dim. "No, not everyone, but most. As for Jesse, yes, she was one of our oldest pack members. Does that change how you feel about her? Does it make her death any less important?"

"No, of course, not." She glared.

"Then why in the hell are you holding it against me?"

Red shook her head. "I don't know what you're talking about."

"Oh yes, you do. When you thought I was just another human, I made love to you repeatedly—and now you can't even look at me, touch me."

"Yes, I can," she fired back.

"Then prove it. Kiss me." Morgan stepped closer until they were mere inches apart. He stared down at her face, searchingly.

Red didn't move. She couldn't for fear she'd bolt.

"Just as I thought," he whispered. "You can't do it."

He began to turn, but she caught his elbow and pressed her lips to his. The spark she'd felt from the start was still there, but different. She released him quickly.

"I have to go," she said.

Morgan stopped her. "Where?"

She wasn't going to lie to him. He deserved to know the truth, if only to prepare everyone for the tactical team's arrival. "Home," she said.

His expression sobered and he returned to sit behind his desk.

She unlocked the door.

"Before you go, there's something else you should know."

"What?" she asked, wondering if he were simply trying to delay her departure. Red didn't think she could handle much more.

"It's about your shirt."

Red's brows dropped. "My shirt?" She glanced down at the front of her clothes in confusion.

"Not that shirt," Morgan said. "The one you dropped off to Jim for analysis."

She stilled, but her heart continued to race. Surely Morgan wouldn't try to blackmail her. She knew he was desperate to keep Nuria's secret, but was he that desperate? "What about it?" Red asked, as panic set in.

"I thought you might like to know how your blood got mixed in with Moira's." He glanced at the crimson-stained wall.

Red followed his gaze. The blood had started to dry. Her mouth watered and her stomach growled with hunger. Something inside of her screamed, refusing to make the mental leap to the most obvious conclusion.

"How?" she found herself asking, despite the pleas in her head to stop.

"You were at the crime scene."

"I know I was. I found you there."

Morgan shook his head. "No, beforehand."

It was Red's turn to respond with refusal, as her worst fears came to life. "That's impossible. It's not like I'd forget to mention it, if I had wandered by."

He continued to stare at her. "You were there. Feeding. You just don't remember."

"Morgan, if this is your way of trying to cloud the issue, it won't work." The word *feeding* finally registered in her befuddled mind. "What do you mean feeding?" Red swallowed hard as her stomach somersaulted.

"It means exactly what you think."

"No!" He was insane. This whole town was insane. Red was sorry she'd ever heard of Nuria and Morgan Hunter. Denial enveloped her, wounding her psyche until she wasn't sure that she'd escape with her sanity. She'd made a mistake getting involved with Morgan. Her emotions had clouded her judgment, making her care when she should not. Damn it! She didn't love this man. Couldn't love him. He was barely human and now he was accusing her of being the same.

He cocked his head and stared at her. "You don't want to understand because the truth is too frightening."

Red's lips thinned as she covered the hurt with anger. "The truth? What truth? You're claiming that I went to a crime scene that I didn't even know about and ate Moira. And you expect me to believe you. Uh-uh, no way. I'm leaving. Now." She turned to the door and raised her hand to open it.

"You're one of us," he said quietly, but might as well shouted at the top of his lungs.

Red whirled around. "What did you say?" Blood roared in her ears as his words pierced her humanity, ripping it away.

He stood, placing his hands on his desk, and leaned forward. "I said, you're one of us. I don't know how you've gone undetected all these years, but I knew it the second you entered the dissecting lab. I smelled the Other in you."

"Is that why you slept with me?"

Morgan gave her body a cold once-over. "It's not the only reason."

"Bastard."

He flinched, but his expression remained cool.

Red backed away. "You are crazy. I am nothing like you. Like the people here in Nuria. I'm a *pureblood*."

Morgan snorted. "I'm sure you wish that were true, but we both know it's not. You're no more a pureblood than I am."

"I know no such thing," she spat, her gaze darting around the room as she searched for a means of escape. He was crazy. They all were. She wasn't one of them. She couldn't be. Could she?

His expression drooped, giving her a glimpse of the disappointment he'd been hiding. "I scented you the second you hit town," he said. "I couldn't believe that an unmated female would waltz into Nuria unprotected. Then when you didn't ask me for protection, I realized you had no idea what you truly were."

"Ask for your protection?" Her brows knitted. "I don't need any man's protection."

"Actually, in this town you do. There are protocols to follow when you enter an alpha's territory."

"You're the alpha of this . . . pack?" she asked.

He met her gaze. "You know that I am. That's one of the reasons that you gave yourself to me. You may not have consciously understood what you were doing, but your instincts did."

"Lies," she hissed. "Nothing but lies."

He shook his head. "Why do you think you can smell a lie? Or heal so rapidly? Haven't you ever noticed how acute your hearing and eyesight are?"

Fear like she'd never experienced sent shivers rocketing down her spine. Morgan couldn't know that. She'd never told anyone—not even her grandfather. She glanced around and the walls seemed to close in. She needed to get out of here. Away from Morgan. Away from this town. She took a step back as numbness settled into her body. Escape was her only option.

"I knew you did," he said.

"I don't know what kind of game you're trying to play here, but I'm not buying. I'm going back to tactical team headquarters and get my warrant, then I'll return."

Morgan's jaw firmed and a muscle began to tic in his rugged cheek. "Do what you need to do, Gina. You can run from me and Nuria, but you can't run from the truth."

chapter twenty-two

Red left Morgan's office with his words ringing in her ears. It took three tries to get into her hydrogen car and she nearly wrecked it leaving town.

She pressed a button and the window opened with a slight hiss. The hot breeze from the desert rushed in, but its arid taint did little to clear her jumbled thoughts. She never wanted to see or smell this place again.

How could she be one of them? She wasn't even sure they'd existed until a few minutes ago. Red had considered the possibility, but that was as far as it had gone. Now Morgan was attempting to force a reality on her that just couldn't be true.

She stepped on the accelerator, ignoring the Republic of Arizona's speed detectors. They flashed, recording her photo image as she zoomed by. Red didn't care. Let them fine her. Nothing mattered but getting home to her grandfather, Robert Santiago. He'd know what to do, what to say to make it all better.

Tears rolled down her cheeks, blurring her vision. She wiped them away and kept driving. She needed to put distance between her and Nuria. She choked as pain fractured her internally.

This could not be happening. There was no way she could enter a crime scene without being detected, much less eat another human being. She gagged at the thought, slamming her foot on the brake. The car skidded wildly before gliding to a halt. Red barely got the door open before she vomited.

Gasping for breath, her mind flashed back to Morgan's transformation. He'd been nearly silent when he approached her and more deadly looking than anything she'd ever witnessed. Was it possible for him to kill someone without leaving a trace? Could she?

Red recalled the animal tracks at the scenes and it triggered her gag reflex. She continued to throw up until there was nothing left inside. Shivers racked her body as an unnatural cold swept over her arms and into her shoulder blades, settling in her chest. Red wiped her mouth with the back of her sleeve and then climbed into the car.

This was a dragon she couldn't begin to slay. She needed a brave knight. She needed her grandfather. Red had been a fool to think this was a simple case of murder and that it would be easily solved in a few days. She was only one woman against a town full of monsters.

Red reached IPTT shortly after midnight. She didn't bother to stop, driving directly to her grandfather's home instead. He'd be asleep, but this couldn't wait until morning.

Robert Santiago's house was one of those newly built two-story replicas of twentieth-century design. It had all the features of a smart home: food dispensers,

A.I. sensors, intrusion alarms with robotic guards, and the latest air-filtration systems that could actually draw water from the atmosphere.

Red knocked on the door, pressing her hand repeatedly on the identification pad. It refused to open. She banged harder, and finally her grandfather, disheveled and yawning, opened the door.

"Gina?" He squinted at her over his hooked nose. "What in the world are you doing here at this hour?" he asked.

"Oh Grandpa," she cried, launching herself into his arms. "I need your help."

His arms tightened automatically. "What's happened?" He glanced behind her, scanning the street.

Red noticed. "It's okay. I'm alone. Sorry it's so late, but I need to talk to you."

He glanced at the time. "Can't this wait until morning?" he asked.

"No."

"Are you harmed?" His gaze swept her.

She shook her head. "No, I'm not injured." *At least not anyplace visible.* "Can I please come in?"

"Of course." He gave the street one more look, then pulled her inside and shut the door, locking it behind them. Robert walked her into the kitchen and sat her at the table. A few seconds later, he pushed a steaming cup of synth-tea in front of her.

"Drink," he said.

Red lifted the cup to her lips with trembling fingers. The tea burned her throat, while the delicate fragrance of lemons tickled her nose. She had no idea where to begin her crazy tale. He would probably force her into taking a desk position after she'd finished.

Her grandfather waited patiently for her to drink her tea, then he spoke. "Tell me what's happened. How did you get here?"

Red glanced at the face she knew as well as her own. Compassion glowed in his eyes as he reached out and grasped her hand. "I drove," she said, shoring up her courage.

"You came here straight from Nuria? At this hour?"

She nodded. "I had to."

"Why, child? What's happened?"

"Oh, Grandpa," she sobbed. "Morgan has told me so many lies that I don't know which way is up."

"Morgan? Are you talking about Sheriff Hunter?" he asked, perking with interest.

"Yes, the sheriff."

"What did he say that's upset you so?" He didn't try to rush her into speaking; instead, he gave her all the time she needed.

"This is going to sound insane." Her eyes met his and locked. "It sounds crazy just forming the thoughts in my mind, but I need you to believe me."

He squeezed her hand in encouragement. "Go on."

"You have to understand. We're talking almost the whole town."

Robert Santiago blinked. "The whole town what, Gina?"

She shook her head. "They're all . . . and he says I am . . . I know he's lying, but I don't know why. It doesn't make any sense. Why would he lie to me about such a horrible thing? It's cruel."

"Honey, I don't know what you're talking about. I need you to make sense. Take your time. Think about what you want to say and tell me. I want to help, but you have to do your part."

Red stood and began to pace. Her boots tapped over the tiles in rapid fire. "I'm not like them. I can't be. I would've known if I were. Don't you think so? It's not something you can keep a secret, at least not for long."

"Known what?"

"He's lying. Morgan has to be lying. Why did I sleep with him? So what if the sex was good. I must have been out of my mind." She stopped. "Scratch that, he's out of his."

"You slept with this man?" His eyes rounded. "When did this happen?"

She glanced his way. "That's not important. I mean it is, but it isn't." She threw her arms up in the air. "I don't know anymore. It doesn't matter. That has nothing to do with this. Well, at least not directly."

"Gina, please sit down. You're making me dizzy and I still have no idea what you're talking about. You aren't making sense."

"That's because I'm crazy. I've obviously gone crazy because I'm seeing things. Things that can't possibly be real. No one can transform from a human into an animal and back again. It's not possible."

"What did Rita have to say about this whole situation?" he asked.

She glanced at her navcom and frowned. "I don't know. I've had her powered down. Do you think I should ask her now?"

"Why did you power her down?" he asked, not bothering to hide his shock. "You've never done anything without her. Not for as long as I can remember and that's a very long time."

Red shrugged absently. "I guess I didn't need her much, while I was in Nuria," she said, continuing to pace.

"Enough! I mean it." He reached out and shackled her wrists, pulling her into the chair next to him. "Now tell me exactly what happened and what the sheriff said to you. Start from the beginning."

Red regaled her grandfather with the story of Morgan's transformation, stopping only to take a breath. She described in detail the attack on her in the share space. She even mentioned Jesse Lindley's untimely death, but for some reason she couldn't bring herself to tell him her suspicions about Kane.

She realized that she wasn't protecting him. He didn't deserve her consideration, if he'd done what she suspected. She was, however, trying to protect Morgan, even though she doubted that he'd believe it. Why would he after what she'd said?

Red continued with her outrageous story, jumping straight to the part where Morgan accused her of being an Other. She knew it sounded insane, even to her own ears. What must her grandfather think? He'd always been understanding and patient with her in the past, but Red had no doubt she'd pushed him beyond his limit on this one.

"Can you believe it?" she asked. "Morgan's obviously delusional." She slapped her hand down onto the table. "I mean really. Me? An Other? Ridiculous! I think we would've noticed by now." She tried to joke, but it came out edged with desperation. She needed her grandfather to refute her story. Tell her everything was going to be okay. Convince Morgan that he'd erred.

Robert Santiago sat at the table, his hands calmly clasped in front of him as he listened intently. The only indication that he'd heard what she said was the whitening of his features.

"Do you love this man?"

She paused. "What?"

"I said, do you love this man?"

Red sat back a moment. "What does that have to do with anything I just told you?"

"Please answer the question, Gina," he said patiently.

Her expression soured. "I don't know. Maybe. It doesn't really matter anymore because I'm never going to go back to Nuria." She leaned closer. "Grandpa, I need you to tell me he's crazy."

He remained so still that Red touched him to ensure he hadn't fallen asleep. He looked up. "Grandpa, please." She sniffled as the cold weight of truth settled upon her narrow shoulders.

"I can't," he finally said, shaking his head. Tears rimmed his tired eyes as he stared into her face. "I can't. I'm so sorry, special one."

Red stood so fast that she toppled the chair. "What do you mean you can't? He's made a mistake. You know it. Why are you lying?"

He shook his head wearily. "Gina, you know I'm not," he said, seeming to crumble before her eyes.

"Not you, too. Why are you doing this to me? Did Morgan contact you before I arrived and tell you to say these things?"

"No, child." He reached for her, but she backed away.

"I don't understand." She ran her hand through her hair, sending loose strands into her face. "This doesn't make sense. Nothing makes sense anymore."

"I should've told you a long time ago. I just didn't know how. You were so young and scared," he said, grasping the cup she'd emptied earlier. He stared into the bottom of it, his gaze growing distant.

Red stopped. "Told me what?" It was as if her nightmares had suddenly sprung to life and were now wreaking havoc on her waking hours.

"About your father," he said softly.

"What about Daddy?" She closed the distance between them.

He glanced at her. "What do you remember about him?"

"Not much." Her gaze dropped to her feet. "I know he died in the car accident."

Robert Santiago shook his head. "That's what we told you."

"We?"

"Your mother and I. You were too young to hear the truth."

Red's throat constricted, nearly strangling her. She could barely focus on his words as a loud buzzing started in her ears. Her vision blurred and she reached out to steady herself using the wall.

"Are you okay?" he asked.

"Fine," she said, pushing away. "What happened to Dad?"

"He was killed."

"I know that," she said, confused.

Her grandfather shook his head and sadness banked his brown eyes. "They murdered him."

Red swayed on her feet. "Who murdered him?" She'd kill them if they weren't already dead. Her hand moved to her weapon, but found emptiness. She let out a sigh. Morgan still had her gun. She'd been in such a hurry to get out of town that she'd left without it.

"The same people who created him . . . and all the Others."

"Created? Dad's parents were from the Floridian Islands."

He laughed, but it held no mirth. "That was the story he told everyone."

"But I don't understand. Why would he do that?"

"Because your father had been created in a lab during the last world war."

She shook her head. "That's not possible. He showed me the vids of when he was little. I saw his parents in the background. He couldn't have been more than thirty-five when he died."

"Forgeries," he said softly. "Some of the Others were created from pure-blood men and women, who had volunteered to help the war effort. They were mainly soldiers. Others, like your father, were developed in test tubes. They aged slightly slower than pure-blood humans, but would eventually grow old and die. Not that your father had the chance . . ."

"You're wrong!" She strode a few feet away, then turned, anger pulsing inside her. "Daddy wouldn't lie to me."

"He had no choice," he said.

Red's world crumbled around her like skeletal twigs in a strong wind. Everything she knew, everything she believed about her life was a lie. Yet even as she denied what was the blatant truth, things began to make sense for the first time in her life.

She'd always been different from the other kids, growing up. Her family had discouraged her from participating in athletic events, saying they didn't want her to get injured. Now she knew that wasn't the case. They didn't want people noticing how fast she was, how agile, how strong . . . how Other.

"Your father did what he did to protect you." Her grandfather's words brought her back from the past.

"Protect me?" *What was he talking about?*

Robert Santiago stood until they were only inches apart. He clasped her chin and tilted her head. Their gazes met. "Yes, to protect you."

"From who? What?"

"The same people who killed him and eventually took the lives of your mother and sister."

Red tried to escape, but he held firm, his grip deceptively strong for someone his age. "If Dad was the Other, why would they murder Mom and—"

"Because they thought your sister was you."

She felt the color leach from her cheeks, flowing down her body until her knees shook and she could no longer stand. Robert guided her into a chair seconds before she collapsed.

"Why did they want me dead?"

He blanched. "Because according to the old government, you aren't supposed to exist."

She took a deep breath and let it out slowly. "What do you mean, Grandpa?"

"I mean, special one, that Others and pure-blood

humans aren't supposed to be able to reproduce. If the public became aware that Others existed and interbreeding was possible, it would expose what those secret labs had been up to all those years ago."

"I thought they didn't exist."

"Oh, they existed like so many other vile places in the world. Fortunately they've long since been destroyed."

"Then why worry?" she asked.

"Because the men behind them didn't shrivel and burn so easily. Their legacy lives on in a new generation. If the knowledge of your birth were to get out, it would put you in danger. There are some people whose entire agenda rests upon the separation of purebloods from the Others."

"Roark," she murmured. "That's why you refused to support him, even though he's considered a hero to everyone on the tactical team." The realization stunned Red. Her grandfather had risked everything to protect her, his position, his reputation—everything.

"He is only the latest of many, but don't underestimate him. Roark can be ruthless. He's had his assistant, Mike Travers, quietly going through the personnel files at headquarters. Roark thinks I don't know, but I do. I had sensors put in place years ago for this very purpose."

Fear seeped in, exposing the weaknesses she attempted to hide. "Did this Travers look at my records?"

"Yes." White lines bracketed his mouth, showing her exactly how much pressure he'd been under.

"Did he find anything?"

"I don't think so. I took great care burying the past, burying *your* past, but I can't be sure. I wish I could, special one, but I'm just not as sharp as I used to be." He swayed, his gnarled hand gripping the back of the chair to steady him.

It was an honest answer, but not the one Red had been hoping for. Her world was disintegrating around her. So many lies, so many secrets, so many senseless deaths.

"I tried to find out more about Mr. Travers, but so far I've turned up very little. It's almost as if he didn't exist until thirty-eight years ago."

"What does that mean?"

"It means that either his real name isn't Travers or he's a lot older than thirty-eight. Let's hope it's not both." Her grandfather's brows shrouded his eyes.

"Why would that be a problem?" she asked.

He met her gaze. "Because that would make him an Other. They're impossible to lose once they have your scent. The only reason I've managed to protect you this long is that the people who murdered your family thought you were dead. If they suspected that you were alive, there would be nothing I could do to stop them." His eyes shimmered with tears as he looked at her. "Not even the tactical team and all its firepower could protect you, if they wanted you dead."

The team might not be able to, but Red knew someone who could . . . if she hadn't blown her chance. Would Morgan accept her if she went back? Then what? It wasn't like some fairy tale where they'd live happily ever after.

She'd be hunted for the rest of her life and so would he. He might be used to existing that way, but she wasn't. How would they survive? How would she, if he turned his back on her like she'd done to him?

Red peered into her grandfather's loving face, gathering strength from his presence. He couldn't help her any longer. She leaned forward and kissed his weathered cheek. "I love you. You know that, right?"

He tapped her nose with his finger. "You know I do. The feeling is mutual."

"Then you understand why I have to go back to Nuria."

"Back?" His brow furrowed. "But—"

"They know the truth about me . . . or at least someone does. Why else would they try to kill me?"

chapter twenty-three

Morgan brushed his hands across his stubbled chin before washing them over his face. He set the book balanced on his chest aside and ran his fingers through his hair as he stood to stretch. Bones popped and muscles ached as he forced the kinks out of his back. He hadn't bothered to go home last night. Morgan hadn't wanted to face his empty rest pad and Gina's lingering scent.

Instead, he'd stayed in his office and scrubbed the blood off the walls and floor. When he'd finished, Morgan had removed "Little Red Riding Hood" from his safe and fell asleep reading it. He glanced at the time. That was thirty minutes ago.

Morgan put the book back and reset the alarm on his safe. He still wasn't sure if he'd done the right thing by shifting in front of Gina, *then* telling her the truth. Her horrified expression remained burned in his mind.

It was too late now. He'd have to live with whatever she chose to do and that included bringing in the tactical team.

Morgan placed a hand on his shoulder and rolled

his head, attempting to dislodge the knots. Like it or not, Gina's suspicions about Kane had taken hold inside of him. She wasn't the type of woman who maliciously accused people of crimes. She was a trained field agent, who also happened to be half werewolf. He couldn't ignore her natural instincts.

Thinking back he recalled several incidents lately where Kane had shown him disrespect. They'd been minor and Morgan had let them go, since he was family, but now he wasn't so sure he'd done the right thing. Perhaps if he'd exerted his position, then none of this would be happening now.

Hell, if it were anyone else, Morgan would've taken the behavior as a direct challenge to his leadership. But this was Kane, his cousin. The man he regarded as a brother. Surely he wasn't still holding a grudge about not being named alpha after the war. Morgan's unease grew.

Kane was normally easygoing, but his behavior had been slowly changing. Morgan had noticed Kane's shortness of temper, the snide remarks, and the lingering eye contact. Taken separately these little things were minor. Together they spelled trouble. But were the changes enough to make the leap to murder? Morgan shook his head. It didn't seem likely. If it was leadership he wanted, Kane could've challenged him directly. There was no need for anyone innocent to die. So why couldn't he dismiss the idea outright?

He needed a second opinion from someone he trusted. Morgan glanced at his watch and grinned. Jim Thornton would still be sound asleep at this hour. It was the perfect time to make a call.

The vidcom chirped endlessly, until Morgan was

convinced that Jim wasn't going to answer. He didn't want to drive all the way out to the dissecting lab director's home, but he would. Morgan glanced outside. Blackness curtained the windows, refusing to give way to the dawn.

On the fifteenth chirp, Morgan heard a click. His gaze shot back to the screen and he waited for Jim's image to appear.

"Hello," the breathy disembodied voice said.

"Jim, is that you?" Morgan asked.

The screen brightened and a closed-eyed, scruffy man came into view. "Sheriff," he said, blinking. "What time is it?" He glanced to the side and squinted, before facing the screen once more.

"About four in the morning," Morgan said, saving him the trouble of trying to read the clock without his glasses.

Jim pried his eyes open. "What's wrong? What's happened . . ." The question tapered off into a snore.

"You still with me, Jim?" Morgan's voice rose in volume.

Jim jumped, his head bobbing as he came awake. "Yes, yes, what were you saying?"

Morgan laughed. "Nothing important, but I do need you to get in here."

"At this hour?" His bushy brows dropped over his eyes. "It's still dark out."

Morgan smiled. "You never seem to have a problem with this hour when you need *me*," he reminded him.

Jim reddened. "I'll be at the dissecting lab in thirty minutes."

"Looking forward to it."

Jim reached to hit the disconnect button.

"Oh, before you go," Morgan said, stopping him. "Could you bring in some of that gourmet coffee you have stashed at home? I don't want that synth stuff."

Jim's eyes widened. "How did you know about—?"

"I have my sources," he said, cutting him off.

"Remind me to have a talk about the definition of the word *secret* with your assistant."

Morgan laughed and disconnected the call.

Jim Thornton arrived at the dissecting lab an hour later. He carried a thermos in his right hand and files in his left. Morgan opened the door for him, then lifted the thermos out of his hands before he could protest.

The cap was off and hot liquid poured into a cup a second later. Morgan closed his eyes and inhaled the aroma of real coffee beans. He tipped the cup to his lips and took a sip. The coffee scalded his throat, but he didn't care because it tasted fantastic. God, he missed real coffee. The synth crap just didn't compare to the bitter deliciousness of the real stuff.

Jim watched him, taking in his appearance from head to toe. "You look like shit. Did you sleep in your office?"

Morgan glanced at him. "Not exactly. I've pretty much been up all night."

Jim glanced around. "Where's Gina?"

"Home or IPTT's main headquarters rallying the troops would be my guess," Morgan said, taking another drink.

"You seem awfully calm. Want to tell me what

happened?" Jim asked. "I thought that you two had hit it off."

"I suppose I have to tell someone."

He nodded in understanding. "Step into my office." Jim guided Morgan through the dissecting lab and into his cluttered office.

Shelves lined the walls, cocooning the room. Specimen jars containing various desert species were stacked three deep and two high. One wrong move would bring the room crashing down around them.

Morgan brushed past an embalmed rattlesnake and sat in one of the two chairs available. Jim didn't seem to notice the clutter. He strode with confidence to the spot behind his desk, brushing synth-papers out of the way so he could sit.

"Now tell me everything," he said, reaching for a dirty cup balanced precariously on the edge of his desk. He dumped the contents into a recycling bin, then poured himself a fresh cup of coffee.

Morgan took a deep breath and let it out slowly. "I told her the truth. The whole truth," he said quietly.

Jim's eyes bugged. "Why would you do something crazy like that? She's a tactical team member." He glanced at the door.

"Don't you think I know that?" He shook his head in disgust. "She left me no choice. She was going to get IPTT to issue a warrant for Kane's arrest."

"What?" Jim leaned forward as if he hadn't heard Morgan correctly. "That doesn't make any sense. Did she tell you why?"

Morgan snorted. "Yeah, she told me why. Gina suspects him of killing those women and Jesse. Can you believe that? Have you ever heard of anything so ridiculous?" he asked, shaking his head. "Kane's a doctor for goodness sake. He saves lives—not takes them."

Jim sat back in silence, his expression completely transparent. Even if it wasn't, Morgan could smell the change in his body chemistry. The sour stench spoiled the aroma of the coffee. "Jim? Don't tell me that you believe her."

"I hate to admit it, but she might be onto something," he said.

"Not you, too. This is Kane we're talking about." The pain of betrayal nipped at Morgan's insides, threatening to rip him asunder. He tensed. Kane and Gina each held a half of his heart. Both had the power to destroy him in their hands. He tipped his cup and drank, swallowing with an audible gulp. Liquid burned his throat, but he welcomed the pain.

"Something's been bothering me about Jesse's death. I mentioned it before, but I have no proof," Jim said, turning the mug in his hands and swirling the contents.

Morgan's breath hissed. "Tell me," he demanded.

"Remember how I said that her throat was injured, but I could find no mention of any medical treatment that could account for the injury?"

Morgan nodded, unable to trust his voice. He wanted to leave, just walk out of here, before Jim said another word. He'd experienced the sensation of being ripped apart every time his body went through the change, but this was worse. This wound wouldn't heal, wouldn't leave him elated. He'd be left with it and his heartache over Gina for the rest of his life.

"I discovered bruising near the carotid artery."

"So?"

"You don't get that unless something presses down or squeezes in. That also explains the petechial hemorrhaging in her eyes."

Blood roared in Morgan's ears. Please let it be anyone else but Kane. "What exactly are you saying?"

Jim removed his glasses and wiped them before placing them back on his face. His fingers trembled as he picked up a few errant folders and stacked them. "I'm saying that if there hadn't been witnesses, I'd swear Jesse had been strangled to death."

"Why would Kane do such a thing?" Morgan asked.

"We don't know that it is Kane . . ." Jim said. "But . . ."

"He was the only one in the room when the nurses came rushing in. No one else had easy access." Morgan stood, unable to keep his frustration contained. "He of all people knows it's an automatic death sentence, according to pack law. What was he thinking?"

"I wish I knew." Jim's gaze dropped and his expression grew bewildered. "But unfortunately, that's a question only Kane can answer."

Red collapsed on her rest pad. She'd swung by headquarter to get another pistol before heading home. It was already late afternoon, so she didn't plan to sleep much longer—just enough to ensure that she didn't wreck her car on the three-hour trip back to Nuria.

Her thoughts went automatically to Morgan when she closed her eyes. She could still see the pain and disappointment in his amber gaze as she shunned him. Red wasn't proud of her behavior, but what had he expected after throwing all that at her? She'd thought it was bad enough watching him shift, but when he claimed she was like him, her world tilted— and had yet to return to normal.

At first she'd been angry with her grandfather when he'd admitted the truth. Always practical, she was over that now, but the hurt remained. She'd spent her childhood and young adult life feeling like an outsider and never knowing why. All it would've taken was one word, one short conversation to change all that. She still wouldn't have fit in on the tactical team, but at least Red would've known why and that would have been enough.

The truth was out now. She just didn't know who else, besides Morgan and most of Nuria, knew about her secret, but she couldn't remain on the team. She was no longer safe. Red sat up and looked around her small sleep space. She realized with perfect clarity as she stared at her food dispenser that she wouldn't be returning here.

Red got out of bed and began to pack what few belongings she owned. She'd shower to wake up. She knew if she left within the hour she should reach Nuria by sunset.

Morgan spent the morning poring over the files of Renee Forrester, Lisa Solomon, and Moira Collins. It had been difficult to keep his thoughts off Gina, but he'd managed . . . sort of. She had been right about the victims' connection to the elder care center. The facility was the only thing connecting the three women.

The "Little Red Riding Hood" fairy tale ran through his head. It was ironic if Kane had picked that particular story from their childhood to follow, seeing as how the Big Bad Wolf died in the end.

Morgan smashed the disconnect button and the screen dimmed. He'd stalled long enough and needed to go find his cousin. He wasn't looking forward to the upcoming conversation. No matter which way it went, the talk would forever change their relationship.

The same as it had with Gina, when he'd revealed the truth.

He pushed his chair back and stood. The coffee hadn't helped much. Morgan still felt tired and shaky. He glanced at his watch. Kane should be starting his shift soon. Perhaps if he hurried Morgan could catch him before he went in.

Morgan rushed out of his office, surprising his assistant. "Sorry about that, Maggie," he said, striding past. "I'm heading over to the emergency care center; if Kane calls, tell him I'm looking for him."

"Okay," she said, then looked askance at his wardrobe. "Aren't those the same clothes you had on yesterday, Sheriff?"

He smiled and kept going. Nothing got past Maggie. "I'll be back later."

Morgan arrived at the emergency care center as the morning crew was leaving for the day. He scanned the lot for Kane's car, but didn't spot it.

Maybe he'd parked in the back. Morgan knew sometimes he did that to avoid the small ten-car traffic snarl that occurred at this time of day.

He shut down his engine and stepped out of the car. He continued to survey the faces, hoping to catch Kane entering, but had no luck. Resolved, Morgan passed through the doors of the care center and strode to the nearest nurse's station. The on-duty nurse glanced up as he stopped before the small counter that corralled the area.

"May I help you, Sheriff?" Nurse Alison asked, giving him a quick smile.

"I'm looking for Kane. Have you seen him?"

She turned to the compunit in front of her and typed in a code. A screen showing employee schedules and check-ins popped up. She scanned the list until she reached Kane's name. "Hmm . . . that's strange."

Morgan leaned over the counter to get an even better look. "What is?"

"According to the schedule, he should be on duty right now, but he hasn't signed in." She doubled-clicked his name and Kane's personal work screen appeared. "That's really weird."

"What?" Morgan asked, trying to figure out what she was talking about.

Alison turned to him. "He's never missed a day before. Not in all the years he's worked here."

Concern lanced Morgan. Where was Kane? Was he ill? Had something happened to him? He refused to believe he was hiding. Why would he? He didn't even know that Morgan suspected anything was wrong.

Alison started to hit a button that would take her to the previous screen.

"Wait," Morgan said, stopping her an inch above the keypad. "Could you look up one more thing for me?"

She shrugged. "Sure thing."

"On the night that Jesse Lindley died, was Kane scheduled for duty?" Morgan asked, sending up a silent prayer that he had been.

Alison pursed her lips and tapped a button that moved the screen up. "Hmm . . . No, it doesn't look like it. I guess we were lucky that he just happened to be around, instead of the part-timer assigned that night. It may not have helped Jesse in the end, but at least Kane's medical expertise gave her a fighting chance."

"Yeah, lucky," Morgan said, thinking it was anything but.

Why had Kane been here? Had he been looking in on Jesse at the time? What were the odds? Not good, he thought. Not good at all.

"Thank you for your help, Alison. If Kane happens to wander in, have him contact me."

"Right away, Sheriff."

Morgan went back to his office to make sure that Kane hadn't turned up. He half expected to have the tactical team waiting for him when he arrived. He wasn't sure if he was relieved or disappointed that they hadn't been. At least then, he would've gotten to see Gina.

He knew he was being pathetic, but Morgan couldn't help it. He missed his mate and wondered, not for the first time, if he'd ever get to see her again. Morgan shook his head. It didn't bear thinking about. He needed to find his cousin and fast. He tried contacting Kane at home, but no one answered.

After two hours with no success, Morgan gave up and decided to drive out to Kane's home. It took an hour to reach the spread. Morgan stared in dismay at the broken windows and splintered door. Kane's house had been destroyed. His hand moved automatically to his weapon as he exited the car and approached the entrance.

Morgan inhaled, but didn't scent anyone nearby. He half expected to find Kane's remains as he kicked in what was left of the door and entered. Glass crunched under his boots as he made a sweep of the home. There was no sign of Kane or of any blood for that matter.

He righted a toppled chair and sat down, staring at the mess around him. The only scent he could detect was Kane's, which didn't make any sense. Why would Kane destroy his own home? Why would Kane do any of this? He'd have to be out of his mind.

Morgan dropped his face into his hands and took a deep breath. He had no idea how long he'd sat in Kane's home until he looked up and noticed that the sun was about to set. The full moon would be up soon. The effects weren't like what folklore described. It wouldn't have half the town turning furry and howling. That wouldn't have helped much during some of the harder battles in the war. Yet the moon's effects weren't exactly harmless, since it did increase desire, the speed at which a wolf could shift, and made them stronger.

With a full moon, a person could be dead in ten seconds as opposed to thirty.

Morgan felt the moon's pull in his blood and growled as his skin began to itch. He pulled himself out of the seat and walked toward the door. He glanced one last time over his shoulder to make sure he hadn't missed anything. Nothing had changed.

Morgan still needed to find Kane and with his house destroyed, he had no idea where to look.

He took a back road from the north into town, passing the remnants of a dead forest. His gaze wandered the tree line, absently staring at the branches. He was still a good thirty minutes away from town when he spotted a vehicle lying in a ditch by the road.

Morgan slowed as he approached. The car came into view, giving him a clear shot at the identification code in the rear window. He swallowed hard as he recognized the number. It was Kane's vehicle. Morgan stopped behind the car and got out slowly. He glanced around, but didn't see anyone. He pulled his weapon and approached with caution.

The car was empty and unlocked. Morgan opened the door and looked inside, but didn't see any blood or signs of an accident. It was as if Kane had driven into the ditch and then left. He shut the door and stepped several feet away so that it wouldn't impair his senses. Morgan inhaled deeply, slowly turning full circle. He caught Kane's scent coming from the woods.

What was he doing out here?

Morgan knew there was only one way to find out. He holstered his weapon and then called in his location. He didn't want to alarm anyone in the office, if it could be avoided, so he told Maggie that he'd found an abandoned vehicle that he needed to check out.

"Location confirmed, Sheriff," she said, via a comlink. "Let us know if you need any assistance."

"Sheriff off," he said, stepping into the woods.

The trail was easy enough to follow, since there was no underbrush or leaves of any kind remaining. It wound around for several minutes, twisting left and right, before opening into a small meadowlike area. Morgan spotted Kane on the other side. Wide circles of sweat dotted his clothes. His normally neat hair was in disarray, clinging to his forehead and cheeks. Stubble covered his chin, giving Kane's face a shadowy cast. He kept pacing and looking toward the sky as if he were waiting for something or someone.

Morgan glanced in the direction he was watching, but didn't immediately spot anything. He approached slowly, purposely making his footfalls heavy. He didn't want to surprise Kane, especially since he appeared to be agitated. The moon was riding him hard, making him jumpy.

Kane continued to wear a path into the ground. "The end is near. Soon the war will begin and the Others will no longer hide in the shadows," he mumbled under his breath. "It's time for me to take my rightful place as alpha." He turned and started back the other direction, showing no indication that he even knew Morgan was there. "She's mine," he said. "The other women were nothing compared to Gina. She's perfect. And soon I will stake my claim."

Morgan listened in shock to Kane's disjointed ramblings. His mind zeroed in at the mention of Gina, and then turned to a red haze when he realized what Kane had planned. No one would claim his mate and live. No one. Not even the man he considered a brother.

He would die before he'd allow that to happen. Gina might not love him, but that didn't change how he felt about her. She was his mate. His heart. The only woman who would ever share his rest pad. His dreams. His wolf's soul.

Suddenly, Kane halted and straightened to his full height of six foot two. A fierce growl rumbled from his chest. He turned toward Morgan and smiled, highlighting the madness in his golden eyes.

"Cousin, I've been expecting you," Kane said, shifting in midair as he launched himself at Morgan.

chapter twenty-four

Red arrived in Nuria at sundown. She'd listened to an edu-disc on the way down that discussed wolves and their habits. It had been a long time since she'd been in school, so she needed the refresher. Red turned onto the main drag. The streets were just as quiet, as when she'd left.

What had you expected? Fanfare?

Most everyone had gone home for the night. She parked her car in front of the sheriff's office and got out. Red didn't know who'd be on duty tonight, but hoped it was Morgan. Shoring up her courage, she entered the building. It was quiet, too. Only Maggie, Morgan's assistant, remained at her desk, manning a small communications console that was attached to her compunit.

She walked up and stopped in front of the woman. "Who's on duty tonight?" she asked, knowing only one or two officers would be on call at night. There wasn't enough activity to warrant more.

Maggie glanced up from the screen she'd been looking at. "The sheriff," she said.

"Is he around?" Red asked, unable to meet her eyes.

"He called in an abandoned vehicle awhile ago. I haven't heard from him since. I've been waiting in case he wants me to send out roadside assistance. For all I know, he may be on his way back. Do you want me to contact him and find out?"

That's odd, Red thought. No one left their vehicles these days with the unknown problem being what it was. You didn't have to with the availability of on-call assistance. To do otherwise was asking for trouble. "Where did the sheriff say he was when he called?"

Maggie relayed the rough directions. Red followed along, mentally mapping the area. Thanks to the time she and Morgan spent questioning townsfolk, she had a pretty good idea where Maggie was talking about. She'd take a drive out there. It might be better to face Morgan away from the prying eyes of the town.

"If he happens to come in, tell him I'm looking for him," she said.

Maggie smiled. "I'll do that. Glad you decided to come back. I don't think the sheriff could handle many more nights of sleeping in his office."

Red couldn't hide her surprise at the announcement, but didn't say anything. So she wasn't the only one who'd had a rough night. Somehow she found that thought comforting. She left after thanking Maggie and had just about made it to her car when a dark-haired man stepped out of the shadows.

"Gina Santiago?" he asked, his accent different from what she'd heard in Nuria.

"Who's asking?"

"My name is Mike Travers and I've been sent here to kill you."

Red's gun was out of its holster and drawn before

the man had a chance to take his next breath. "Thanks for the warning," she said.

The man—Mike—watched her carefully, but made no move to disarm her. "I wouldn't do that if I were you," he said calmly.

She laughed. "You aren't me."

"You're correct. I'm not near as *special* as you are."

The emphasis he put on that one word had Red's hand wavering, but she didn't lose her aim. He knew the truth. He knew what she was. He'd found the hidden information despite her grandfather's efforts. She had to do something to stop him. If he was here to kill her, then she'd take him out first. But was he really sadistic enough to warn her ahead of time?

She decided not to wait and find out. Red raised the pistol a couple of inches higher until it was level with his head. Her finger brushed the trigger. A breeze hit her a second later, or at least Red had thought it was a breeze until the gun began to turn direction.

"What the hell—?" she shouted, struggling to force the gun back toward him. Her gaze shot from the muzzle to his face. "How are you doing that?"

He shrugged carelessly and whatever had been fighting her for control released its hold. "All that matters is that I can."

Red's gaze swept him, taking in his dark suit, pasty skin, and red lips. "What are you?"

He smiled then, flashing startling white teeth. "An ally."

His response shocked her. That was the last thing she'd expected him to say. "Why should I believe you, when you just told me you're here to kill me?"

"Good question. Let's just say an old friend has shown me the error of my ways," he said, glancing over his shoulder.

Raphael Vega appeared out of the shadows and nodded in her direction. His presence did little to ease her concerns. She glanced back at Mike, who looked at her as if she'd grown four heads.

"What?" she snapped.

His lips quirked. "Your appearance is deceiving. You look so normal—so human."

She recoiled at that last statement, but held her ground. "Well it's obvious that you are anything but. I'm surprised Roark Montgomery hired you, what with his pure-blood platform."

It was Mike's turn to flinch. So he had a secret, too. She almost laughed at the absurdity of the situation. "Yes, I know all about you," she said. "You didn't think that you could break into the IPTT records without being detected, did you?"

"I must be losing my touch," he said, more than a little amused.

Maybe he was telling the truth. There was only one way to find out. Red lowered her weapon, but didn't holster it. "If you're not here to kill me, then what do you want?" she asked.

"I've come here to warn you that Roark has someone working for him other than me."

"Who?"

"I don't know, but he may be angling for my job."

"Your job?"

Mike shook his head, but his matted black hair didn't move. It was as if it were painted on his scalp. "It's not important," he said, talking more to himself than to her. "I'll take care of whoever he has in mind. We have a bigger issue to worry about."

"Such as?"

"A war."

Red frowned. "The IPTT won't allow the republics to go to war. Everyone knows that. It's the team's main purpose for existence."

He grinned. "That's where your untimely death comes into play."

"I don't follow."

"He wanted me to kill you in order to gain IPTT support."

Red threw her head back and laughed. She laughed so hard her shoulders shook and tears came out of her eyes. When she'd finally managed to pull herself together, Mike was staring at her with a bemused expression upon his face.

"I don't see what's so funny."

She wiped her eyes. "The joke is that the only person who'd miss me or even care that I died is my grandfather. And he isn't about to throw support behind Roark Montgomery. In fact, if anything happened to me, he'd do just the opposite."

Mike frowned. "I don't understand."

"I'm so special no one wants to work with me. As far as the tactical team members are concerned, I'm a social pariah."

"I see," he said.

She holstered her gun. "I have one more question for you."

"Which is?"

"What are you going to tell Roark when he finds out I'm still alive?"

"I'll—" A buzzing sound interrupted his answer. Mike tapped his ear. "Sir? I can hardly hear you over the noise. What is that?" He straightened to attention.

Red wished she could hear what was being said. Mike's expression soured, then his color drained more, if that were even possible.

"Yes, sir. I'll get there right away." He hit the device again, then glanced at her. "I have to go."

"Was that Roark?"

He nodded. "Yes. He's waiting for me north of town in a clearing. He's there with the sheriff." He started down the sidewalk.

Red's mind blanked. There was no reason for Morgan to be with Roark Montgomery. No good reason. "I'm coming with you."

Mike turned back to look at her. "We can't go in there together. He'll suspect."

He was right of course, but that didn't make her feel any better. She would've preferred to keep an eye on him now that she'd had a sample of his power. She shivered at the memory of his mind, pushing at hers, forcing her to act against her will. "Fine," she said. "I'll meet you there."

He nodded and then disappeared, moving faster than she could visually track. Red's heart slammed against her ribs as she jumped in her car and sped out of town. The minutes ticked by slowly, even with the pedal pressed to the floor. She pulled behind Morgan's car twenty minutes later.

So much could've happened in the time it took her to get here. She climbed out of her vehicle and glanced at the full moon hanging low in the sky. Any other time, she'd stop to admire the beauty of a night like this, but not tonight. She took a deep breath and held it, listening for any sound that seemed out of place.

A cry came from the woods.

Red started sprinting before the sound died on the wind. Her blood thundered in her ears as she raced along a well-worn trail. The sounds were growing louder now, bone hitting bone, if she wasn't mistaken. Morgan . . .

Red broke through the clearing and cried out at the scene before her. Blood covered the ground and two men were fighting, except they weren't men at all—they were werewolves. She recognized Morgan instantly from seeing him transform yesterday.

He looked in pretty bad shape. His head was bleeding profusely and his back had strips of flesh torn away. She glanced at the other figure and realized that it was Kane. Red didn't know how she knew it, but she did.

Morgan circled Kane with his arms held wide, preparing to strike. Kane leapt at him, but Morgan stumbled to the side, barely avoiding the razor-sharp talons aimed at his abdomen. Red screamed before she could stop herself, momentarily distracting both men.

A twig snapped to her left and she saw Roark Montgomery step from the shadows. He stood near a hydrocopter, watching the melee like a spectator at a sporting event. His gaze shot to her at the sound of her cry, and then he glanced behind him. Mike Travers walked forward, his head bowed in submission. Roark's face scowled in disapproval and he looked away.

Kane took that moment to strike. Morgan bellowed as claws raked his right arm. It now hung nearly helpless at his side, shredded and bleeding. His gaze met Red's and held for a split second.

In that moment, an understanding passed between them. One that did away with their differences and focused on their similarities. They may not fit into each other's worlds or know what the future held, but they wanted to face it together.

Red remembered what she'd learned about wolves. They lived in a pack culture that was based on dominance. The alpha was the leader. Morgan had been telling the truth. He wasn't just the sheriff of Nuria. He meant much, much more to this town. Meant more to her.

If the fight ended badly and she had to kill Kane, Red needed Morgan to know ahead of time how much she cared. She slowly lowered her eyes in respect . . . in submission. Morgan let out a triumphant howl, then jumped forward with renewed vigor, landing on Kane's back.

Morgan's jaws clamped down on Kane's neck while he slashed Kane's chest with his good arm. Kane yelped in pain, but Morgan kept up his assault. The clack of bone and muscle ripping filled the air.

Red's stomach roiled and she fought back the urge to vomit. A flash of movement out of the corner of her eye drew her attention away from the carnage. She saw Roark Montgomery raise a laser rifle into the air.

His prowess with a gun was legendary. He still held the record with his marksmanship. Red didn't have time to think or even to breathe. She pulled her charged pistol out of its holster and fired. Laser light snaked out, hitting Roark's trigger hand, severing three of his fingers.

He shrieked, dropping the weapon in order to clutch his smoldering injury. At that moment, something to her right snapped loudly. The wet twist was followed by a gurgle of breath. Someone's last breath. Please don't let it be Morgan. Red turned in time to see Kane's body drop to the ground, twitching as his lifeblood seeped into the dirt.

She glanced back at Roark and saw Mike Travers helping him into the hyrdocopter. The machine started and began to lift off. As soon as it cleared the trees, it shot forward with blinding speed. Within seconds Roark Montgomery and Mike Travers were gone.

Red watched Morgan's ravaged body fall. She rushed forward. He was already shifting back into his human form. She dropped to her knees when she reached him.

Blood covered every inch of Morgan's skin, making it difficult to lift his torso off the ground. Her quaking hands slipped twice before she succeeded in pulling him onto her lap. Breath rattled in his chest. He was dying.

Red hit a button, waking Rita from her long snooze. She prayed the navcom didn't take this moment to malfunction. "Rita, I need your help" she said, hearing the panic in her voice.

"Gina, I detect foreign material all around you. I will run a scan immediately to determine the extent of your injuries."

"No! I need you to please contact the emergency care center in Nuria. Tell them that Morgan is hurt bad and to send help. The sheriff's station has our location."

"Affirmative."

Red brushed Morgan's wet hair away from his face. There was so much blood that she didn't know where to press first to stop the bleeding. It had already soaked into her shirt and through her pants. "Please don't die," she begged, pulling him closer and rocking. "You have to hang on."

Morgan's eyes opened and closed, but he wasn't able to focus. Red began to cry. "Help me, please somebody. Help me!" A hand touched her shoulder. For a second, she'd thought she'd imagined it, then she looked into Raphael Vega's concerned face. "He needs help."

"Let me take him."

"Can you get him to the emergency care center?" she asked, afraid to let Morgan go.

"I can do one better than that," he said, nipping his wrist until it bled. "But you have to let me have him for a moment."

Red nodded and reluctantly released Morgan. Raphael lifted him as if he weighed no more than a child. He leaned in close to Morgan's ear and whispered. Red couldn't make out what he was saying, but Morgan's eyes opened and fixed on Raphael's face.

"Drink," he said clearly, placing his wrist to Morgan's mouth.

Morgan latched onto his arm and sucked, pulling Vega's blood into his mouth.

Red frowned in confusion. "I don't understand how that's going to help him. He needs a doctor." Her own words reminded her exactly how much was lost this night. Her gaze swept to Kane's tattered body. He, too, was back in his human form, even though pieces of his flesh were scattered over the arid meadow.

"This will keep him alive until help gets here," Raphael said, drawing her back. "Although I'm not sure Morgan will appreciate the *gift*." He smiled as if amused by some inside joke.

"You're not hurting him, are you?" Her hand moved without thought to her pistol.

Raphael watched her, but didn't release Morgan. "That would not suit my purposes."

"You hurt him and I'll kill you," she said, glaring at him.

"Once help arrives," Raphael continued as if she'd never spoken, "I'll take care of this." He fluttered his fingers in the direction of the mess. "I'm sure Jim Thornton will be grateful to receive the body."

He glanced down at Morgan, then whispered something else in his ear. Morgan released his wrist. His breathing had evened out and he didn't seem near as pale. Raphael lowered him to the ground, then motioned for her to take his place. Red stepped forward and sat next to Morgan, his head resting on her lap.

"Help is coming," Raphael said. "They'll be here in a few minutes."

"How do you know?" she asked, looking at him.

He smiled, flashing fangs. "I can hear them."

The emergency care rescue unit arrived a few minutes later via hydrocopter and shuttled Morgan off. Red rode with them, refusing to leave his side. Morgan's heart stopped twice, but they resuscitated him both times. By the time they reached the center, the medics had him stabilized.

They rushed Morgan into surgery, leaving Red to pace outside the nurse's station. Three hours later he was settled in a private room with half the sheriff's department standing outside in the hall, fighting over who would stand guard first.

Red let them fight as relief washed over her. The doctor had said that if Morgan made it through the night, then he'd live. She sat in a chair next to his bed, willing his heart to beat and his lungs to fill with air. Tears spilled down her cheeks as she watched his pale face wince from the pain.

She couldn't bear the thought of losing him. When had he stolen her heart? Red thought about the first time she'd seen him on the vidscreen. She had known in that moment that he wasn't like the others.

She stood and leaned over the bed, until her lips touched his ear. "Morgan, this is Gina. I don't know if you can hear me, but the doctors say you're going to be all right. Do you understand? You're going to be fine. And I'll be waiting right here until you open your eyes." Red sniffled. "I love you. Don't you die on me, damn it!" She kissed his forehead and sat back down.

Red drifted off while watching Morgan sleep. She woke shortly before dawn to find him looking at her. She yawned and stretched, rising slowly.

"You're awake," she said.

"Thanks to you," he said, his eyes brimming with emotion.

Red shook her head. "It wasn't me."

Confusion twisted his features and he winced. "Then who?"

"Raphael Vega. He gave you some of his blood."

Morgan's eyes widened and his color paled to three shades lighter.

"Did he do something to hurt you? I told him I'd kill him if he did, and I meant it."

"I don't know for sure." Morgan glanced at the window. "Is the sun up?"

"What?"

"The sun," he said. "Can you see it?"

Red walked over to the window and opened the automated blinds. Sunshine poured into the room. "Yep, it's up."

She looked back in time to see Morgan throw his arms up and curl his body forward in defense.

Red drew her pistol. "What's wrong?" she asked, glancing outside. She scanned the sky and the ground, but saw nothing amiss. She holstered her weapon.

Morgan slowly lowered his arms and inspected his skin.

"What are you looking for?" she asked, concern growing. Had Morgan's injuries gone beyond the physical, affecting him mentally?

He stared out the window, then met her gaze. "Nothing's wrong." He smiled. "Everything is just fine. I didn't mean to worry you."

"Right," Red said, not believing him for a second. "Sometime soon you're going to have to explain to me what just happened."

Morgan grinned. "I'll do that, but right now I'd like a kiss."

Red pressed her lips to his gently. Heat from his body seeped into her, telling her without words that he was going to be all right.

"I have something I need to do," she said, staring into his eyes.

"Do you need help?" he asked, throwing the covers back.

"Oh no, you don't." She grabbed the blanket and pulled it over his legs, tucking it against his chest. "You're staying here until the doctor says you can leave."

The mention of the word *doctor* brought pain to Morgan's eyes.

"Morgan, I'm so sorry about Kane." Red clasped his hand, giving it a small squeeze.

His jaw tightened. "He made his choice and left me none. The rules of the pack are clear."

"I know, but he was still family," she said.

Morgan met her gaze. "You're my family now."

Red's heart swelled at his words. She kissed him again, then stepped away. "I'll be back as soon as I can. In the meantime, there are a lot of people outside who'd like to say hello."

"Where are you going?"

"IPTT headquarters. I have to take care of something."

He nodded. "I'll be here when you get back."

She laughed. "You'd better be."

Morgan watched Gina leave, his heart light and elated. She'd come back. Even after learning the truth, she had returned. He only remembered bits and pieces of what had occurred during and after the battle with Kane, but one thing Morgan did know was that Gina hadn't left his side.

He grinned to himself as his mind scrolled through a future that until yesterday he hadn't dared dream would exist.

Sheriff Hunter, I'm so glad to sense that you are awake. I was beginning to wonder if I'd been too late.

"Raphael?" Morgan bolted forward at the sound of the vampire's voice. "Where are you?" He glanced around the empty room, then leaned over the side of the rest pad to check underneath.

Is that any tone to take with the man who saved your life?

"Man?" Morgan snorted. "Why can I hear you so clearly?"

That is the question, isn't it? Let's just say that my blood is the gift that keeps on giving and giving.

"What in the hell is that supposed to mean?"

That your ability to hear me in your mind is only the beginning.

"You're going to be sorry when I get my hands on you. Raphael, what have you done?"

Done? Moi? Why Sheriff, I'm hurt that you would think such a thing. Would I do anything that would cause you discomfort?

"Hell yes!"

I'll be in touch. Tinkling laughter followed the statement, then slowly faded away.

Morgan groaned and fell back onto the pillows. "Terrific," he muttered under his breath. That damn two-legged bat would never let him live this down.

Red strode into IPTT headquarters. She dropped her weapons off and stepped through the scan. This time no booties awaited her on the other side. She walked to her desk and opened the drawers, searching for anything that she might want to take. Satisfied that there was nothing she needed, Red strolled down the hall toward her grandfather's office.

She stopped at the door and waited to be scanned. A second later, the door popped open. Her grandfather sat behind his desk like usual. She glanced around the room at the holo-images and the old tomes. She was going to miss this place, but not as much as she was going to miss the man behind the desk.

Her grandfather glanced up from his paperwork. "Gina," he said, smiling. "You're looking well."

She laughed. "Yeah, a lot better than the last time you saw me."

He waved a hand. "Please take a seat. To what do I owe this unexpected visit? I thought you were going to spend a few more days in Nuria."

Red sat in the big chair and swung her legs back and forth, feeling like the little girl who used to play in this building. The same little girl who'd become friends with a navcom named Rita.

She glanced at her wrist and slowly unhooked the device, then placed it on top of her grandfather's desk. She fingered the strap lovingly for a moment, before moving her hand away.

He looked down at the navcom and frowned. "Why did you remove Rita? Is she broken again?"

Red smiled. "No, she's fine."

"I don't understand."

"I won't need her anymore."

His brows lowered. "I see. Is there anything else?"

She took a deep breath and placed the two synth-documents beside Rita.

"What are these?"

"Just read them."

His eyes scanned the first document, then he quickly glanced at her, concern marring his weathered features. "All this transpired in Nuria?"

"Yes."

He picked up the second document. "Gina, this is your resignation."

"I know, Grandpa."

He shook his head. "But why?"

She smiled again. "You know why I can't stay. Not now. Not after everything I've been through. The truth won't remain a secret forever. Roark doesn't know, but he suspects. It's only a matter of time. I love you and respect the tactical team too much to take a chance that I might somehow damage its reputation. I'm sorry that I won't be here to take over as commander, but that was your dream, Grandpa. Not mine."

Robert Santiago opened his mouth to speak.

"You know I'm right."

He closed his mouth and sat back, his eyes taking in her features as if he were memorizing them. "What are your plans?"

"Would you believe I don't have any?" She chortled.

"No," he said patiently.

"Other than going back to Nuria to check on Morgan, I really don't know what I'm going to do. Until now, my whole life's been planned out for me."

He glanced at her resignation. "I've never known you not to have plans."

"Yeah, it's a first for both of us." She laughed. "Well, I need to get back."

Robert came around his desk until he was standing next to her. "Are you sure about this? Really sure?"

She rose and stepped into his arms, hugging him for all she was worth. "No, I'm not sure about anything right now."

He pulled her back until he could look into her eyes. "You always have a home here for as long as I'm commander."

"Thanks, Grandpa. I love you, too." She gave him one more hug, then released him and headed toward the door before she did something embarrassing like cry.

"You will visit, won't you?" he asked quietly.

Red stopped and glanced over her shoulder. "Nothing could keep me away."

"I'll hold you to that promise, special one," he said, sniffling.

"Thank you, Grandpa."

"For what?" he asked, his eyes glistening with unshed tears.

"For everything."

Red stepped through the door and waited for it to close, so that she could get one more whiff of her grandfather's office before she left. Her body trembled as her mind registered the magnitude of the decision she'd just made. The tactical team was her life, all she knew how to do. Fear of the unknown nearly propelled her back into the commander's office. She forced herself to move away from the door instead. She'd made her decision and she'd live with it.

She was so wrapped up in her thoughts and tumultuous emotions that Red almost didn't see Roark Montgomery and Mike Travers enter the front of the tactical team building. Before she could think or even breathe, Red rushed forward and met them at the door.

"How's the hand?" she hissed under her breath, glancing at his bandages.

He looked around at the other team members, then lowered his voice. "You'll pay for this," he said, indicating his injury.

"I know what you've been doing," she said. "The only reason you're not under arrest is because I don't have enough proof."

He smiled a politician's smile and waved at someone over her shoulder. "Good luck getting it."

"I'm going to be keeping my eye on you. You won't be able to shit without me knowing about it," Red warned.

"That's nice. Wonderful idea," he said loudly. "I'll do the same for you. Thanks again for your support. We always appreciate the opinions of the female officers on the team." He reached out and clasped her hand with his good one and shook it, squeezing until she had to bite the inside of her mouth to keep from crying out.

Red pulled back and wiped her palm on her pants, feeling suddenly dirty. "This isn't over."

"You're absolutely right," he said. "This is only the beginning," Montgomery added for her ears only. With that he stepped around her, giving Red a wide berth, and continued deeper into the building.

Mike Travers followed a safe distance in his employer's wake. He met Red's gaze as he passed her and a tiny smile flitted over his bright red lips, before quickly disappearing.

Red strolled out the door, grinning from ear to ear. With Mike's help, she'd always know what Roark was going to do next. That realization made leaving the tactical team somewhat easier.

She walked down the steps toward her car, her mind taking in the details of her surroundings to be stored in her memories for later examination.

A shuttle let off a group of cadets. They raced past her toward the facility, their training almost complete. One female officer stopped a few feet in front of her and stared, waves of power pouring off her. Red froze and held her gaze. There was something different about this woman. Something *Other*. Red waited to see what would happen. The woman's eyes widened, then she bounded up the steps.

Red continued down and was halfway to her vehicle when she spotted Bannon coming up to start his shift.

He passed her, then stopped. "Well, well, well, if it isn't the great white hunter," he said, sneering.

"Hey do you know who that woman is?" Red ignored his comment and pointed at the crowd of cadets.

Bannon squinted against the sun. "You mean the redhead?"

"Yeah, that's the one."

"Her name is Catherine Meyers. Her fellow cadets call her Chaos. Apparently, she's almost as weird as you."

Red had no doubt after sensing the woman's power. She wondered if Catherine knew the truth. She debated whether to approach her and decided against it. It wasn't her place to out a fellow Other. Eventually, Catherine would come looking for the truth and Red would be there to help her.

"By the way, how's the wild animal chase going?" Bannon asked, interrupting her thoughts.

"Fine," she said. "I bagged one. I'm going back now to get me another." The single step Bannon had taken made their height difference colossal. Red didn't care. She'd never allowed Bannon's size to intimidate her before and she wasn't about to start now. Besides, she didn't work here anymore.

"Shouldn't you be reporting for duty?" he asked, glancing at her civilian clothing.

Red shook her head. "Not today. Like I said, I have more animals to catch. You'd be amazed at what I discovered while I was out there by the boundary."

"Yeah, I bet," he said, staring at something at the bottom of the steps. He grinned and an evil light filled his blue eyes. "In fact, I think I could guess one thing you found in Nuria."

Red frowned and glanced over her shoulder. She saw Morgan at the foot of the stairs, propped against a car, covered in bandages. She'd never seen anything more appealing in her life. Her heart tripped in her chest, then swelled. Morgan smiled and gave a little wave with his good arm.

"I guess I was wrong about you," Bannon said.

Red turned to look at him once more. "What do you mean?"

"You did remember how to spread your legs." He nodded toward Morgan. "If his whipped expression is any indication of what occurred between you two. Looks like he's been between your thighs a few times and barely survived."

Anger surged inside of Red and her hands fisted. She struck Bannon in the abdomen before she had time to think about it, then followed the blow with a kick to his face. He dropped back onto the steps, holding his bleeding nose.

"You're going to be sorry for that. An attack against a superior officer can get you relieved of duty or kicked off the team," he said with a slight nasal inflection.

"Too late." She smiled. "I already quit." Red continued down the stairs without a backward glance and stopped when she reached Morgan.

"What was that all about?" he asked, nodding in Bannon's direction.

"Needed to settle an old score before I left." Red shrugged. "What are you doing here?" she asked, taking in the blood that had started to seep through some of his bandages.

"I thought you could use a ride," he said, motioning toward the car.

"You should still be in the hospital. There's no way they released you with all these injuries."

"They aren't so bad."

Her eyes narrowed in suspicion. "How did you get out?"

He grinned. "Snuck."

Red shook her head. "You're insane. You know that, right? You nearly died yesterday. I can't believe you've healed this much."

Morgan tried to shrug, but couldn't. "That was then, this is now. I'm feeling much better—thanks to Raphael's *gift*. And let's not forget that I'm not wholly human in the first place."

"Yes, I recall."

He shifted to prove his point, but a muscle ticed in his jaw as Morgan attempted to hide the pain.

"Okay, tough guy, I believe you. Now stop, before you do even more damage." Red stepped forward and touched his shoulder. "What am I going to do with you?" she asked, pursing her lips.

"I can think of a few things." He winked. "But first what are your plans?"

"Not sure. I just resigned from the team. Can't exactly work here, knowing what I know now. And Roark Montgomery isn't likely to stop until he succeeds in either killing me, starting a war, or both."

Morgan leaned forward until they were nearly touching. "Then we'll just have to make sure he doesn't succeed."

She snorted. "How are we going to do that? It isn't like Roark's overt about his plans. And we can't just walk up to him and shoot him, no matter how tempting the prospect."

"We'll form our own tactical team, so that we're ready for him," he said.

"Just like that, eh?" She snapped her fingers. "You think we can form a team to compete with IPTT and not encounter any problems."

"I didn't say it would be easy, but yes, we could. The major difference is our team will be made up of Others like us."

Red ducked her head. "I wasn't sure there was an 'us' after all that passed between us."

Morgan grinned. "You didn't think I'd let you get away that easy, did you?"

"I'd hoped not." She tilted her head and kissed him. Morgan yelped.

Red jerked away. "Sorry, I forgot for a second that you were hurt."

"Get back here." He grabbed her, taking advantage of her surprise to deepen the embrace. Morgan kissed her long and hard, until they were both gasping for breath. "Just so you know, I'm never *that* injured," he said, his eyes sparkling gold in the sunlight.

"Thanks for the warning." She smiled and started to laugh.

"Hell, beautiful, it's not a warning. It's a promise."

"Do you really think we can do this?" she asked, warming to the possibility of having her own tactical team. It would take a lot of work and they'd have to clear a lot of hurdles, but it could happen.

"Yes, I do." Morgan pulled her close and brushed a kiss over her forehead. "Together we can do anything." He grinned devilishly. "Besides, no one is stupid enough to mess with Red and the Big Bad Wolf." He laughed.

Red hoped that was the case as she briefly met Morgan's gaze. She turned and glanced up the stairs at the IPTT entrance where Roark Montgomery had passed only moments ago. He was one man who might be dumb enough to try.

TOR
ROMANCE

Believe that love is magic

Please join us at the Web site below for more information about this author and other great romance selections, and to sign up for our monthly newsletter!

www.tor-forge.com